SHEILA'S TREE

SHEILA'S TREE

Malcolm D. Crawford

FEB. 2006

Best Wishes,

Enjoy a good Western read.

Malcolm Crawford

iUniverse, Inc.

New York   Lincoln   Shanghai

SHEILA'S TREE

iUniverse, Inc.

For information address:
iUniverse, Inc.
2021 Pine Lake Road, Suite 100
Lincoln, NE 68512
www.iuniverse.com

ISBN: 0-595-32963-2 (pbk)
ISBN: 0-595-77793-7 (cloth)

Printed in the United States of America

To my three brothers, Dan, Dave and Steve

For their inspiration, encouragement and, more often, disparaging laughter.

Contents

▼

PROLOGUE 1

SHEILA'S TREE

DISCOVERY 13

CITY HALL 17

THE GEOLOGIST AND THE COWBOY 27

WORK HAZARDS 31

CATTLE RANCHING AND THE OL' SWIMMING HOLE 37

STAKING THE CANTEEN CLAIMS 46

ADVENTURES AT THE COUNTRY CLUB 49

THE URANIUM BROKER 59

PRELIMINARY INVESTIGATIONS 62

MILO CASHES A CHECK 67

STRANGERS AT THE BULL RUN 72

THE SHOWDOWN 77

HIGH STAKES POKER.. 83

DARK OF NIGHT 90

BARBECUE AND DIAMOND DRILLS 96

WORK AND PLAY AT THE ROUNDUP................................. 99

URANIUM RUSH AND POLITICS 103

TROUBLE ON THE BENCH 110

YELLOW CAKE AND PASS ROAD 112

BACK AT THE RANCH 117

POLITICS 119

ALL KINDS OF NEW DEVELOPMENTS 122

HIGH FINANCE AND COUNTER CURRENT
    DECANTATION 125

THE HAUL ROAD 128

ALTERING HISTORY 130

I'LL SEE YOU IN COURT 133

MILO'S MISERY 135

WINTER OF HARDSHIP 139

FRUSTRATION AND WORSE 143

GOSSIP 146

REVELATIONS AND CHALLENGE 149

RESCUE 155

DARK DREAMS 157

DEATH WATCH 159

THE SHOOT-OUT AND AFTER EFFECTS 166

RECOVERY AND HOPE 176

PANIC AND POOR JUDGMENT 180

COLLIE'S REVOLT 183

BREAK-IN 186

SEARCH AND RESCUE 189

NATURAL CONSEQUENCES 193

THE LAST SUPPER..196

CRY "HAVOC!" 198

CLOSING IN 204

JUSTICE SERVED 206

EPILOGUE..209

ABOUT THE AUTHOR 213

PROLOGUE — 100 YEARS
BEFORE THE STORY BEGINS

▼

August 1853

Westward progress of the wagon train was halted. Booney Krantz, a tough old German scout well known on the frontier for his wide knowledge of western lore, talked his boss, Wagon Master Dorsey Fuller, into pausing for a few days in order to replenish community food supplies. Krantz swore that he could bring in a two-month supply of bison meat if given six good men and a couple of freight wagons. Fuller led the long caravan of immigrant wagons from Independence, Missouri towards the rich agricultural lands of southern Oregon. Five days earlier they had left Fort Laramie, Wyoming Territory, low in provisions because of earlier weather delays and the Wagon Master was worried about the long trip ahead over South Pass and the salty deserts of Utah and eastern Oregon. Dorsey was discovering the truth in rumors circulating around St. Louis while he was preparing for the difficult journey, that game was getting scarce along the well-traveled Oregon Trail. In four previous trips across the high grass country of central Wyoming Territory, Dorsey had been accustomed to bountiful herds of buffalo and pronghorn antelope but by 1853, after a decade of predation by processions of wagon trains, changes were gradually becoming evident. Game was scattered and less plentiful and plains Indians, once friendly and open handed, were showing resentment and desperation in increasingly hostile encounters with the flood of aggressive intruders from the East. The Wagon Master passed word back along the dusty line of wagons to break down for an extended rest and circled the train to a halt near Independence Rock on the Sweetwater river. There was plenty of grass and water for the livestock and the area was relatively safe from Indian harassment because of lack of game in the vicinity and the frequent passage of other parties making their way westward. Dorsey was aware that safety in numbers was a good rule when traveling through Indian Territory.

Several men of the company, including two mission Indians of the Shoshone tribe who had joined up with the train at Fort Laramie and were riding along as far as the Green River country west of South Pass across the Continental Divide, took two heavy freight wagons and headed north in search of bison. Dorsey Fuller decided to go along and command the expedition himself, though Krantz and the two Indians, one of whom spoke English to a limited extent, were expected to locate the quarry.

"Three days ride Nort und der Powder river we shall zee," Booney told Dorsey. "Der we finden lots buffalo."

On the first day the heavily built but lightly loaded oaken wagons, each drawn by four sturdy draft horses, traveled at a good pace over broad low hills of grassland until by evening the party could see glints of setting sunlight on peaks of the Big Horn range scores of miles to the north. As the men set up a dry camp and began heating coffee, boiled red beans and salt pork for supper, a lone rider cantered into their midst with a jaunty halloo of greeting. It was Dorsey's tall, red headed daughter, Sheila Fuller, a strong, good-natured, courageous girl who had traveled across country with her father several times since early childhood. Though only seventeen years old, she was an expert rider, faultless marksman and as saddle tough and fit as any man in the group. She had been furious at her father's decision to leave her out of the hunting party and refused to be left behind in camp.

"Daddy, you jest hush now," she admonished. "You aint gonna leave me behint whilst you men have all the fun. I only kilt that one buff'lo last year an' I want to git in on a big hunt this time."

"Sheila girl, I'll whop you like a stepchild iffen you don't do like I tell you," Dorsey stormed. "You git back on board that pony an' head south right now, an', by God, iffen them hostiles git you, hit'll be no more than desarved."

"Oh phooey! Them Injuns been quiet as mice ever since the Council of '51 an' you know it. You jest want to put a short hobble on me 'cause I'm a girl."

"Hit aint no joke, now, an' you don't know what yore talkin' about," Dorsey answered. "Them 'Rapaho and Crow is gittin' meaner all the time. We're goin' right up to the Powder River country where we're sure to meet up with some of 'em, an' God only knows iffen they'll make a run at us or not. An' iffen it aint the

Injuns, h'itt'll prob'ly be a big ol' grizz that'll git you. Jedediah Smith damn near got ate by one just a little way north of here some yares back."

"You' Vater ist right, Missy," growled Booney. "We gonna zee plenty saviches 'round dem buffalo. Dey, maybe, don't like it, we shooten der beasts."

"Then what the Devil are you all goin' up there for iffen you expect them Injuns to come down on you? I reckon you could use my carbine as well as Judd's or Tom's or Rudy's," she gestured towards the other men around the fire.

"You keep a civil tongue in yore haid," Dorsey scowled. "Iffen yore pore daid Ma knowed how I was araisin' you she'd come back to ha'nt me for sure." Dorsey faced up to the inevitable outcome of almost all differences of opinion against his daughter's willful disposition. He had lost many similar arguments in the past.

"I'll tell you the truth, child, we don't really expect no trouble. The Cavalry has been patrollin' up north some, an' them savages has got the fear of the Lord into 'em. Iffen we keep our eyes peeled an' show a strong party, we won't have to shoot nuthin' but a bunch of buff'lo an' then git the hell back down to the Sweetwater with the meat." The hunting party was augmented by one.

Two days later they reached the uninspiring muddy bank of the Powder River, a northward flowing major tributary of the widely branching Missouri river system. The placid waterway cut through the prairie in wide sinuous curves, its course marked by cottonwoods, willow thickets and eroded bluffs seldom more than sixty feet above the silt laden water. Some twenty miles to the west of the river, another impressive natural feature dominated the prairie scene. Paralleling the general northerly trend of the river, a great escarpment of red and gray layered cliffs jutted abruptly from the undulating umber plain of prairie grasslands. Looming behind the colorful cliff wall in jagged profile against the western horizon rose the thirteen thousand-foot peaks of the Big Horn Mountains.

The party of hunters had come across no sign of Indians but evidence of buffalo was everywhere. John Iron, one of the mission educated Shoshones, told Booney that they were approaching a place called Su-mini-cum where a good-sized tributary, called Framboise creek, flowed into the Powder River. A deep canyon in the tall rim face to the west showed where the creek had eroded through resistant layers of rock during the passage of geological ages. The tributary waterway, named by French Canadian trappers for its slow moving raspberry colored flow across the prairie, tumbled onto lush grassland from the shadowy canyon mouth, meandering in languid russet boils along its cottonwood lined pathway to the North fork of the Powder river. John Iron said that the joining of the two streams was a good place to find buffalo and that the location was marked from a great distance away by a huge lone pine tree which towered above the low bluffs and relatively featureless topography of the grassy plain.

By mid morning the landmark tree was sighted and Fuller found a good spot along the Powder River to set up camp for processing buffalo meat. Fire pits were dug for smoking and curing, wooden tripods of driftwood were erected upon which to suspend carcasses for skinning and butchering and quantities of firewood were collected from along the riverbanks.

Booney Krantz and Drasco, companion of John Iron, cautiously rode up to the confluence; followed the smaller Framboise stream valley and eventually found a herd of several hundred buffalo some three miles to the west. Leaving the lethargic animals undisturbed, the scouts cut back across country to the butcher camp to make plans with the rest of the hunters.

Since only a few of the animals could be used, it was decided to send Booney, the two Indians and Sheila, because she begged so ardently, to sneak up on the herd and make the kill. Dorsey and the other four men were to come behind with wagons to help load and transport the animals back to the temporary butcher camp.

As planned, the four hunters painstakingly approached the herd from a brush filled depression that offered cover to within one hundred feet of the ponderous ruminants. Booney carefully pointed out exactly which individual beasts each person would aim at so that only the tenderest yearling calves would be killed. Each marksman was responsible for two animals. Booney told Sheila that buffalo often would not run away even when fired upon, provided that movement or scent of hunters did not alarm them. She was told to aim for the spine close behind the massive skull, insuring a quick kill that would not damage any meat. Leaving horses tethered to gangly shrubs of tall sagebrush, the four deployed behind rocks and brush awaiting Booney's signal to fire. Sheila smelled dust and manure stirred up by splayed hooves; saw shaggy hides plastered with mud from a recent wallow and felt the excited thud of her beating heart as she carefully brought her rifle to bear on an intended target. In surprisingly easy fashion the first volley dropped four animals to the ground with a dusty thump while the remaining herd began bawling and milling in confusion. At the second shot three more collapsed immediately but John Iron struck his target high in the hump of shoulder muscle well above its spinal column. The wounded animal plunged through the herd bellowing and frothing which set off a frantic stampede. The buffalo herd bolted away from the hunters, turned for higher ground within a few hundred yards, and disappeared over the horizon of the shallow stream valley in a cloud of powdery alkaline dust. With shouts of excitement the hunters ran out to examine their trophies. Sheila could hardly believe that her rifle had dropped the huge beasts, as she looked for nearly invisible wounds in their heavily maned necks. The two young animals killed by Sheila lay practically side by side where they had fallen without a kick, both instantly dead.

At that moment the triumphant hunters suddenly became quarry in their turn. Sheila looked up at a cry of alarm from Krantz, to see a flying wedge of ten or twelve mounted Indians galloping towards them from the same direction in which the buffalo had fled. Sheila sprinted in terror for her horse, getting there just as the three men mounted and whirled away down the creek towards the Powder River. By the time Sheila followed, the Indians were less than one hundred yards behind and their savage screams sounded frighteningly closer. Her horse was a tall gelding with good speed and stamina, allowing her to overtake the less well mounted Shoshones and ride up beside Booney.

"What are we gonna do?" she screamed.

"Ride like fury und keepin' down der head," he cried. "We get to d' trees und maybe fight 'til you' Vater und der boys comin'."

Over the three-mile chase to the river Booney and Sheila gradually gained ground. Their mounts seemed infused with the terror of their riders and flung themselves with desperate energy over rocks and through whipping limbs of shrub and brush. The inferior horses of Drasco and John Iron could not keep pace. Sheila looked over her shoulder in horror as the two men were ridden down one after the other. John Iron tried to turn away as leaders of the pursuit closed in but a long flint tipped lance thrust under his arm and through his chest. Drasco was overtaken as he galloped. A large warrior buried an obsidian war ax between his shoulder blades with a wild round house swing. Screams of fierce triumph rang after the two fleeing whites as each victim fell.

"Oh God," thought Sheila, as her horse plunged across shallow turnings of the creek bed, "I never even knowed the name of that one pore Injun. Oh, don't let them murderin' devils catch us up," she half prayed.

The streambed broadened as the riders came closer to the Powder River. Sparse stands of Fremont poplar, aspen, willow and alder stood along the water course, filled in with buck brush, choke cherry, elder berry and other tree-like shrubs, so that horses were forced to weave single file along game trails through the heavy thicket. The following Indians soon lost sight of their intended prey but Usho, a minor Chief of his tribe and leader of the foraging group, with a wave of his hand, sent three riders to the left and three to the right around the narrow wooded area while the rest clambered directly on in screaming pursuit. Usho was quick to take advantage of an opportunity that seemed to favor his men. Surprise and superior manpower were strong factors in his decision to attack aggressively. He was usually very wary and tentative upon encountering white men. In his experience things almost always turned out badly for his people when confrontations occurred with these strange beings and their little understood culture.

Booney was watching alertly for a spot with some natural cover or protection against which he and the girl might hope to make a stand. He needed a barrier at his back with limited field of fire in front to have any chance at all to hold off an attack. He thought maybe Fuller and the other men would hear gunfire and come to the rescue. Unfortunately no such temporary haven was found and they soon broke out of the wooded area onto a wide graveled beach that sloped gently several hundred yards to the edge of the Powder River. A huge ponderosa pine tree nine feet or more in diameter at the base with a flourishing crown one hundred and eighty feet above their heads was the only vegetation contained in the confluence basin other than scattered patches of sage and yellow blooming rabbit brush. The Indians were too close to allow escape by riding up steep bluffs to the right or left. Either way would find them cut off and ridden down in the same fashion as their Shoshone companions. They were in a trap and Booney could see no hope of escape. He rode up to the base of the giant tree and dismounted in a cloud of dust, signaling Sheila to do the same. Turning towards the howling pursuers, he held his rifle up in both hands, took half a dozen steps towards the Indians and threw it down in a gesture of surrender. Sheila had not removed her rifle from its saddle scabbard. She leaned against the tree overwhelmed with fright as Krantz stood with empty hands outstretched.

The Indians reined to a stop about thirty feet in front of the two whites, pausing for a moment as if savoring the end of the chase.

"What are we waiting for Usho?" asked the Lieutenant, T'nun. "Let's kill this trash like we did the other two."

"No," grunted Usho. "These Whites are pretty scared but they are tricky. Let's all dismount and walk up slow and easy. If that old dog tries anything you put an arrow in him quick, Sagus. And you, Ishota, keep an eye on the small one by the tree." The Commander of the Indians was noted for his prudent awareness of the white adversaries' strength and cunning. He seldom took unnecessary chances.

Booney stood with arms extended as the Indians cautiously approached. Sentaway and Golgat each grabbed an arm and twisted the old scout to his knees. T'nun leaped forward and dealt a swift blow with his already bloodied war ax that crushed the man's skull. Sheila screamed and crouched against the tree waiting for her turn.

"What the hell did you do that for, T'nun?" demanded Usho. "You always get in a big hurry about everything."

"You know why I did it," answered the muscular Lieutenant bitterly. "That is only a little return to these white killers for what they did to our village over on Antelope Creek last year."

Ishota pointed at Sheila kneeling with her head in her arms against the tree. "Look at that cowardly one. These whites have no dignity. We better make this one sing a song for Coyote and North Wind to call attention to our victory here today."

"He is ready to sing already," laughed Asotin. "Look at him shaking over there."

Golgat and Sagus had already stripped Booney's body and, after T'nun had taken the fringed buckskin shirt that was much too small for his broad torso and Usho acquired the long Colt pistol, others divided up the remaining booty. Sheila shivered and sobbed in anticipation of a cruel end she feared was near. She would not look at the Indians as they mauled Booney's remains but their clicks, grunts and dissonance sounded grimly in her ears.

"Well, Usho, what are we going to do with this sniveling horse shit?" asked T'nun.

"We could bury him up to his neck in the sand," answered Usho.

"That would take too long," observed Sagus. "We have to get back and skin out those buffalo they killed. That's going to be plenty of work."

"How about dragging him behind your horse back to where they killed the buffalo?" asked Crolo. "Then we could finish him off later."

"We could take him clear up to Canyon Village and let the squaws have some fun. My woman was telling me what some Arapahos did to a white soldier they caught. I think she'd like to try it," said Golgat.

Asotin laughed. "Golgat, you think that female wolverine in your house will leave you alone for a while if she has some white man to torture?"

Golgat stared darkly and arose with his hand on an iron skinning knife at his belt.

"Listen, fat fool, at least I have a woman. You sleep with your horse."

"Enough!," barked Usho. "Let's take Crolo's idea and drag him back to the buffalo place. We have to get back there and camp by the meat tonight anyway. Strip him down and make sure everybody gets a souvenir."

As three of the warriors roughly followed Usho's order, the discovery of Sheila's sex caused a sensation.

"Look at this," shouted Sagus. "This is a white female. I never saw one before."

Ishota and Crolo each took an arm and pinned Sheila's naked body against the rough bark of the towering pine. Her tanned neck and hands contrasted starkly with the white skin of her body. The pubic triangle was a blaze of dark red.

"Look at that bright red cho-cho," T'nun almost whispered in awe. "It looks like somebody built a little fire on her belly."

The Indians were reduced to silent contemplation as they stood around, unsure what to do, gazing at Sheila's pinioned form.

"Well, we could all rape her like we did to that skinny Crow woman over near Ten Sleep Pass that time," said Usho.

"Not me," hastily disclaimed Asotin. "It looks like you could get your tool burned off between this big woman's legs. Besides that, she stinks."

"I agree," said Ishota, who was still holding one of Sheila's arms. "She smells like a Mama bear coming out of winter sleep."

"I don't want to drag a woman behind my horse," said Usho. "We might as well just get rid of her right here and have it over with."

He drew an iron knife and advanced towards Sheila. She saw the glistening, nearly naked savage approach with the knife in his hand and knew that her moment had come. She closed her eyes and raised her face to the sky.

"Dear Lord, accept my soul and let Daddy find me for a decent burial," she whispered through clinched teeth.

"Wait," yelled Golgat, impressed by her stoicism. "She can still sing to Coyote and the North Wind. There's no use killing her too quick. Why not torture her for awhile? Those buffalo can wait."

"That gives me an idea," said Crolo. "Let's tie her to this big tree and start a little fire between her legs. That red cho-cho looks like it's on fire already. She might burn good like a piece of bear fat."

The Indians quickly tied her to the tree and set about gathering a small pile of brush, bark and pine needles, which they mounded up between the girl's spread-eagled legs. Realizing her terrible fate Sheila began screaming and writhing in panic. Ishota laughed excitedly as he struck flint sparks into cattail lint and other shreds of flammable material extracted from a small leather bag tethered to his waist. The Indians arranged themselves in a comfortable semi-circle and prepared to enjoy a long concert of agonized suffering as the poor girl slowly burned.

The grim events unfolding beneath the giant ponderosa were being observed by someone else. Dorsey Fuller, aware that no sign of Indians had been reported by his men, decided to ride along the western bank of the Powder river looking for more firewood and scouting the area which he had never visited before. He recognized the risk in his solo trip of exploration but had confidence in his ability to avoid trouble if Indians were encountered. The other four men were sent with wagons towards the hunting grounds. They all expected to meet back at the butcher camp by the river within two hours. Dorsey rode up on a bluff overlooking the confluence basin just as Booney and Sheila came galloping furiously out of the Framboise Creek drainage to make their final stand under the tree. He spotted the Indians coming through and around the strip of trees and brush and saw the terrible trap closing on his daughter and the old scout. He watched with tears and curses as Booney died and his daughter was bound against the tree. He thought it impossible to rescue Sheila by himself and he realized with bitter regret that the others were too far away to be summoned in time. Even from three hundred yards away the girl's screams of panic were rending his brain.

Quickly wiping tears in order to clear his vision, Dorsey laid his powerful buffalo gun across a flat ledge of rock and took deadly aim. With an echoing clap of thunder that seemed to reverberate from all directions in the river basin, the heavy bullet slashed through the right side of Ishota's neck. The group of men sprang to their feet in confused consternation, unable immediately to locate the source of the rifle fire. Ishota rose from the dust and ran around and around in a small circle as blood fountained from his wound. He soon fell across the body of Booney Krantz and the two men sprawled side by side in death. Reloading the single shot rifle at top speed with the new recently acquired smokeless powder cartridges and firing carefully, Dorsey was able to drop two more men in a few seconds. The Indians were quickly demoralized by the accurate fusillade which seemed to strike from an unknown and undetectable location. Those left unhurt sprinted in panic to their nearby horses and galloped speedily for the scanty cover along the creek bed. As soon as they were out of the confluence area the frightened Indians cut for the north slope of the creek bed and rode out onto the prairie. From his elevated location on the south edge of the low valley Dorsey watched their retreat and saw that the whole party had taken flight. Only the four dead bodies on the blood soaked ground and Sheila's slumped form against the tree were left to mark the massacre site.

Dorsey descended quickly to release his daughter who was nearly unconscious from fright and shock due to the appalling events of her captivity. The two were able to find the other four members of their unlucky hunting party without further incident and eventually returned safely to the wagon train on the Sweetwater. The mighty tree that almost served as Sheila Fuller's pillory became a famous landmark in Wyoming Territory. During the next few decades, as Native Americans were rounded up on reservations and white immigrants filled the area, the exceptional old pine became widely known as Sheila's Tree.

Only seventeen years later, in 1870, an adventurous young rancher named Everett Lee Palmer drove a herd of Texas longhorns into the Powder River country and began building one of the first great cattle ranches in Wyoming Territory on the banks of Framboise creek.

Early in the twentieth century the huge lone pine tree succumbed to forces of nature in a raging winter storm that splintered its decaying trunk. Another Sheila's Tree was already growing in the same location.

SHEILA'S TREE

AUGUST 1953

DISCOVERY

Tom Regelstorp was on his regular weekend quest. He went prospecting for uranium during time off from a greasy little café where he toiled weekdays before a huge black griddle. It usually took most of Saturday and Sunday before the smell of bacon fat and lard was expunged from his nostrils by the clear air of Wyoming high country. Regelstorp was not a skilled geologist; in fact, he searched almost at random among the plains, foothills and mountain ridges surrounding the small city of Sheila's Tree. He had a secret weapon that he believed could locate a radioactive orebody by magical powers like the X-ray vision of Superman in comic books. He carried a radiation counter that he had ordered from old Uriah Rodich's hardware store. Tom was one of a small army of adventurous dreamers intent on making a bonanza uranium strike the same as a few lucky prospectors had already done in New Mexico and Colorado. Uranium fever was a common ailment among many professional and amateur prospectors in the mountain western states.

On this sun ripened summer Saturday he had driven west of town to talus slopes at the foot of Red Rock Rim. He spent two hours climbing up through steep declivities and terraced cliff faces of the high wall in order to reach the gently sloping grassland at the top of the rim which locals called The Bench. The twenty mile wide plain, gradually rising in elevation towards the west until sharpening hillocks and deepening gullies merged into thrusting white capped peaks of the Big Horn Range, was a semi-desert sedimentary plateau of grass, sage, and wild flowers; full of animal life, hidden springs of clear icy water; patched by small pockets of conifers and quaking aspen. The ribbon of bench land fronting the mountain range was almost completely isolated from the prairie and ranches to the east by the imposing eroded fault scarp standing hundreds of feet above the relatively flat land below. Red Rock Rim was a spectacular geological feature rising precipitously from the prairie to form a mighty fortress wall running north and south for more than forty miles.

Regelstorp stood at the top of the rim looking east across a wide prairie landscape. Shallow drainage patterns etched dendritic incisions on a sage and grass blanket of tan and purple sweeping ocean-like to the colorless horizon. A scarcely visible north-south line in the middle distance marked the state highway and the Great Northern railroad track that paralleled the rugged escarpment and the Powder River on its lazy course. Regelstorp caught an occasional glitter of sun reflected from the windshield of a car or truck. Some distance to the south he could see a smudged dark line of cottonwood trees starting at the foot of the rim and meandering across the grassland to a point almost due east of where he stood. The trees marked the course of Framboise Creek from its emergence out of a deeply notched canyon carved in the face of Red Rock Rim to its end point within the city limits of Sheila's Tree where it met the Powder River. The confluence area above the high water mark of Chopstick reservoir was the location of Su-mini-cum Memorial City Park with a bronze plaque relating the story of the pioneer heroine, Sheila Fuller. Tom knew that the headwaters of the Framboise rose on the snowy flanks of Big Horn peaks, danced rapidly across the sloping Bench, through high pastures of the Palmer Ranch, then dropped in a foaming cascade over Garnet Falls into Palmer Canyon from whence it flowed with energy spent for a more sedate journey across the plain. After passing through the town of Sheila's Tree, the stream made quiet union with the muddy waters of the Powder River and the man made lake. Tom calculated his position on the rim at about five miles south of Palmer Canyon, which would put him close to the fence line of Palmer ranch. He wanted to work upwards across the Bench towards the mountains where national forest land bordered private landholders.

If you're going to make a strike it might as well be on public land, he figured.

Still perspiring after climbing some five hundred feet up rocky breaks and eroded crevices in the steep precipice, he paused to take a long drink from his canteen. Tom had two oranges and five or six biscuits stuffed with bacon and cheese in his pack, but decided to wait until later for lunch. His eyes followed a colorful red tail hawk circling carefully along the crest of the rim. The Geiger counter on his hip ticked and muttered with ubiquitous background radiation, counting tiny sub-atomic missiles as they flashed through the ionization chamber.

He turned and strode westward, sighting on one prominent peak among the serrated points of the high range. He followed the rounded crest of a broad ridge covered with ring shaped patches of low growing beaver-tail cactus, clumps of wheat grass, cheat grass, fox tail and brome between thickets of pungent, shoulder-high sagebrush in areas where available moisture encouraged growth. He often paused to pick up glossy opalized pieces of silica or chunks of fissile mudstone which parted easily into plated sheets, sometimes containing fossil fish scales or brown imprints of fern leaves like ancient bouquets pressed between the pages of Earth's diary. None of the rock specimens changed the monotonous tempo or intensity of his clicking Geiger counter.

By early afternoon Regelstorp was seven miles west of the rim, almost half way across the Bench. He was tired and hot from the long hike and decided to work northward towards the inviting cold clear waters of upper Framboise Creek. He knew there was a good jeep trail down off the Bench through Palmer Canyon which would be a much easier route back to his old pickup truck parked miles away below the rim. There was a chance, Tom thought hopefully, of running into some of the Palmer ranch outfit on the road who might give him a ride out to the truck. The canyon pass road was the only vehicle route from the plains up onto the Bench for at least twenty miles in any direction and it was gated a number of times by Palmer fences.

An hour later he was following a dry, though seasonally flowing, tributary of Framboise Creek no more than a mile from its meeting point with the main flowing stream. As he walked along the crest of a steep embankment bordering the flat bottomed dry wash, a startled bobcat bolted from a shadowy hiding place twenty feet below and scrambled nimbly away, dodging rapidly through brush, debris and rock piles until it quickly disappeared. Regelstorp ran a few steps along the crest of the bank in an effort to maintain his view of the beautiful animal. His water canteen became dislodged from its clip to his belt and the round container bounced and rolled over the bank, then slid into a narrow crevice cut a few feet deep into the hard sandstone floor of the gully below. The canteen lay in plain sight at the bottom of the dry watercourse, twenty feet away down a vertical cliff of crumbly, soft sedimentary gravel deposit. He stood looking down at his last few cups of water, undecided whether or not it was worth finding a way down to pick up the canteen. He was thirsty and not quite sure how much further he had to walk before coming out on Framboise Creek. Proceeding along the bank for a short distance he came to a spot where the thick sedimentary deposit had crumbled away forming a steep ramp into the gully. Tom sat down, digging his heels into the soft gravelly soil, and slid easily down. The bottom of the old watercourse was wide and flat with a shallow, narrow channel eroded into the surface of a hard underlying sandstone formation. The erosional feature was the beginning of a process that would eventually devour the hard rock and scour out a steep canyon as slow millennia of rain and storm worked over the ancient surface of the planet.

Regelstorp walked rapidly back to the spot where the canteen lay and vaulted clumsily into the V shaped ditch to pick it up.

When he first heard the frantic crackle of sound from his Geiger counter Tom thought the test button had been accidentally pushed, activating an audio signal. He lifted the counter out of its leather case on his hip, examining the settings and calibration carefully. The chatter slowed as he raised the instrument away from the rock. He lowered it slowly, watching the dial swing wildly; hearing the tiny speaker merge random clicks into a buzzing crackle once more. He could hardly believe his ears. There was a strong source of radioactive emission locked somewhere within yellow, brown and ochre striations of the sandstone formation. The activity came from a narrow band a couple of feet above the bottom of the ditch. Three feet on either side of the hot spot only normal background count was detected, though the rock looked exactly the same.

His canteen still lay at the bottom of the channel precisely in the middle of the mysterious strip of radioactivity. He picked it up and climbed back out of the shallow cut. The Geiger counter immediately fell silent, but it had already exposed the location of radioactive minerals that were the rainbow's end for Regelstorp. He felt like John Marshall at Sutter's Mill or Carter at the first glimpse of Tutankhamen's tomb. He was happily ignorant of the difficulties lying ahead for himself and others who were soon to struggle with the reality of the uranium discovery and its impact on the people of Sheila's Tree and the rest of the State of Wyoming.

CITY HALL

Collie Winston poured a pitcher of water into fluffy potting soil supporting a tall, thick stemmed, but struggling, dieffenbachia plant. The deep hexagonal redwood planter beside her desk turned slowly dark at the seams as a few beads of moisture trickled down, dripping soundlessly onto the beige carpet. She had many tasks awaiting her attention on this warm summer day at her desk in City Hall but she had learned that patience and tolerance were valuable assets in her job. She had learned a number of interesting lessons since being elected Mayor of Sheila's Tree two years previously and the education continued each busy day.

The sign on the door of her small office in the City Hall wing of the Galena County courthouse read, "Colorado Palmer-Winston", because the Palmer maiden name was an important one in Wyoming. Her grandfather, Everett Lee Palmer, had driven cows up from Texas back in 1870, six years before the Custer massacre, and established the Palmer spread on Framboise Creek as one of the first and most successful ranches in Wyoming Territory. Collie remembered E.L.—he was known to everyone only by the initials—as a small, sun wrinkled, wind burned man with a big western hat. His story was one of pioneer hardship and the civilizing of the West. There were Indian fights and rustlers and sheep wars in the history of Palmer ranch. As a child Collie was saturated with the lore and tradition of every story, having heard them all on the bony denim covered knees of her famous grandfather. At the age of fourteen, two years after her grandfather's death, she had shot an antelope with E.L.'s shiny old model 94 Winchester rifle which was known to have been used for more serious matters when it was newer. The trials and adventures of those early days were legend in the community; time having dimmed somewhat the often squalid reality of greed and brutality in favor of a more romanticized and sanitized version of history. Collie's maiden name had always been a significant benefit to her political aspirations. Though she may have felt the need of the well-known Palmer name as an aid to election, the Mayor, in her own right, was a woman of charm, intelligence and physical grace. In addition to the uncommon natural beauty of her regular Nordic features, healthy complexion and full athletic figure, she also possessed calm self-confidence and her Granddad's share of ambitious drive. Colorado Palmer-Winston had exuberant goals and firmly believed in their achievement but at the age of thirty she was subliminally aware of vague unease and conquests as yet unmounted. She experienced an inner feeling, unvoiced, perhaps mostly undiscovered, but persistently felt, that something was missing.

Her present energy was focused on the affairs of Sheila's Tree and the needs of her constituency in the blossoming city of six thousand souls on the western edge of Wyoming's eastern plains. In a state that counted a total population of only four hundred thousand, Collie's city was an important center of commerce and agriculture.

The Mayor's secretary, Louise Greene, knocked twice and stuck her head into the office.

"Want to hear about your day, Collie?" They were good friends and wasted no time on formalities unless trying to impress someone from outside.

"Sure. Fire away. Just remember I need a couple of hours to work on my remarks for the Country Club dedication next week. Do you think this plant is going to make it? Maybe I'm watering it too much."

"Don't ask me. I couldn't grow fuzz on a peach. My boyfriend, Jake, told me last night how his Mom used to grow tomatoes and squash and beans and stuff; then make preserves to eat all Winter. I don't know how to do all that housewife junk, Collie."

"Well, I think Jake Walker is an old fashioned sort of guy. Policemen are usually social conservatives. It preserves the status quo and makes for a safer more regulated society."

"He is conservative all right. He thinks Ike Eisenhower is some kind of Pinko because we let the North Koreans off so easy. I think he wrote in MacArthur on the ballot last year. Well listen, do you want this Philip Stover guy from National Ammunition Company to come in at 10:30? He called yesterday and said he would drop around about that time if you are going to be here."

"Oh yes, I'll see him then," replied Collie. "Did you call Patrick in Cheyenne to find out if Stover is talking to anybody else about a location for this new factory?"

Collie had been writing and calling for weeks attempting to persuade the ammunition-manufacturing firm to consider building a plant in Sheila's Tree. She pointed out that there was an adequate work force available and plenty of room for an explosives maker to find physical isolation while still being close to the railroad for shipping. Her friend, Patrick McCall, in Cheyenne was a legislative lobbyist for the Association of Wyoming Municipalities, and would know if other cities in the state were also wooing the company.

"Patrick said Stover was looking at Rock Springs and Laramie both because they are on the proposed new interstate highway," Louise answered.

"My Heavens, they haven't even begun building that highway yet and our railroad provides an immediate shipping point. Well, what else?"

"Mr. Winston called and wants to have lunch with you over at the Bull Run. Said he could be in town by noon." Louise, like almost everyone else, referred to Collie's husband as "Mr. Winston", despite a small town propensity towards calling most people by their given name. Delvane Winston, himself, did not find it unusual or distasteful to be formally addressed. He tried hard to retain a semi-British accent which he had picked up in England during the war, in the belief that it added something to his personal image. He usually wore riding boots and britches, a tweed hunting jacket and even carried a riding crop. Less of a caricature than it sounds, he carried off the affectations with convincing charm and dignity. The fact that he managed the Palmer ranch since the death of Collie's parents added to his prestige.

"Okay, lunch it is." She gave a small shrug of her shoulders. "I thought we were going to spend the weekend at the ranch...wonder what's up," she mused.

"You've got to be back by 1:30, Collie," Louise directed. "The Rodeo and County Fair Committee want to talk you into getting the city to help them out with the Frontier Days program this year."

"Oh yes, well, we can provide parking attendants and take care of traffic control for the parade, I guess. Remind me to call Chief Bertie on that will you, Louise?"

"And the last thing...Ballard Crown out at the D-Z called just before you came in. He asked if you would call back after 3:00 this afternoon."

Collie noted the time on her desk calendar wondering what Ballard had on his mind. He was owner of the D-Z ranch bordering the south side of the Palmer spread and had been a close friend of her parents.

As Louise withdrew to her desk in the outer office, Collie's eyes turned to a picture of her father and mother on her own desk. It was an enlarged snapshot of her laughing parents as they stepped into a light four-place airplane with Palmer Ranch emblazoned in bright red and white letters on the fuselage. The picture was only three years old. Soon after it was taken the plane had plunged into a Colorado mountaintop only a little way from the Denver airport. Collie blinked hard as she pulled out a yellow legal pad, forcefully turning her mind to the coming festivities for the opening of a new country club and nine hole golf course overlooking the river.

A little more than three hours later Collie wheeled her modest Plymouth coupe into the parking lot of the Bull Run Cafe and Lounge. The Bull Run did not have fan-folded cloth napkins, wine glasses and formal place settings on every table as did the old Cielo Grande Hotel on Main Street but it did have the best food in town. The fare was simple; chicken fried steak with garden vegetables, Salisbury steak with gravy and canned mushrooms or steak and eggs for the lunch crowd. Iris Patton, owner and manager, insisted on quality and cleanliness. She served good food, maintained a friendly, home-style atmosphere, and made most of her profit from the lounge. It was the most popular bar in Sheila's Tree and specialized in serving cowboys who came to town on weekends after payday looking for a juke box, a cold beer and a good time. She ran a decently quiet establishment with good pool tables and a running poker game in the back room. There was a small dance floor usually favored with live music on Saturday nights; occasional fights; sometimes, single women in for a look around. The place was an asset to the business community of the town.

Del was nowhere in sight as Collie, ten minutes late, looked around the dining room. Waving and smiling at nearly every face in view, she moved swiftly to a corner table of the large country and western decorated room. A young waitress came over immediately with a glass of water and a menu.

"Howdy Miss Winston. You alone today?"

"No Jeannie, I think my husband may be in the lounge. Would you mind telling him that I'm here?"

"Oh sure, Ma'am. Right off."

The girl hurried over to a leather padded, swinging door with a small red neon BAR sign overhead. She returned shortly with another glass of water and menu.

"He's playin' a game of snooker with another gentleman, Ma'am. Said he'd be right in quick as he's done."

Jeannie dashed off among the red checkered tables as the dining room rapidly filled up. Collie scanned the room over the top of her menu while waiting for her husband. She recognized Milo Harris coming through the door followed by a nice looking towheaded young man whom she had never seen before. Everyone else in the room recognized Milo also. He was one of only a few Negroes living in the community and the only black person commonly seen in downtown business establishments. There were one or two other colored families living in town that Collie knew of, but they worked for the Great Northern Railroad Company and were seldom seen on Main Street. Milo, Foreman at Ballard Crown's D-Z, was a tall athletic man who could ride down any wild bronco or outfight any man in Galena County. That was his reputation at least, though Collie had never heard a first hand account of his doing either one.

Del came in jauntily with bright eyes and a flushed face. "I beat poor old Frailey three racks in a row and I haven't played snooker in a year or more," he laughed. "Sorry to keep you waiting, Pet, but the old war horse must answer a challenge, what?"

Delvane was only one year older than his wife but he often spoke as though she were much younger than he was.

"You were playing with George Frailey, the real estate broker?" She tried to appear interested.

"Oh yes. Picked up a quick fiver and got an offer of forty thousand on the town house if you ever want to sell," he replied.

"I can't believe that, Del. My folks paid twenty three thousand in 1949 when we got married. That's almost double in four years."

"Well, Frailey said quality homes like ours located on the bluff are going out of sight. We're property rich and cash poor, my dear."

Collie was surprised that he would mention the depleted condition of their bank account even to her. He usually put up such a solid front of middle class opulence that he seemed to fool even himself, she thought. We are not rich by any means, she reflected, but the ranch is worth plenty and provides a good income. She saw that his tongue was loosened by several drinks.

"You know that I have to live in town since being elected Mayor," she said. "If you spent more time here instead of out at the ranch house, having two homes wouldn't seem such an extravagance. That reminds me, I thought we were staying out at the ranch for the weekend. Why did you come into town this morning?"

His dark eyes took on a somber and intense look as he glanced at her. "Oh God, Pet, I've got several appointments tomorrow and a lodge meeting tonight. I must stay at the town house, my dear, but no need for you to miss an outing. I know how you enjoy a good ride."

She frowned. "I will not go out there if you're staying in town, Del. We haven't been together since you came in to the Smith's party two weeks ago." She looked sideways from under arched eyebrows. "Wouldn't you rather I stayed?" She spoke in a lowered voice.

"Of course I've missed you awfully, Baby." He reached across the table and took her hand in his. She had always liked his hands, strong and firm, yet clean and manicured. "But I really need for you to look things over up the canyon before roundup time," he continued. "You can't believe the terrible luck we've had this year. The herd doesn't appear to have gained much weight and we only got about half a cutting off the hay meadows. It's going to be a tough winter and we may have to buy feed. I thought you could go out and take a good look at things this weekend so that we could put our heads together later. You're always trying to tell me how to run the place, anyway."

She was not quite ready to turn her attention to problems at the ranch, though his request for her opinion was almost unheard of.

"Del, don't you remember how it was at Berkeley before the war? We were so close and you were so young. We were just two country kids in the big city," she reminisced.

"Sure, I remember. You were set for grad school and I never even got to finish my bachelor degree," he remarked bitterly.

It was galling to him that she possessed a Masters Degree in political science from the University of California while he had not been able to complete a four-year course. World War II and military service had come along while he was still an undergraduate. Events after the war had precluded a return to school and, now, at the age of thirty-one, it was all behind him. They were married in 1949 with a huge affair in Sheila's Tree and then the death of Collie's parents had left them with a ranch to run. His own family in Napa Valley, California did not have a ready place for him in their vineyard and wine business so it was natural that he and Collie stayed with the Palmer ranch. Collie knew much about cattle, horses and ranch economics, having heard little else for the first seventeen years of her life, but it took only a short while for the two of them to learn that they could not work harmoniously together. Del had a natural flair for command, enhanced by military officer's training, and some agricultural experience from the California vineyards, but the problem was, he could not defer to any opinion of Collie's. He ended as manager of the ranch while she turned to a career of public service begun in Sheila's Tree during and after the war years.

Their minds were following different paths.

"I meant the two of us," she smiled. "Remember how it used to be? Are we growing apart?" She squeezed his hand gently.

"Collie, I've got problems. How many times have I asked for your help in the past four years for God's sake?" His voice was flat and neutral, not responsive to her mood. "That damned crew of wranglers out there is incapable of doing the least task on their own; the weather and hay crop have been abominable and now you refuse to go out and take a look at the place while I have a load of work to do in town. One man can only do so much, you know!" He shook his head; mouth a grim, compressed line.

"But Del, beef has been a terrific price the last three years," she said. "I thought we were coming out well."

"I took this ranch over to build a premium herd to replace those scrubs your father used to run. I sold just about every head on the place during the first two years and have been building the purebred Shorthorn Hereford stock ever since. You were the one who thought the purebred herd was such a great idea, remember? This should have been the pay off year but the yearlings haven't gained the way they should. Carl Mansfield down at the University at Laramie told me these calves would gross six or seven hundred pounds by roundup but most aren't much over five hundred, I bet. Besides that we lost close to fifty head that died off this summer for one reason or another. While you play Queen of the May in town, I'm out there at the ranch busting my ass for nothing! Well, the games are over and now you're going to do something for me, by God. Remember how oily-sweet old man Smith was at the party last month? I have borrowed forty-five thousand dollars over the last three years to buy cows, fertilizer, irrigation pumps and I don't know what all for your damned ranch! Now that fat bastard won't give me another penny without some paper with your name on it."

Delvane was flushed and panting from the emotional outburst. It was not all fury, however. He eyed his wife apprehensively while waiting for her reaction to the long pent up revelations.

Collie was stunned. A tumult of related thoughts poured through her mind as she sorted and classified this unpleasant array of new perceptions. I knew he was impractical at times but how could it be so much? Would the bank really have financed him without my knowledge? What could he have possibly spent so much money on? Why couldn't he tell me?

They both sat staring at each other, food cold and ignored, while Collie began to grasp the possible implications of Delvane's story. Debt was a foreign word in her vocabulary. In all her previous experience money came from beef sales or savings accounts or a small salary from the city; never from charge plates or mort-gages. She finally spoke.

"Are you telling me that you have spent forty-five thousand dollars of some-one else's money?"

He was waiting for an opening, a chance to vindicate his position; to transfer some of the anxiety and worry of three years growing failure onto her shoulders.

"It was my money, by God! The bank lent it on my signature to finance my ideas for the ranch. Smith bought it all the way and then when he found out the fall sale is not going to pan out so good, all of a sudden he starts talking paper on the ranch. Collie, we can pay the loan off and the bills, too." His voice dropped as he muttered the last phrase. "All we need is a break on the price and some grass next Spring. I could sell five hundred head at twenty cents per pound on the hoof and we could gross sixty or seventy thousand in a breeze."

Collie had performed in public too often to stay rattled for long. She had received a psychic blow from a totally unexpected direction, but already her sense of balance was returning and logic was beginning to take over from emotional reaction.

"I'm sorry, Del. I'm sorry. You must realize this is a shock for me. I thought the herd was doing fine. I certainly never realized the things you were doing on the ranch were so costly."

She looked at him again and read a shadow of uncertainty, a possible evasion, in the way he was observing her.

"I will go out to the ranch this weekend. I've been too wrapped up in city affairs," she said. "I haven't taken a really good look at the place in months. Don't worry about all this, Del. There must be some way we can make things work out as you say."

She wondered if her gelding, General, would still recognize her. Suddenly she wished it were Saturday already and longed to be in the saddle again with the sights and sounds of her childhood. Thank heaven it's Friday, she thought, I'm going straight out to the ranch as soon as I close the office tonight.

"I must get back to the office," Collie said. "Find out all you can from Orville Smith about this mortgage and we'll see what has to be done."

Delvane never said a word as she gave his hand another encouraging squeeze and slipped out of the booth. After she was gone he tossed the five-dollar bill he had won from Frailey onto the table for the waitress and stalked into the bar. There was only a slight tremor in his hand as he picked up the first shot glass.

When Collie got back to the office she had little time to think about her per-sonal problems. The Rodeo and Frontier Days Committee wanted detailed commitments from the city, which Collie supported, but she was unsure about budget limitations. In 1940, at the age of seventeen Collie had reigned as Rodeo Queen and also won the barrel race on her registered quarter horse mare, Winnie Winkle. Committee members knew she would be involved in the annual celebration to the extent that the city could afford because of her personal interest. They came with a long list of items for her consideration.

After that interview, City Councilman, Bill Spielman, dropped by to discuss at some length his critical evaluation of the city's Department of Public Works. Spielman was a construction contractor and builder who held strong views on the overly rigorous engineering standards imposed by the 'bungling bureaucracy' as he usually phrased it. Collie, quite used to discussions with irate constituents and opinionated Council members as well, managed to diffuse the Councilman's frustration yet another time.

By 4:00 p.m. activity at City hall wound down so that Collie found time to return the telephone message from Ballard Crown.

"Oh Ballard," she said, "It's so good to hear from you. Why don't I ever see you anymore?"

"Well Honey, you got the best of me on that. I aint gone nowheres. You just got real busy with town doin's, I reckon."

His familiar voice was like the man, she thought, firm and resonant but softly modulated and clear. The Crown brothers, Ray and Ballard, had migrated to the growing state of Wyoming in 1914 as young men. They came from Texas, bringing with them plenty of cash money. Ballard purchased the D-Z ranch from its original owner, Deuteronomy Zwitzer, while Ray opened the doors to his Crown Publishing House by starting the first weekly edition of the Galena Journal. Both men were good managers, level headed participants in community affairs, and unmarried by profession. Though often pursued by designing women, and sometimes caught, neither man had been brought to the altar. Ballard, a close friend of the Palmer family, had helped supervise Collie's upbringing on the ranch practically to the same extent as her own parents and was second only to E.L. Palmer in early influence on her.

"Child, I don't mean to toss my sombrero on a peg where it aint wanted," he hesitated for a moment, "but I've been thinkin' you, mebbe, need some talkin' to. If this aint none of my business just say so." He paused again for a long moment but Collie did not say a word. I know what this is going to be about, she thought.

Ballard continued, "Since you and the Dude parted ways on who was going to run that ranch things aint improved none, Honey. I've bit my tongue over some of his new fangled ideas, like the one where he had the crop duster from Riverton fly ten tons of fertilizer on the northwest range last year, but this last one just takes the cake. He never put his bid in on the BLM grazing land this Spring and Tommy Jutes over at the Tip Toe ranch has got the Palmer grazing rights now. Hell, ol' Delvane has run three or four head to the acre on your range all summer and it's lucky to support a cow an' calf pair on a good year. Did you know all this, Girl?"

"Yes, Ballard," she sighed, "we did discuss dropping the Bureau of Land Management lease, and, frankly, I objected strongly. But Delvane said we could save seven thousand a year in rent while making up the lost grazing by improving our own rangeland. The Agricultural Extension Agent, Mansfield, from the University at Laramie told him that every ounce of fertilizer applied to that grass would yield a pound of beef by Fall."

"Well, if you believe that, Child, you're the one ol' P.T. Barnum was lookin' for. I don't think it's pannin' out too good by the look of them scrawny yearlin's."

She tried to be loyal. "We have to give it a chance. It's been a dry year but Del says things will turn around."

Crown had said his piece and was noncommittal on Delvane's opinions.

"Why don't you call Juno for a chance to take a passeo around your spread this weekend? She was tellin' me a while back she wanted to do some ridin' but I been busier than a red fox amongst the Banties tryin' to get ready for the roundup and shippin'. It might do you good to palaver with her some anyhow, Collie. She's damn near as smart as you are."

Juno Castle was a close friend of Ballard's, and rumored to be even more. Ten years older than Collie, Juno owned her own accounting business and was a devoutly independent feminist. Her father was Judge Vincent Kerby; Juno's last name, Castle, being the sole remnant of a short and superficial marriage of her youth. She and Collie were acquaintances from childhood but had never been close friends.

"The minute I hang up this phone I'm heading for the ranch," Collie evaded. "I hate to call Juno this late. I'm sure she has her weekend planned."

"Well, no, I'd guess she was just waitin' for your call, mebbe," Ballard commented dryly.

"Oh—oh, I see," Collie saw. "All right you old busy-body, but next time you have a lecture to deliver come do it yourself."

"I reckon things 'ull come out okay if you wake up and fly right," he drawled.

"I love you, Ballard." She hung up the phone thoughtfully.

THE GEOLOGIST AND THE COWBOY

Ryan Baker and Milo Harris entered the Bull Run at about twenty minutes past noon into a crowded, clattering dining room. Ryan noticed curious eyes following the big black man ahead of him as Milo moved gracefully between tables to a vacant booth. He was still surprised that Ballard Crown's foreman, whom he had met a few minutes earlier, turned out to be a Negro. No reason why not, Ryan assured himself, except that he had never dealt with a black person before outside a hotel lobby or a passenger train. This fellow was dressed like a cowboy, acted like a cowboy, and Ryan was beginning to accept him as a cowboy.

"Ballard says you might be the man to help us out on this stock pond construction." Milo's deep voice enunciated each word clearly with only a slight western articulation of the vowels.

Ryan was again somewhat surprised, despite himself, at the lack of conformance in this man to the black racial stereotype of the time.

"I'm a professional geologist, Mr. Harris. I believe Mr. Crown heard about me through my sister-in-law, Susan Baker. I arrived in Sheila's Tree only last week from Climax, Colorado where I had been employed at the molybdenum mines. For reasons of my own I decided to come here and establish a consulting business. I have a degree from Colorado State and a Masters in mineral processing technology from Colorado School of Mines at Golden. I have worked for several years in the field of applied geology and have a fairly comprehensive background including work in soil stabilization. I believe I can be of service in evaluating the dam location and soil bearing properties."

Ryan made a sales pitch out of the formal presentation of his qualifications. Although he still had nearly two thousand dollars in the bank, he needed the work and was anxious to begin acquiring some clients who would spread the word on his availability in the area.

"Was Harlan Baker your brother?" Milo asked. "I knew him pretty well. We used to fish together sometimes up on the North Fork." Seeing Ryan nod in agreement Milo continued, "Sure sorry about the accident—what?—two years ago now? He was a hell of a nice guy. I never knew your sister-in-law though."

Ryan acknowledged the sympathy with a grim nod. He had been very close to his younger brother, Harlan, whose sudden death in a water skiing accident on nearby Chopstick reservoir had been a blackening sadness for everyone in the family. Concern for the care and security of his brother's family was another reason that Ryan had come to Sheila's Tree.

"I understand there was some preliminary work done on your project last year which didn't turn out well?" Ryan returned to the topic at hand.

"The pond will only cover about five acres," Milo related. "I suppose you could store about fifty or sixty acre-feet of water with a dam one hundred and twenty feet long and, maybe, twelve feet high. The thing is, it's mostly gravel in the bottom of the gully and we couldn't get it to hold for us. We only put in a little levee about five feet high, figuring we'd add to it this year but she washed right out on us before hardly any water backed up."

A pleasant looking, freckle faced woman dressed in a mannishly cut western suit complete with a turquoise squash blossom bolo tie approached their table. She laid her hand lightly on Milo's shoulder with a smile.

"There's a seat saved for you at the poker table tonight, Mr. Harris, if you're goin' to be in town."

Milo did not turn his head but Ryan noticed the corner of his mouth twitch with a suppressed smile of pleasure as he said, "Howdy Iris. You know the payday of every outfit in the county don't you?"

He winked at Ryan and turned to face the lady.

"This here is Mr. Ryan Baker, new in town and probably more fodder for that gin mill of yours next door. Mr. Baker, this is Miss Iris Patton, Chief Cook and Petty Officer of this establishment. She happens to own the place."

Ryan found he could not stand up in the booth, but crouched forward, awkwardly extending his hand. Her hand was lean and brown, surprisingly firm and strong as she shook.

"Howdy Ryan. Welcome to the Bull Run. I admire your taste in food but can't say as much for the company you keep."

Ryan could tell by her expression and bantering tone that the exchange of insults was a long-standing gambit between his two new acquaintances.

What Iris saw was a sunburnt, blonde, tousle headed man with widely spaced hazel eyes and a fascinating cleft chin. He looks just like Jack Armstrong, the All-American Boy, she told herself.

"Won't be in town tonight, Iris," Milo casually mentioned. "I brought the flatbed into town to get a new set of mud grips on it. Have to get it back so Shorty can haul salt blocks tomorrow."

"Like every other dang thing on that D-Z spread, I reckon the headlights don't work so you can't go home after dark, can you?" She was laughing at Milo who sadly shook his head in acquiescing silence.

"You boys enjoy your lunch. Glad to meetcha, Mr. Baker." She moved away, pausing for a greeting or a joke at each table of diners.

"I need to examine the dam site to evaluate problems of construction and take soil samples," Ryan continued the business discussion. "When would a field trip be convenient Mr. Harris?"

After regarding the geologist for a thoughtful moment, Milo answered, "I would say the most convenient thing would be for you to begin calling me Milo for a start. As to the other thing, I suppose tomorrow would be too soon for you?"

"Sooner the better," Ryan grinned, sticking his hand across the table for a friendly shake. "My friends call me Ry sometimes. I guess Ryan is too long. Listen, Milo, if you have time to go over to my place, that is, my sister-in-law's place where I'm staying, I could throw a pack together and ride out to the ranch with you this afternoon. That way I could get a good early start in the morning. Could you put me up in the bunkhouse?"

"You bet," Milo answered. "I can show you around Saturday and Sunday too if you need more time. There's always somebody coming back to town about every night so you don't have to worry about a ride home."

As they slid out of the booth Ryan nearly collided with a lovely auburn haired woman only an inch shorter than his own five foot ten inch height who brushed rapidly by with a preoccupied look on her pale face. He started to apologize but realized that she had not even been aware of him. Obviously, her mind was fixed on more important matters than dining room traffic.

"That's her Honor the Mayor of this village. Name's Colorado Winston and they say she is usually friendlier than Hector's pup," Milo whispered, as she hurried up to the cash register ahead of them.

"I'd vote for her every time," Ryan murmured to himself.

WORK HAZARDS

Early on a cool beautiful Saturday morning Ryan and Milo rode out of D-Z headquarters, starting their horses up a narrow man-made switchback trail towards the top of Red Rock Rim. They were full of bacon and eggs and biscuits to a state of repletion unaccustomed by Ryan, though Milo had put away at least twice as much.

Yesterday afternoon they had made an easy trip from town to the D-Z on dusty county roads in the old flatbed truck. Crown's wood framed ranch house was built in a grove of aspen, cottonwoods and ponderosa pine against the foot of a towering rock wall, near where a year-around spring flowed 2000 gallons per minute of pure icy water in an unfaltering stream. The barn, shop, bunkhouse and other outbuildings were unobtrusively placed among the trees close to the big house.

The final six miles of the drive was through D-Z property where Milo pointed to fields of irrigated pasture filled with fat steers. Milo told Ryan that Ballard had given orders to start trucking cattle down off the summer range on the Bench several weeks ago in an effort to hurry the animals to market. They were to begin shipping Monday because Crown had a feeling that several years of exceptionally high beef prices were about to give way to an inevitable economic down cycle. Milo informed Ryan that his boss was seldom wrong in these business assessments and had built a small fortune based on his hunches.

Ryan had felt like a character in a Zane Grey novel as Milo showed him to an army cot in the sleeping loft of the bunkhouse. There was a crew of twelve, including Milo and Ballard, who operated and maintained the ranges, trails, fences and animals of the seven thousand acre D-Z ranch. Six of the men were unmarried and lived in the headquarters bunkhouse. Ryan met Shorty, Pop, Cowboy, Louis, Raoul and a shock-haired youth called Squirrelly, whose dormitory home he invaded at Milo's invitation. As foreman or "Ramrod" of the outfit, Milo rated a tiny one-bedroom cabin in a row of similar residences that housed the other four married men and their families. One of these wives, a hearty, red-faced woman of thirty years named Heidi, was cookie for the bunkhouse men. The food, both for supper that night and for breakfast at dawn the next morning, was as good as it was plentiful.

The creak of leather and grunting snorts of climbing horses were occasionally seamed by the scream of a gracefully maneuvering red tail hawk cruising rising air currents on the face of the rim. The trail was comfortably wide enough for two; cut in solid sandstone cliff face for much of the hairpin passage upwards.

"There's three trails up like this one," Milo commented. "In the old days they used to drive whole herds of cattle up and down these chutes because there was no other way up to the Bench where the summer grass is at. Now-a-days we truck 'em up or down Shovel Creek road twenty miles south of here, or through Framboise Creek Canyon on Palmer ranch which is just a couple of miles over that way," Milo gestured northward along the rock face.

"Have you ever noticed any outcrop of coal or layers of black strata around the area?" Ryan asked. "I think there is a good possibility that Wyoming will prove to be a rich source of coal. In fact, that's partly what brought me over here from Colorado. There is a big market, right now, for additional coal supplies for power generation. I have a notion there may be a lot of it in this very area"

"Nope, I haven't run across anything like that as I can remember. I tell you, though, I never took much interest in the rocks. Maybe you can teach me something"

"Well, it's a big country and it looks like you can see most it from right here," Ryan admired.

The view was almost that from an aircraft as they worked higher and higher up the cliff. The burnt umber prairie rolled outward below them, growing lighter in the distance until merging almost imperceptibly with the white sky of early morning. Ryan read millions of years of history in exposed layers of rock. Mostly hard yellow and red sandstone, the rim was interbedded with thick layers of shale and coarse gravels which eroded at varying rates, forming narrow benches and shallower slopes at intervals along the steep climb. At one point about half way up, there was a sheer ledge of gray limestone marking the ancient bed of a shallow inland sea. The limestone was only about twelve feet thick but formed an easily identifiable marker bed, which persisted in the cliff face as far as Ryan's eye could follow. As the geologist pointed out various physical features and described the creative processes by which they arose, Milo began to see the familiar landscape in ways he had never before recognized. It was an enjoyable trip for both men during which each discovered interesting and admirable resources within the other.

They reached the Bench at an early hour, then swiftly covered an additional four miles over the sloping, eroded rangeland. The Big Horn peaks, rising before the two riders, sparkled crystalline epaulets of snow on furrowed purple shoulders. The mountains appeared to be much closer than they actually were.

When they arrived at the broad shallow canyon, which was the site of the proposed stock watering pond, Ryan went to work. He unpacked a Brunton compass with which to measure angle of dip from the horizontal and direction of strike of exposed rock formations, a geology hammer with long chipping point, cloth sample bags and a triple lens magnifying glass for examining rock specimens. He carried a hardbound notebook in which he scratched meticulous notes as he methodically moved over the area. He knew the exact length of his normal comfortable stride and so measured accurate distances by counting steps. He filled half a dozen small cotton bags with gravel and rock chips from various locations; drew an accurate map of the visible features and then climbed up to the highest knoll at the edge of the dry watercourse. He sat quietly studying the whole panorama as his mind extended the view to ribbed bones and marrow of rock structures beneath the surface of the earth.

After about ten minutes he collected his equipment and strolled over to a twisted old juniper tree where Milo rested easily, whittling on a thick stem of sagebrush. The two horses were placidly grazing nearby where Milo had staked them out with his braided leather riata.

"Not going to be an easy task, Milo," Ryan said. "This gravel is well washed with very few fine particles to make it impermeable. Water runs through it like a sack of marbles so I'm not surprised you had a washout. Even if the small dam had not washed away, all the water would have leaked out of the reservoir. I'm going to have to study these samples but I've done about all I need to for the time being."

Milo glanced at the sun instead of his watch. "It's barely ten o'clock, my friend, and you're done already. I'll tell you what, I've got a couple of bamboo fly rods in my pack and we're only about two miles from some of the best trout fishing in Wyoming. Let's head over to Framboise Creek and pull out a few brookies for lunch."

They mounted up and moved northward across low ridges and shallow valleys. Several small herds of antelope were seen regarding them curiously from a distance with telescopic eyes or fleeing at startling speed if approached too closely. There were abundant flocks of big gray sage grouse, which moved slowly and stupidly aside as the walking horses passed.

"How do these birds survive?" Ryan asked. "They don't appear to have good sense."

"They don't seem too bright," Milo agreed, "but Mama Nature helps them out. They smell just like sagebrush which is about all they ever eat and they move slow and easy so they're mighty hard for hunting coyotes or bobcats to spot. They will fly, though, if somethin' spooks 'em."

It seemed like no time before the rumble and tumble of flowing water was heard, then seen, as they approached the rushing snow melt stream, hardly recognizable as the lazy little creek running through Sheila's Tree some thirty miles to the east.

Hungry trout snapped at their floating lures. Within five minutes they caught several fat, brilliantly mottled Eastern Brook trout with distinctive, white edged belly fins.

"Holy smoke, Milo, this stream is full of them. We're going to have to quit or else file the barbs off the hooks," Ryan expostulated happily.

"They're not too big," Milo nodded in agreement, "but plenty of action. Doesn't seem to matter what fly you use, these babies grab everything that comes down the stream."

They continued to fish downstream, releasing the fish and taking turns walking the horses along the grassy bank. After a busy and absorbing hour Ryan could hear a louder, deeper rumble above the normal splash of running water.

"We're coming to Garnet Falls at the head of Palmer Canyon. The falls are only about sixty feet high but in the spring when there is more water in the creek she really boils and thunders," Milo said. "We can get down a horse trail on this side or else cross over and take the Pass Road. It's a well-graded gravel road all the way through the canyon and into town from here. Palmer ranch has it fenced, of course, but lots of people drive up on the Bench this way and Winston usually doesn't object. They lock the gates up, though, in the fall so hunters can't pour through."

"You mean we can get back to the D-Z this way?" Ryan asked.

"Sure. We just ride out the canyon; turn right at the foot of the rim and we're only about five miles from the ranch," Milo replied. "I'll tell you something else. Below the falls there are some nice size Rainbow and Brown trout in the pools of the canyon. Doesn't get fished much but I got permission to go in there any time. Wait until you hit one of those five pounders! These little ol' pan size Brookies are fun but they're only a warm-up for the lunkers in the canyon."

In August the volume of water over the falls was near its annual minimum but still produced a beautiful and inspiring spectacle. A smooth sheet of water twenty five feet wide flowed over a flat sandstone ledge, descending sixty feet in shimmering white streaked veils to a catch basin of boiling, smoking water. As they led the horses carefully down a narrow, muddy trail into the mossy, cool canyon depth, a rising plume of atomized water particles hung overhead. The luminous cloud of vapor scintillated with spangled rainbows of dispersed sunlight. Crashing tons of water made conversation impossible but an appreciative Ryan could think of no appropriate comment, anyway. The humid, protected environment of the canyon floor encouraged rank growth of ferns, wild grape vines, reeds and willow trees along the confined borders of the stream.

When they reached the floor of the canyon Milo motioned Ryan to make a cast into the foaming milky water of the circular caldron at the base of the falls near its overflowing outlet. The tiny artificial lure hardly dimpled the surface of the pool when a silvery trout flashed at the surface of the water. It was a thick-bodied Rainbow; the largest Ryan had ever had on a rod. He gently pulled upwards to set the hook in the bony ridges of the fish's jaw then grunted in dismay as the line tautened sharply, then snapped with a twang easily heard over the roaring water. Ryan had forgotten to loosen the drag on his reel after tightening it down previously when his hook caught on the rocky floor of the creek. This large fish had hardly exerted itself in breaking the four-pound test monofilament leader on its first run for freedom. Milo rocked with laughter at the ambiguous expression of amazement and disappointment on Ryan's face.

"Ol' Granddad took lure and all," Milo chuckled. "Lots more in the pools on down from here," he shouted, motioning Ryan to take the trail away from the falls.

Since they were both fishing the same side of the stream, Milo let Ryan start out several minutes ahead. He was more familiar with physical features of the creek and believed that he would be able to work some hiding places that Ryan might miss. The geologist, an experienced outdoorsman, was having the time of his life. The staccato shriek of a belted kingfisher winging swiftly down the watercourse and the bobbing figure of a little gray American dipper diving in and out of the foaming creek were welcome sights and sound in the beautiful isolated canyon. Ryan had caught and released several large fish when he came to a minor division in the flowing water. The main stream eroded a wide gap through the gray limestone marker bed which Ryan had observed earlier in the morning but a resistant core of rock diverted a portion of the stream to the side and across the slanting surface of the smooth, hard streambed. The smaller flow had worn a concave trough some twenty feet long in the sloping rock floor which led down to a vertical fall of eight or ten feet into a pool below the ledge. Ryan could see the top of a spreading willow tree peeking over the shelf of lime rock but the drop-off obscured his view of the pool below. There was less than a foot of water in the trough-like streambed, however it raced with great velocity down the slippery chute. Leading his horse across the limestone shelf, Ryan decided to cross the smaller stream in favor of following the main watercourse. With one negligent foot placement the world turned upside down. Both feet went flailing from under him on the slick, wet rock. Grasping desperately for the horse's reins to catch his balance, Ryan crashed to the ground and rolled on his back into the shallow, rushing water. The bottom of the narrow channel was covered with an alga growth that lubricated the rock surface more effectively than axle grease. He lay in the water half stunned with blood spreading over his face from a contusion on his forehead, careening backwards, headfirst, down the water slide on his way to the waiting pool below.

CATTLE RANCHING AND THE OL' SWIMMING HOLE

Collie and Juno sat in comfortable lawn chairs at a patio table drinking strong, aromatic coffee. The Saturday morning sun was making an appearance over tall canyon walls which rose in many hued cliffs and wooded slopes above the Palmer ranch buildings. A western meadowlark triple tongued his effortless melody to the cloudless blue sky. The two women had been up for some time but had slept considerably later than usual for either one. With small talk behind them conversation begin to turn towards that area which Juno and Ballard had previously rehearsed in hopes of alerting Collie to their growing fears about mismanagement of the ranch. Ballard, especially, felt obligated by long friendship and the best of intentions to come forward. It was not a common thing for friends to pry into each other's business, but, feeling that Delvane's inability, so obvious to Ballard, warranted an intrusion on neighborly privacy, Crown had hit upon sending Juno to have a serious woman to woman discussion. As a diplomatic, if somewhat obvious ploy, the game was working. Collie found Juno to be both knowledgeable and sympathetic, besides bearing practical advice.

"I know what Ballard's opinion is of many of Delvane's decisions," Collie said, "but, honestly, there was good sense in improving our herd and range land."

"I agree completely," Juno replied. "I have seen the benefit of improved breeding pay off for many ranchers in the last few years. I think Delvane's trouble may be tactical rather than strategic, if you know what I mean?"

"The long range ideas are fine but the way we carried them out leaves something to be desired?" Collie asked.

"Exactly, at least that is Ballard's opinion and he has heard quite a lot of critical talk among the men."

"But Juno, look at this place. Does it look run down or neglected?" Collie asked rhetorically.

The buildings were all in good repair and freshly painted, as were hundreds of feet of whitewashed wooden horse fences separating pastures and lining driveways among the outbuildings. Grass and shrubbery beds were neatly mowed, trimmed and tended so that the headquarters yard was more typical of a Kentucky racehorse farm than a working Wyoming cattle ranch.

Juno smiled in agreement. "It is beautiful. There was never a more lovely setting, with the creek running by and the trees and the hay meadows. . it looks like a storybook place."

"It was so wonderful to grow up here," Collie gazed about. "E.L. almost raised me until he died when I was twelve. I spent all my time riding and exploring and working the cattle. My poor Mama hardly ever saw me once I got saddle-broke. Mama came from Denver, Colorado before she married Daddy. She was the one that named me. She said I was going to be a little reminder of home for her. She learned to love this ranch more than any of us, I think. The hardest part of growing up, for me, was learning to be a town girl."

"Do you suppose that's why Delvane wanted you to come up and look things over this weekend?" Juno asked. "I think he respects your judgment and needs your help more than he is ready to admit."

"He was so aggressive and positive when we took over the ranch after the plane crash that I felt I had to back away," Collie replied. "I made my decision to continue working in town and got out of his way with regard to the ranch. He really would not tolerate any advice or suggestion from me, Juno, so the best thing was to find an interest elsewhere. After I won the election in 1951 I was too busy to bother Delvane anymore. He did share his activities and plans to a large degree, however, so I believed the ranch was doing well. You really can't imagine how upset I was yesterday when all these problems came to light."

She appeared uncomfortably close to tears, though that was an emotional relief seldom indulged by Collie. Tears of sympathy or joy brightened her eyes on many occasions but she despised self-pity or despair.

Corvey Hansen, one of Palmer's cowhands, brought two mounts up the driveway from the barn and stable complex.

"Here's General all rarin' to go, Miss Collie, an' I got ol' Rollo saddled up for Miz Castle." The gray bearded old cowpuncher had been a member of the Palmer outfit since before Collie's birth in 1923.

"Thank you, Corvey," Collie smiled gratefully. "Guess you think I'm too soft to toss a saddle for myself these days?"

"Hell, Miz Collie, we're all a bunch of Goddamned daisy farmers around here nowadays!" He shook his head sadly. "It aint like it was in the good ol' days."

General did remember Collie, prancing and bridling sideways in anticipation as she lifted smoothly into the saddle. The big gelding immediately took the bit low towards the ground, crowhopping stiffly several times to see if she were really well seated on his powerful back. Collie laughed delightedly as she swung her body in perfect easy rhythm with the horse's movements, then gently pulled his head up and pranced to a stop beside the more orderly Rollo. The two women cantered away at an easy gallop, backs straight, hair ruffled in the wind, both completely at home and comfortable as they rode up the canyon.

The day was a long series of disappointing revelations and discoveries for Collie. They were hardly out of sight of the ranch house when she began to see subtle signs of neglect and disrepair. The upper hay meadows were patched with fluffy ranks of invading Canadian thistle which crowded out grass hay and used up valuable soil moisture. She remembered the long streamside benches as grassy fields completely free of noxious weed growth. Fences were down in some places allowing nondescript range bulls to get in with purebred Shorthorn cows whereupon they were not reticent in making friends with the pedigreed ladies. There would have to be a rigorous culling at next year's spring roundup to maintain purity of the herd registry. Examination of two irrigation pumps used to lift water from the creek to higher pastures on the flanks of the canyon floor showed signs of neglect. Small oil reservoirs, which kept bearings lubricated, had been allowed to run dry and a magpie nest provided stuffing for an open electrical control panel on one pump.

Worst of all to Collie's eyes were tall hedges of lacy water hemlock topped with flat umbels of tiny white flowers growing profusely along the wet stream bank. Her Grandfather had told Collie how the juice of this plant had been used in 399 BC for execution of the Athenian philosopher, Socrates. Collie was sure the deadly plant was responsible for the loss of more than one head of stock.

As the pattern became more and more clear, Collie felt a demoralizing wave of recognition force its way into her consciousness. A long repressed realization about her husband seemed to crystallize into a fully developed idea, as if her unconscious mind had been aware and working for a long time. The ranch is just like Del, she thought, manicured and handsome with painted fences and colorful landscaping, but neglected and beginning to spoil from the inside. It's a perfect reflection of him. She was ashamed of the thought but pursued it grimly. He has been drinking too much for a long time and all those trips to Laramie, Denver and San Francisco were evasions of responsibility—not business. He was never really ready to take over the ranch and become a working manager like Daddy or Ballard. I loved him for what I thought I saw. We were so long apart during the war and he was so brave and handsome...I never really knew him, she confessed to herself at last.

None of these sad thoughts were shared with Juno but her companion could see a growing awareness and impatience in the younger woman, which was not difficult to interpret.

By early afternoon they were far up the canyon and had seen more than enough to satisfy Collie's curiosity, while underscoring Ballard's warning. It was an unusually warm day even for August, making sweaty horses and flushed faces on the riders. They were hungry, thirsty, hot and Collie was emotionally drained.

"We're almost to the swimming hole, Juno. Have you ever come up here before?" Collie asked.

"I haven't been this far up the canyon on horseback before, though I've driven through on Pass Road lots of times," Juno replied.

"Well, there's this hidden pool separated from the main stream by a hedge of willows and stinging nettles where I used to swim all the time. It's a perfect place for lunch and I could use a cool dip," Collie explained.

Thick cold chicken sandwiches, garlicky potato salad and a quart thermos of iced tea were soon laid out on a picnic cloth spread beneath the umbrella-like limbs of a shaggy willow tree. A small waterfall cascaded over a twelve-foot high ledge on the upper end of the quiet pool as a flock of brilliant canary and black goldfinches trilled and fluttered through the brushy enclosure. A tiny yellow, black capped warbler busily worked among the branches of the willow unconcerned with human intruders.

"Oh, Collie, it's absolutely perfect. We might as well be in the Garden of Eden," Juno laughed happily.

Both women had folded their clothing neatly on the grassy bank and slipped into the cool, placid water. The floor was sandy, gradually sloping to a deeper channel down the middle.

"I've had so much fun here in the past," Collie reminisced. "There's a long natural rock slide on the ledge above just like a carnival ride. I've spent hours climbing up that little trail."

As she pointed upward at the lip of the rocky ledge a flailing apparition sailed over the edge of the waterfall, catapulting with a mighty splash between the two startled women. Juno took two swift strokes and hit the shore running. She swooped up her clothes and disappeared into the brush before Ryan ever broke the surface of the water. Collie was on the wrong side and had further to go. The man bobbed up in front of her, blood streaming down his face, which displayed a dazed, uncomprehending stare from wide open eyes. As she started to speak he again sank pliantly beneath the water without a struggle. Collie did not have to dive under. She grabbed the back of his shirt, clearly seen in the transparent water, and quickly pulled his sodden weight up to the edge of the pool.

"Juno help me, he's hurt," she gasped, struggling to drag him out on the bank. She picked up a bandanna with which to wipe blood and water from his face. His eyes were open but he seemed stunned and in shock as he lay unmoving. Collie was completely unaware of her own condition, bending over the man, feeling for pulse in his neck and wondering frantically how badly he was damaged. She would have been in shock herself had she known what was going through Ryan Baker's mind as her bare breast swayed inches above his face. He was not at all sure he had not died and gone on to some Houri-inhabited Heaven.

Don't let anything change, he thought,…just keep still and nothing will change…as she knotted the sodden bandanna about his injured forehead.

Suddenly Collie realized she was looking into a very aware and conscious pair of hazel eyes. Despite her embarrassment and a belated rush of modesty, she almost burst out laughing at the melting expression of awe in those same eyes. She calmly gathered her clothing and walked behind the willow tree leaving the wounded Ryan to roll over groaning and coughing for breath.

Milo and Juno broke upon the scene simultaneously; he crashing through the brushy hedge from the main trail with two balky horses in tow; she from the tall growth on the opposite side of the pool, scratched and disheveled but fully dressed. Ryan was standing by the water's edge disconsolately wringing out his shirt and glancing apprehensively towards the willow tree.

"What the Hell happened, Man? You okay?" Milo barked. Ryan's forehead was still oozing blood from under the blue bandanna.

"Yeah, yeah, I'm fine now. Frankly, Milo, I don't really have a clear idea what did happen." Ryan's look of comical puzzlement was somewhat reassuring.

"What in the world are you doing here, Milo Harris?" Juno stood akimbo, frowning at both men.

Milo, finally catching his breath and equanimity, swept off his Stetson and made a small bow of greeting.

"Miss Castle, it's a great pleasure to see you again. My friend and I were fishing and I reckon he figured to take a little swim." Milo was unaware that the women had also been in the water.

"Sorry to interrupt your lunch," Milo apologized, looking at the picnic spread.

Collie strolled around the tree, a picture of refreshed loveliness with everything in place and perfectly arranged. Her short hair was clustered in tight, damp curls but otherwise she looked as if she had just stepped off the train.

"Who is this drowned rat that has come floating down my canyon, Mr. Harris?" she smiled sweetly at Ryan.

Ryan stood bare chested with the twisted shirt dangling from his hands, staring at Collie as if she were the reincarnation of Helen of Troy. It was obvious that he was totally incapable of speaking for himself. Juno began to giggle, quietly at first, then in uncontrollable waves and spasms. Milo did not have a clue to the humor of the situation but it was easy to see that there were no hard feelings, at least.

"May I present Mr. Ryan Baker of Colorado, Mrs. Winston? Mr. Baker is setting up in Sheila's Tree as a geological consultant and we are on a business excursion today for Ballard Crown," Milo explained.

"A bu-bu-business excursion?" Juno strangled, "Oh my God!"

Collie walked up to Ryan with perfect composure and extended her hand.

"I'm charmed to make your acquaintance Mr. Baker. We must see more of each other in the future."

As he dumbly stuck out his hand and shook in robot-like jerks, the howls of Juno Castle echoed in the secluded glen.

The four sat down on the shaded riverbank to share lunch and laugh again at the lucky, for Ryan, accident of their unexpected encounter. Ryan soon felt comfortably a part of the group, acknowledging a forgiving smile from Collie with a rueful grin of his own. Conversation moved with the flow of exchanged views and ideas from a discussion of the colorful pageantry surrounding Queen Elizabeth II's coronation, to a critical commentary by Ryan on Hemingway's latest novel, The Old Man and the Sea, to a marvelous description by Milo Harris of the successful climb of Mount Everest by Edmond Hillary and Tenzing Norkay. All four proved to be literate and expressive on topics of individual and mutual interest. Collie and Ryan found themselves repeatedly in agreement on most of the issues that came up so each thought the other exceptionally perceptive and well informed. For the first time in many hours Collie was laughing and relaxed with financial and marital clouds drifting at the back of her mind.

She was very interested in Milo's opinions and perspective on the subjects under discussion because she rarely, if ever, had the opportunity to converse casually and in candor with a black person. There were very few Negroes living and working in Wyoming. She made an effort to draw him out.

"Did you serve in the military during the war, Mr. Harris? she asked, following a comment by Ryan on his own Navy tour in the Aleutian Islands. Everyone knew "the war" meant World War II, not the Korean conflict currently dominating the radio news reports.

"No Ma'am, I didn't. I was one of those 4-F slackers who stayed home with the girls," he smiled but with a hint of chagrin at the admission. "I had a foot injury as a kid and couldn't pass the military physical."

Ryan and the two women looked expectantly as if encouraging further expression so Milo decided to go ahead and narrate a short version of his personal history.

"Well, I was brought up by my Mama in Oakland, California. There was six of us living in a two-room apartment and, thinking back, I don't know how the poor woman managed to keep us all going. My two older brothers brought in some cash once-in-a-while but mostly we lived off her little wages and a welfare check. One day when I was about fifteen my oldest brother, Jonaldo, sneaked a six pack of beer home when Mama was out. I swiped a bottle when he wasn't looking and took it out on our little balcony to drink. He caught me and we started scuffling and next thing you know I got pitched over the balcony and fell about twenty feet to the alley. I probably would have been OK but I bounced off a big ol' iron trash bin then hit the concrete. It broke a bunch of those little bones in both feet. The right foot healed up fine but the left one kind of toed in and turned over instead of healing straight. It was three months before I could walk again and then I got physical therapy for a long time and all kinds of wedges and braces in my shoes for years. I still wear built up arches in my left boot but I'm perfectly good to go now. Anyhow, that therapist, Eddie Whallin, who worked with me for almost a year, he came from up at Worland, and all I heard was how beautiful Wyoming was and how friendly the folks were. I got to reading stuff about cowboys and Indians and the many Negroes who made a name for themselves in the early days on the frontier as scouts and cowboys. By the time I was about eighteen I just pulled up and hitchhiked out for Worland to see if it was anything like Eddie described it. I guess it kind of was. They were so short of men, then, 1943 was the year, that I got a job out at Mrs. Corpening's Flying W even though I had never even been on a horse before. You talk about a city kid being out of his element—I never knew which end was up for a good while."

"Why, I know Julia Corpening well," said Juno. "I see her at the Cattlemen's convention every year down in Cheyenne."

Milo continued. "I was willing to work and first thing you know this ol' Indian named Fatback Red Feather took me under his wing and started teaching me the trade. He showed me how to give a horse confidence and how to treat cows like friends. After a while I got so I could ride and rope with the best of them. I didn't realize it but ol' Fatback taught me a lot of natural history and biology and botany all at the same time. During the next four years he gave me a real good post-graduate course in cowboying. Eventually I found out Fatback had a powerful weakness for DeKuyper Creme de Menthe. Real late one night he was all drunked up driving his old Dodge flatbed out to the ranch and wrapped it around a railroad overpass abutment doing about fifty miles an hour. It was almost like losing a Daddy for me. I sure was broken up about it and ended by taking off from the Flying W for good. By then, though, I loved the work and knew I couldn't go back out to California. I came down here to Sheila's Tree and got a job with Ballard Crown and fit right in at the D-Z. He and I seemed to hit it off real good from the start. When Dennis Enright, Ballard's foreman, got retired by a violent run-in with an unsociable ol' range bull a few years back, Ballard made me Ramrod and I been happy as a clam ever since. I guess that's a lot more than you wanted to hear, Miz Winston," Milo flashed a self-deprecating smile.

"I must say that's an interesting and creative way of finding your vocation," Collie answered, "and I have heard you are very good at what you do."

When the time came to pack up and ride home there was a feeling of comradeship and easy understanding between the four picnickers. Bantering and chatting, they walked their horses over a shallow ford through the stream, across a narrow hayfield and up to Pass Road. The miles passed quickly, soon bringing them within sight of tall Lombardy poplars and ponderosa pine surrounding Palmer Ranch headquarters near the mouth of the canyon.

At the top of the final pasture they overtook a walking figure loaded down with a bulky back pack, dusty and perspiring but with a vigorous, almost bouncing, stride.

"How much is that doggie in the window? Woof, woof! That dog with the waggily tail…," The walker sang lustily and surprisingly on key. He gave them a wide toothy grin and generous wave as they rode along side. The long shanked scruffy walker recognized Collie, having seen her picture often in the Galena Daily Journal.

"Howdy, Miz Winston. My old truck is parked on your line fence down below the Rim. I'm just takin' the easy way out, havin' hiked in the back way," he explained his presence.

"You are welcome to use the road," Collie nodded. "Looks like you have quite a load there." It was almost a question.

He glanced at each of them, then smiled disarmingly and swung the pack down with a shrug. "Just some moss agate and pretty rocks I picked up on the Bench, Miz Winston. Don't amount to nothin'"

"You look tired," Collie observed. "I'll send Corvey up with the pickup when we get to the ranch. He will give you a ride out to your truck."

"Oh Lordy love you Miz Winston, I'm plumb obliged to you. I am about tuckered out and in a hurry to get back to town, too. My name is Tom Regelstorp, Ma'am, an' I won't be forgettin' your kindness."

"You are welcome. Just sit tight for a few minutes and you will be on your way," Collie replied, as the group rode on towards the ranch.

"That guy was in a mighty good mood," Milo commented. "Acted like he had Dark Star at twenty-five to one in the Derby." Milo had bet on Native Dancer. . .

"He wasn't just a casual rockhound," Ryan said. "That was an expensive Geiger counter on his belt. He is another of these uranium fanatics looking under every rock in the West. Too bad he hasn't got a counter to sniff out coal deposits. That is where the mining future of Wyoming is going to be."

Ryan and Milo bid goodbye to the ladies and cantered on towards the mouth of the canyon where Framboise Creek, emerging at last from Red Rock Rim, wandered onto the prairie in search of the Powder River. Ryan, unaccustomed to horseback riding; his head throbbing painfully, began to look forward to arrival at the D-Z and a long, hot shower. He was also having a great deal of trouble trying to think of something other than the enchanting image of a tall, auburn haired beauty disappearing around the knarled trunk of an old willow tree.

STAKING THE
CANTEEN CLAIMS

Days following his discovery were busy times for Tom Regelstorp. He spent the next day, untypically, in his tiny apartment absorbed in plans for carrying out his dream. Conversations with Ringo, a wiry tiger striped tomcat, honed his thoughts.

"First off we got to get some claims staked out over that uranium rock. I'll need a batch of two by fours about five feet long with points hatched on 'em so's they can be drove in for claim corners and a bunch of Prince Albert cans to hang up my discovery notices. Better get me a compass and Government quadrangle map so's I can make some kind of a location. Listen Ringo, how'm I gonna get them samples assayed? You reckon I could mail 'em off to the University at Laramie, or where?...We got to keep this quiet, cat!" Glancing about as if searching for listening ears, he poured a saucer of pasteurized milk from a glass dairy bottle for the cat and a muddy, black cup of coffee for himself.

"Oh don't you know we're shittin' in tall cotton now?" he leaned back in the old wooden kitchen chair with eyes closed ecstatically. "I'm goin' back to Paris, France and look for some of them Mamzells that were so glad to see us."

He had spent the most memorable night of his life in the arms of a young French girl shortly after the World War II liberation. Tom could think of nothing more valuable on which to spend the untold riches he expected to harvest from the uranium find. Regelstorp was geared for the search, however, not the finding. He had read adventure pulps about exotic mineral discoveries yielding fabulous fortunes overnight from the jungles of Brazil or the Colorado plateau. Regelstorp knew how to stake and file a legal mining claim but had no conception of how to proceed with development after that. Uranium was an unusually difficult mineral to deal with. Few were familiar with mineralogy or characteristics of its natural occurrence in the earth, let alone mining and processing techniques. The industry was too new. Tom was not aware that mining, refining and marketing of the radioactive metal were all tightly controlled by the United States Government through the Atomic Energy Commission. Tom's deficiencies might soon be exposed but he glowed all day Sunday in the warmth and wonder of having his dreams come true.

He happily quit his job at the Big Pine Cafe by the simple method of not showing up for work at 5:00 AM on Monday morning. Instead of reporting at his griddle, Tom drove over to Copeland Lumber Yard and filled the back of the truck with pointed two by four posts. Next stop was the Safeway store where he purchased twenty cans of Prince Albert pipe tobacco, carefully placing the contents into an empty coffee can at home. Other purchases at various stores in town were groceries, beer, a map, compass, heavy waterproof paper and a six-pound sledgehammer. By noon he was driving up Pass Road on his way to the Bench.

The lode mining claims were staked in approximately twenty-acre rectangles measuring six hundred feet wide by fifteen hundred feet long. A stake was pounded in at each corner and a discovery monument built close to the center of each claim. The discovery monument was another stake driven in the ground with a small cairn of rocks piled up around it. A tin tobacco can, serving as a note repository, was nailed to the discovery stake. A folded note of waterproof paper in the Prince Albert can contained information about the mining claim and would remain at the discovery point of each parcel so that no one else could come along and over-stake or dispute ownership of the claimed area. The same information was later taken to the County courthouse in Sheila's Tree to be legally recorded for a small fee. The discovery notice contained the date; location, based on Section, Township and Range, if known, or simply distance and compass direction to a recognizable landmark; the name and approximate dimensions of the claim and finally the signature of the claimant.

Tom returned to the well-remembered radioactive hot spot, building his first discovery monument close by. He named the first mining claim Canteen One, then proceeded to stake out twenty more claims in the shape of a huge cross. One arm of the cross covered the axis of the dry wash in which the discovery had been made; the other arm striking at right angle from the point of the find. He staked out Canteen One through Canteen Twenty-one with the material he had brought along, taking five days of hard labor. The layout plan was systematic but, of course, unrelated to physical occurrence of a possible ore body because Tom possessed no such knowledge. He found no further indications of radioactivity. After returning to town and filing on the claims at the county courthouse with John Steen, Galena County Recorder, Tom began to run out of ideas. The radioactive fragments of sandstone that he had chipped out on discovery day still lay undisturbed in his knap sack. He possessed mineral rights to four hundred acres of National Forest land, which might or might not contain an economical ore body but his cash supply was down to thirty-two dollars and a brass teapot full of pennies.

"Cat, I reckon what we need is a partner. Somebody we can trust, for damn sure, who kind of knows what's what with this here uranium game." He was leafing through the Galena Daily Journal looking for Alley Oop and Ooola. The word, uranium, leaped out of an article headline on the business activity page. URANIUM MONEY PROMOTES GOLF DEVELOPMENT. The story was a fawning tribute to local real estate developer, George Frailey, who was promoter of the Sheila's Tree Country Club and Golf Course development. The newspaper listed fairway lots available starting at two thousand dollars. Frailey's business acumen and philanthropy were lauded in the story, which recounted his investment in New Mexico Mining Corporation on the advice of his brother-in-law who was an officer in the company. Having generated a small fortune in stock profits, Mr. Frailey was eager to turn a larger one from real estate in Sheila's Tree. Besides qualifying George Frailey as humanitarian of the year, the newspaper article also described his close ties by marriage and investment with the uranium industry. Tom Regelstorp read the answer to his problems.

ADVENTURES AT THE COUNTRY CLUB

Collie Winston drove her Plymouth to the country club grand opening. Delvane was late getting to town from the ranch but had promised to dress and meet her in time for the banquet. He remained self-righteous and defensive at her recital of deficiencies following the weekend inspection of the ranch. There had been no compromise or offered solution to their problems. Collie would not agree to the bank mortgage but she could not find an alternative either. Worse yet, there was no satisfactory communication with Del. A wall had been built stone on stone almost without notice since the early days of confrontation over management of the ranch. His absences had gotten longer as the months passed until Collie finally found herself uncomfortable and crowded on the infrequent occasions spent together in her double bed. She was used to sleeping alone but missed their former intimacy and regretted growing isolation and indifference.

I love the spotlight of political office and public activity more than I love Del, she thought guiltily. When this term is over I'll become the kind of helpmate a man deserves. As Juno said, Del needs my support and help, not criticism.

Juno had said no such thing but Collie was casting among the ashes of self-blame and guilt for perspective and identification of her role in their personal problems. She was a bemused young woman, not at all comfortable with seldom-experienced insecurity and confusion.

She pulled into the spacious parking lot, already half full of chrome-bright, finned monsters. The simply designed natural stone building consisted of a pro shop with double locker rooms on one wing and a banquet room and large bar on the other, overlooking a tranquil embayment of Chopstick reservoir. There was a full kitchen, newly staffed and prepared to open for public dining after the evening dedication ceremony.

Collie checked her short fur jacket and walked into the milling, chatting crowd. She felt the warmth of familiarity and belonging among these people. She had known almost every one since childhood or at least since returning home from college six years ago. John Delaney, operator of Eternal Rest Gardens and his wife Naomi were standing with the banker, Orville Smith and his wife, Julia, and Dr. Gregory Smith, Eye, Ear, Nose and Throat, and his wife, Rosalie. Denton Eldring and his wife, Leah Anne, were also part of the group. Eldring was a flamboyant young lawyer who was making a great name for himself with several notable cases that were getting attention far beyond the city limits of Sheila's Tree. The group was discussing the next dinner and bridge party for their monthly social to be hosted by the Delaneys. Both male Smiths, in no way related to each other, were on the City Council and greeted Collie warmly.

"Isn't it a lovely building?" commented Naomi Delaney. It was the standard opener for the evening, not really a question.

"Sheila's Tree is catching up with the Joneses," Collie smiled.

"I'd say we have probably passed most of the Joneses at two hundred and fifty bucks a membership," frowned Dr. Smith. "You would think they could have a tennis court for that kind of money."

"And there's not even a card room for my ladies pinochle group," lamented his wife, Rosalie. "The Elks club over at Casper has all that in their lodge and the dues are cheaper than this."

The banker, Orville Smith, put his arm around Collie and patted her shoulder. "Our little Mayor has done her best on this one, Greg, as you well know. She took my advice and got this development annexed into the city limits two years ago." He smiled pompously, "Now Collie, where's that husband of yours? He was supposed to bring you around to the bank last week."

Though Collie was used to condescension from most of those with whom she dealt, this issue was a bit too personal for easy acquiescence.

"You are too kind, Orville. Delvane is going to be here in time for dinner; I'm sure he will find a spare minute for you. Oh, pardon me please. I must see Ray Crown over there, if you don't mind." She smiled at the circle and turned her back gracefully.

Raymond Crown, publisher of the Galena Daily Journal and owner of Crown Publishing Company, had brought Susan Baker to the dinner dance. They had been seen in company for several months so their association was old gossip by this time. Ryan Baker had come with them at Crown's invitation, although he had found an apartment of his own and was no longer staying with his ex sister-in-law. District Court Judge, Vincent Kerby, was also a member of the group, which parted to include Collie at her approach.

"Isn't it a lovely building?" commented Susan with the icebreaker.

"It is a nice facility. I hope the food is good," Collie responded. "We could use another good place besides the Bull Run."

"Good evening, Mrs. Winston," Ryan Baker smiled boyishly. "May I get you something to drink?"

Collie suddenly realized it was Ryan she had come to see in this group. "My goodness, Ryan, surely we are on first names after last weekend. I can't think when I've enjoyed a picnic or swim more." This time her smile was genuine and happy.

"Yes, please, a nice martini with plenty of vermouth."

Ryan turned rapidly towards the bar as a flush darkened his sun-tanned face. A slight abrasion could still be seen on his forehead.

Betty Spielman stuck her head in the spot vacated by Ryan.

"You know why the Little Moron stood on the corner of Hollywood and Vine waving two slices of bread?" she asked winsomely. Little Moron jokes were in vogue. "He was waiting for the traffic jam," she squealed with laughter. "Isn't that too cute? My daughter, Connie, told me it yesterday."

She was a petite, brunette woman of thirty-six who had never retired from the highschool pep squad. Her husband, Bill Spielman, was a construction contractor who spent eighty percent of his time out of town on business. Betty spent most of her time looking for excitement.

Ray Crown glanced at Susan with a wicked grin and then addressed Betty. "I heard a great Knock-Knock joke the other day, Betty. You start."

Betty giggled happily, "Okay. Knock, knock!"

Crown looked very attentive and delivered the ritual, "Who's there?"

A long pause ensued as the group waited for the punch line response from Betty which she was, of course, unprepared to deliver. Betty stammered confusedly setting a personal record for silence. "Oh, Raymond, you old ass!" she spluttered.

Ryan returned with the drinks as everyone was recovering from extended laughter. Even Betty had joined in at last, though not with her usual energetic gusto.

"Mr. Baker, you associate with a group of cruel hoaxers," She tapped his chest familiarly, though they had never been introduced, and whirled away into the crowd.

"Here you are Collie," Ryan handed her the drink. "Two olives."

"Oh yes," Judge Kerby raised grizzled eyebrows in a deadpan glance at Collie, "this Kinsey fellow claims olives are a potent aphrodisiac. That's why Spain and California are both becoming overpopulated."

Collie had only heard radio commentary on the recently published <u>Kinsey Report on Sexual Behavior of the Human Female</u>. Susan Baker, a highschool Home Economics teacher, had already studied the book thoroughly.

"Judge Kerby, it says nothing of the kind," Susan admonished. "It certainly says lots of other things, however, equally unbelievable to me. I bet half those folks they interviewed just made up the wildest stories they could imagine."

"My guess is that if we are ignorant of group norms in any area it would be sexual behavior," Ryan commented stiltedly.

Crown chuckled, "We three are damned poor representatives of the average male." He glanced at Ryan and the elderly Judge. "Only Vince has been married and he had the good fortune to gain his freedom long ago."

Actually, the Kerby split-up had scandalized the town back in 1929 before divorce was common. Vincent's wife had run away with an itinerant portrait painter, leaving the young lawyer to raise his sixteen-year-old daughter, Juno. His daughter's many accomplishments were one of the town's success stories.

Susan smiled to herself without comment. She had been married to Harlan Baker, Ryan's younger brother, for seven years before his death and had two children from the marriage. But she had never been so excited and sexually stimulated in her life before knowing Ray Crown. Though thirty years older than her former husband, the man had a power and sensuality that demanded her richest response. What fun it was!

"If nothing else, Dr. Kinsey has made a major contribution to cocktail conversation," Collie said.

Conversation flowed on in the smoke filled room. Jokes got funnier, voices more shrill and inhibitions relaxed. By the time dinner was served many of the guests had already drunk too much. Food slowed the process of inebriation somewhat but it resumed quickly after dinner. Collie's speech was short, spiced mostly by golf jokes, which were new to Sheila's Tree. Her main theme centered on progress achieved by the little city since the war and pointed towards goals of the future. She proclaimed the next milestone to be construction of a new City Hall and jail, both of which were currently shared with Galena County Government.

A plaque of walnut and bronze was presented to George Frailey in appreciation of his entrepreneurial talents in founding the country club facilities and he made a self-congratulatory speech of thanks. Delvane had breezed in towards the middle of dinner in a maroon dinner jacket, not behind anyone in alcohol consumption.

Frailey returned to his seat at the head table well pleased with the evening. He had two more prospective lot sales in the Country Club subdivision which, if closed, would put him months ahead of his tentative sales schedule. Money was already starting to come in and the town was pinning medals on him. He sat down beside Delvane Winston who was as dapper as ever but seemed more relaxed than usual.

"George old man, you're better at speeches than snooker." Delvane laughed and slapped him on the back a bit harder than necessary. "Bye the bye, I met an acquaintance of yours loading alfalfa pellets over at the feed mill the other day. You remember Toby Swanhunter, of course. Surprised you didn't mention him just now. He was sort of a business partner was he not? Or did you buy him out at a fair price, Frailey?" Delvane's face was close to Frailey's. He wore a deceptive grin but his eyes were dangerously narrowed and a high flush colored his cheek.

Delvane was drunk and belligerent enough to mention an aspect of the country club development that everyone was aware of but few were concerned about. The property had long been owned by an Arapaho Indian rancher named Toby Swanhunter who maintained a small cattle buying and feed lot operation. The two hundred-acre parcel, located close to highway 94 and the railroad on the bank of Chopstick reservoir, presented aesthetic problems for the city. The sight, sound, and smell of the feed yard had been a source of irritation at the front door of Sheila's Tree for years and grew constantly worse as the easterly limits of the city moved closer to the man made lake. Proprietorship by a Native American made the situation all the more intolerable. When Frailey was finally in a position to make a move, it was a simple matter to get Galena County officials, backed by the Real Estate Board and the County Health Department to pressure the operation out of business. Frailey bought the ground for a fraction of its value from the financially drained Swanhunter and immediately started the Country Club development. The community generally applauded the transaction except for a few like Delvane who had done business with Toby and admired his industry and honesty. Those attributes were seldom credited to Indian people whether deserved or not. In Delvane's eyes the bureaucratic contrivance that broke Swanhunter amounted to a monstrous injustice and his resentment had simmered subliminally for two years. Frailey's fatuous remarks coupled with several drinks too many brewed sudden truculence.

"Well, what of it, George?" Delvane demanded. "I don't see Toby here tonight. Maybe he doesn't have a tuxedo. What do you think, George?" By this time Delvane was stabbing his index finger at Frailey's chest and his voice had risen in pitch and volume.

"You're drunk Winston. Leave me alone goddamn it." Frailey half-rose and tried to retreat but fell backwards over his chair in an awkward heap. Collie and Frailey's wife, Coral, quickly helped the overweight Frailey to his chair. Delvane had turned away in search of another drink at the bar.

"I'm so sorry George. Please accept my apologies for Delvane. That was whiskey doing his talking for him, I'm afraid. I've never seen him act like that," Collie pleaded.

"I should have knocked the cocky bastard on his ass," Frailey blustered.

The tables were cleared and friendly groups were reforming as Goldie Evan's band began playing dance music. There were laughing comments about George Frailey's fall at the head table but few had seen or overheard Winston's part in the scene. Collie was moving unobtrusively through the crowd looking for her husband when Louise Greene hailed her to a table.

"Hey Collie, come on over for a minute," Louise called. "I loved your golf jokes, Kid."

Louise's date, Jake Walker who was a Wyoming State Highway Patrolman and Porky Noonan, a State Highway Department Engineer and his wife Elsa seconded the applause.

"Thank you." Collie, always conscious of her political image, sat down for a minute. "Have you seen Del, Louise?"

"Nope. You want Jake to put out an APB?"

"Oh, it's not important. I just haven't seen him for a few minutes." She looked around, wondering if he had left the party entirely. Porky Noonan told a long golf joke, the punch line of which was a roared "Gotcha"; the only part Collie heard. The swing band played a lively version of "Hernando's Hideaway" as several couples Tangoed gracefully and the rest performed the Sheila's Tree Two Step.

"…and with the big family we need more space anyhow. Don't you think it's a good investment, Collie?" Elsa was looking at Collie expectantly.

"Yes," Collie responded automatically, "Oh, I mean I didn't hear you, Elsa. What was it?"

"We're thinking of buying a lot over on the ninth fairway to build on," Elsa repeated.

"It's going to be a lovely development I'm sure," Collie replied. She wondered how the woman coped with her four youngsters and, now, another on the way. She felt a momentary flicker of regret at her own childlessness.

"Jake is talking about buying a lot too," Louise said excitedly. "When we get married next Spring the house would be all ready to move into, if we can afford it?" She looked questioningly at Jake.

"You're not going to work after we're married, my Girl. I'll make the living for my family," Jake proclaimed.

Collie felt a tap on her shoulder and looked up at Ryan Baker standing behind her chair.

"Excuse me, Collie. Would you like to dance? I'm not very good," Ryan admitted.

Ryan felt awkward and school boyish as they moved between tables towards the dance floor. He looked well finished enough, though he wore a dark two piece suit instead of a dinner jacket. The feeling of discomfort was a matter of his inexperience. Ryan had almost none where women were concerned. Though thirty-three years old he had never been seriously involved with anyone. There had been few opportunities in his profession to meet women. He had gone straight to a remote naval outpost in the Aleutian Islands for the duration of the war and to equally isolated mining projects after his discharge. Ryan was far better acquainted with the Paleozoic fossil array than with the ways of modern womanhood. A few neophyte experiences with college and military sex had left him more mystified and curious than knowledgeable. His exposure to Collie Winston had all the more devastating effect because of his essential innocence. Her self-assurance and beauty overwhelmed him. He knew that she was married and, therefore, out of reach but his fascination was a powerful influence. He had not analyzed his feelings towards Collie, yet he constantly wished to be close to her. He was infatuated but without any conscious component of serious pursuit. She was a dream; not well enough known to come alive in his thoughts and plans.

Goldie Evan's clarinet carried the gentle melody of '<u>Hey There</u>' as Ryan stiffly clasped her waist and hand, trying to establish some semblance of rapport with the beat.

"What do you think of Sheila's Tree by now, Ryan?" Her eyes were not quite level with his.

"A town seems to be what the people make of it," he replied. "I've met some very nice folks here." He hoped his smile personalized the statement. "You are so natural and assured in front of all these people. Your jokes were funny, too. How do you do it, Collie? How did you get to be Mayor?" he asked with sincere interest. Ryan remembered delivering a technical paper at a convention in Denver as one of life's harrowing moments. Collie was used to drawing others out rather than talking about herself. She found pleasure in reciting some details of her political career.

"I came back to Sheila's Tree during the war with a Masters Degree in Political Science from University of California at Berkeley. With all the men gone to war it was easy to get a job as administrative assistant to Mayor Berwold. I worked directly with the City staff and City Council for two years until I just got disgusted with their policies. I mean, there was no planning or foresight at all and they wanted to run everything on a shoestring." She had moved closer to Ryan and laid her head on his shoulder as she talked. He found himself relaxing as she gracefully flowed with his movements. His arm encircled her waist and they moved comfortably in a close embrace. Though he did not know the name, Ryan would never afterwards fail to recognize the scent of Arpege perfume in her hair.

She told him of quitting the city job for a stint as Staff Assistant to Wyoming Senator, Wyatt Paige, in Washington DC and finally the return to Sheila's Tree and marriage to Delvane. Collie was reciting the circumstances of her parents death in an airplane crash when the band once more picked up a Latin beat which was too much for Ryan's limited skill on the dance floor.

Collie, enjoying her own narration, was stimulated by Ryan's close attention. His arms about her felt strong and solid and, though she was not consciously flirtatious, she was happily responding to his open admiration.

"It's so hot and smoky in here. Lets step out the side entrance by the driving range for a minute," she suggested.

There was a short concrete patio and long graveled walk with rubber matted stations for golfing practice. The walk was backed by a thick hedge of tall arbor vitea planted to protect players from errant shots off the adjacent fairway. The air was cool and Ryan removed his jacket, placing it over Collie's bare shoulders as they walked along the path. She had gotten to the point in her personal history where conflict with Del forced her away from the ranch and back to a renewed interest in the politics of Sheila's Tree. Loyalty to Del glossed over marital problems as Collie felt reluctant to discuss personal details despite her growing amity with Ryan. She was telling him of her campaign to unseat Mayor Berwold in the 1951 election when she was interrupted by a commotion on the other side of the looming evergreen hedge. The crunch of running footsteps approached, then the sound of a sliding stop and heavy breathing. A lighter step ran up and collided with the first runner.

"Give me back that bra, you rat. I'm going to freeze my boobies."

Feminine laughter and muffled struggling. Collie instantly recognized the voice of Betty Spielman but Ryan did not. Collie put her finger to her lips in a signal for silence and pantomimed a laugh at Ryan's obvious discomfort. He shrugged and shook his head resignedly. There was a good deal of moaning and shuffling going on behind the hedge. Ryan was thankful that darkness masked his blush.

"Ya want more? Ya want more? Come an' get it, you rat!" More squealing laughter and both footsteps ran on down the hedge.

"Come on quickly," Collie said, "let's get back inside before they come around the end of the shrubbery. My God, it doesn't take the country club set long to live up to their reputation does it?"

They hurried back inside and went over to the table where Ballard and Juno were seated with several other couples.

Juno spoke to Ryan. "Ray and Susan got a call from her daughter, Cheryl, and had to leave. We told her we would be glad to drop you off at your apartment. It was nothing important. I think the baby sitter got sick or something."

"Oh sure. Well, thank you," Ryan said. He turned to pull out a chair for Collie. Her face was a pale mask of shock. She put a hand on his shoulder for support and whirled around as if to run.

"What is it?" he cried. For God's sake Collie, what's the matter?"

Juno jumped up and tried to put her arm around Collie who looked quite stricken.

"Are you ill, Dear?" Juno whispered. "What is it? What's wrong?"

"No, no, I'm perfectly all right," she rasped huskily. "Yes, I mean, I don't feel well right now. Oh Ryan, please drive me home." She shrugged off Juno's arm and walked rapidly away towards the front door.

"Okay, Juno, okay. I'll take care of her," Ryan nodded to the table. "If she is really sick I'll get her to a doctor. I think she'll be all right." He backed away motioning them to stay seated, then turned and followed Collie out. He never noticed Delvane Winston and Betty Spielman moving between tables on their way to the long polished bar for a refill.

Ryan reached the parking lot in time to see Collie entering the passenger side of a gray Plymouth coupe. He walked to the driver's door and slid in behind the wheel. Collie was staring at the windshield; clinched fists held, shaking, before her.

"I'm so angry! So angry! What a ridiculous fool I am. I'm so angry!"

Ryan extended a tentative hand, touching her shoulder. She turned to look at him as if only suddenly aware of his presence.

"Oh Ryan, there's nobody, just nobody to turn to. I'm su—su—such a fuh—fuh—fool." She began to cry, leaning towards him as he rather clumsily put his arms around her.

He held her close, muttering a low, "Sh, sh, sh, sh," into her hair as the sobs quickly subsided. Ryan found himself caressing her bare back and kissing her hair. She lay still and silent against his chest for some time.

Collie had been stricken with furious anger when she saw her husband come in the side door behind Betty Spielman. She wanted to scream and strike out but was forced to run away instead. By the time she had walked to the car and sat still for a moment the rush of adrenaline began to fade. Anger was replaced by dismal humiliation and at Ryan's sympathetic touch her pride crumbled a little. She was absorbed in her own feelings; not thinking of the impression she was making on Ryan, as she leaned into his embrace. Resilient as ever, she quickly regained her composure, pulled back and dabbed her eyes with tissue. She noticed the claim check for her fur jacket in her tiny sequined clasp purse and asked Ryan to go in and pick it up.

"The car keys are in the coat pocket," she explained. "If we want to go home you better bring my jacket, please." She managed a smile. By the time he returned to the car she had moved over to the driver's side.

"I'm feeling much better now. I can drive fine. Hop in, I'll drop you off," she seemed almost cheerful. "It was nothing. Just a reaction to the heat or something, I guess. I almost passed out but I feel okay now." She did not look at him.

Ryan was not extraordinarily socially adept nor well at ease with beautiful women but he was a moderately sensitive and aware man. He knew perfectly well that Collie had just suffered some kind of severe emotional stress though the cause eluded him. By the time his own reaction became clear, the coupe pulled up to the driveway of his apartment building. He did not get out immediately but sat watching Collie until she slowly turned her head to meet his eyes.

"Collie, I admire you very much. I have never had a woman friend before," he looked away for a moment, "but I want you to know that I am your good friend. If you ever..." he looked back steadily into her eyes..."If I can ever do anything for you I'll be ready any time."

He got out and walked to the stairs leading up to his rooms without looking back.

THE URANIUM
BROKER

George Frailey was sitting at his desk looking out the wide picture window of his second story office when the private telephone rang. The unlisted phone was usually the bearer of good news since only friends and trusted business contacts knew the number. Of course, sometimes it was only his wife, Coral, but often more exciting calls came in on it.

"George, this is Marion. Got the assay back on those ore samples you sent down last week." It was Marion Reinhardt, Vice President in charge of mineral exploration for New Mexico Mining Corporation, and husband of George's sister, Ruth. "There wasn't much material there but it certainly is low grade uranium ore. It seems to be a complex of alumina, silica and uranium oxides similar to some stuff that has been found in Utah. Are you sure your man is on the level with his location? We get a lot of scams in this business you know."

"Well, I'm convinced he thinks he's got something," George replied. "The guy is just a dumb fry cook with a Geiger counter. I doubt he has the imagination to try an' pull anything. I went out and looked at the deal with him a couple days ago. You can't see a Goddamn thing but his clicker goes crazy on that spot where the samples come from." George decided not to mention the twenty-one claims already filed by Regelstorp. He also neglected to mention that Regelstorp had spent two whole days in his outer office waiting to see him. George was completely convinced upon hearing Marion's test results, that he was sitting on a million-dollar bonanza. His reaction was predictable.

"Listen Marion, who the hell knows what we got? It's a real long shot but you never know. Whyn't you fly up here sometime and check it out just for the hell of it?" he tried to sound casual.

Reinhardt recognized the subterfuge in George's voice and immediately became alert. On the other hand, he had seen hundreds of leads turn out to be worthless. The fact that Frailey was interested plus the preliminary test results made a check worth while.

"Tell you what, George, Ruth and I will drop up there next weekend for a couple days and I'll take a look at it. If it looks like it could amount to anything the Company will be interested. One thing—you better not mention it to anybody, including Coral or your prospector. If he calls around just say you're still waiting...no, say the tests were negative but the Company might send somebody up to look at it, okay?"

"Sure Marion, no problem. I'll just sit tight 'til you get here," George said. "Thanks for the call. See you next week."

The phone receiver hit the cradle and George hit the floor at the same time. He had Regelstorp's address at an old auto court near the railroad tracks. Tiny kitchenette cabins had been made into dilapidated rentals when newer motels began to attract the overnight tourist and travel business.

"Hello Tom," George gave him a big salesman's smile and shook his hand. "Just dropped around with some good news. I know you've been anxious to hear what the Company thinks of your prospect."

"Sure Mr. Frailey. Come on in an' have a cup of java," Tom motioned to the wooden kitchen chair.

"No, no time, by golly. I got to get right along." George ignored a skinny, yellow striped cat rubbing his ankles. "Those rocks of yours have got interesting traces of some hot minerals, Tom, but they can't tell whether it's worth anything. Said they might send a man up here sometime this winter just to see how the country looks, you know. I guess they get rocks like this sent to 'em all the time, you know. Not much ever turns out."

"Oh, this here is the real thing, Mr. Frailey," Tom exclaimed. "Hell, I know this here uranium. You get those clicks on the ol' counter and you can bet it's the McCoy, all right."

"Well, the assay never showed nothing of any importance and, by the way, you know you got to put in one hundred dollars a year for development work on each of them twenty-one claims in order to keep 'em? You got two thousand dollars ready money to take a gamble like that, Tom?" Frailey was solicitous as the bearer of bad news.

"I figured somebody would want to make me a deal on all that uranium, Mr. Frailey. I never figured on puttin' up no development money. Maybe I better call up Allied Nuclear down at Grand Junction. They might take an interest in me." He looked slyly at Frailey on the last sentence.

"Well sure, you better do that then," Frailey smiled cheerfully. "Maybe they'll get a different answer on that assay, Tom. Good luck to you. I gotta go on out to the Country Club."

He backed out the door, pausing to straighten his turquoise string tie and fasten the top button of his suede jacket. He almost made it to the front end of his Cadillac.

"Uh, Mr. Frailey. Say, I don't reckon I should spread this all over creation 'fore we know e'zactly what's out there. How soon you say these glory boys from the Company supposed to be here?"

"Shouldn't be long before we know one way or the other. Tell you what, Tom, if you want to do business with me, I 'spect I better show a little good faith on my part. No use you worrying about that two thousand dollars for claim work. Whyn't you come on back to the office with me and I'll draw up a little contract to protect your interests? You done all the work so far, though, of course, the real money starts now but that'll be up to me. What do you think's fair, Tom?"

Tom had already given it some thought.

"I'll take fifty and give you fifty, Mr. Frailey. We'll go right down the middle with her if you go the expense from here on out."

"Hop in the car, Tom." Frailey went around to open the door. "I guess I better tell you how these things usually work."

Tom got his first ride in a 1953 Cadillac. Two hours later he emerged from Frailey's office building clutching the first fruits of his uranium strike. He had a check for five thousand dollars which was at least one and a half years of earnings for him and a guaranteed royalty contract for ten percent of the gross proceeds from any minerals sold off his Canteen claims. It must have been a good business deal because both Regelstorp and Frailey were jubilant over the results.

PRELIMINARY
INVESTIGATIONS

Marion Reinhardt circled towards the Sheila's Tree airport in a wide turn over Chopstick reservoir. The twin engine, eight passenger aircraft felt a bit tail heavy on the approach as he eased down towards the asphalt runway. Marion had enjoyed the flight up from Gallup, New Mexico in the big Company plane. He did not often have an opportunity to pilot for himself since becoming Vice President. Usually a Company pilot chauffeured business trips but in this case he had billed the flight as a weekend jaunt for himself and his wife. He taxied in past a row of open aircraft shelters where a variety of single engine planes were tied down, rolling to a stop at a spot near Stellmon Aviation Service hangar and shop.

"Give her a check and fill her up," he told the mechanic who emerged with clipboard in hand as Marion and his wife pulled overnight bags from the plane. "Check the stabilizer and tail surface fabric too. She felt a little logy coming in. I may want her this afternoon for a short hop and then we'll be pulling out Sunday afternoon," he instructed.

It was a cool early Friday morning in mid-September. Reinhardt wanted to look at the uranium prospect as quickly as possible for two reasons. If it turned out to be worthwhile the secret would only keep for a matter of days, perhaps hours, after which a frantic rush of fortune hunters and exploration companies would inevitably crowd the scene. Marion had been both an observer and participant in more than one such hectic competition and knew the importance of early arrival. Secondly, if further testing were called for he wanted some time to work before the severe Wyoming winter closed in. Marion had been exceptionally successful in finding and acquiring valuable properties for New Mexico Mining Corporation, particularly in uranium interests. He was a risk taker who believed that expedience was the most valuable attribute towards achievement of goals. He could swallow anything so long as it led to the proper result. Reinhardt was intelligent, aggressively political and usually had common sense, which was the glue that held the collage of his strengths and weaknesses in order. He was also a user of people, situations or any resource available to promote his ends. At age forty-two he was a fast rising star in the mineral industry, though feared as much as respected by close associates.

That afternoon Marion and George flew over the Bench so that the discovery site and local terrain could be pointed out. Red Rock Rim was as impressive from the air as from the ground. Marion immediately saw the significance of the great natural barrier in relation to development of a mining operation on the Bench. It formed an impassable wall forty miles long, broken only by Palmer Canyon and Pass Road. There were faintly visible traceries of cattle trails on the Bench, mostly following shallow ridges in parallel rows towards the foothills of the Big Horn Range. North-south travel across the erosional features was obviously more difficult, with gully crossings almost impossible to spot from the air.

The drive up Pass Road next day accentuated the importance of the access bottleneck.

"How come these cowboys have the road fenced?" Marion asked.

"It's private ground all the way through the canyon and maybe five miles on above," George replied. "They keep it open most of the year when it's not snowed in."

"You can't run a fleet of ore trucks over private roads if it comes to that," Marion commented. "We'll have to see what we got here."

Once above Garnet Falls the road quickly faded to a weedy rutted trail with forking branches wherever topography permitted. The main road, though seldom used and in bad repair, continued westward, crossing and recrossing Framboise Creek over shallow rocky fords. Far up in the foothills the road found its' destination at the abandoned site of the old Cielo Grande silver mine. Frailey and Reinhardt did not drive the pickup as far as the old mine. Just past the Palmer ranch high fence line, Frailey angled away from Framboise Creek following a dry wash along a track shown to him by Regelstorp the previous week. The site of Tom's discovery was marked by a wooden stake with a red bandanna flag fluttering in the cold wind. Marion took Geiger counter readings and chipped more sample material from the sandstone. He examined the claim marker for Canteen One and read the discovery notice that Regelstorp had placed in the Prince Albert tobacco can.

"Your man, Regelstorp, seems to know the fundamentals of claim staking," Marion said. "I don't suppose you checked to see if he filed at the courthouse?"

"Oh yeah. I forgot to mention that part," Frailey smiled. "He staked twenty-one claims up here and filed on 'em right away. Course, I moved in and tied him up soon's I got word on those assays."

"You mean you already made a deal on these claims?" Marion asked incredulously. "Christ, George, there's still only one chance in a hundred that this is an economic uranium deposit. You can get traces in almost any rock you pick up on this side of the Rocky Mountains. These complex oxides are called aura minerals because they are secondary indicators of the primary uranium source. They sort of surround the main deposit and give off a lot of radioactivity mostly from uranium daughter products. They can travel a long way dissolved in water or even in gaseous form sometimes. If we do find the uranium deposit, it usually turns out to be too small or too low grade to bother with. What kind of a deal did you make with this guy?"

"Don't worry," George was slightly disconcerted by Marion's information. "I got ninety percent and gave him ten percent royalties. Course, I did give him five thou' to close but that's peanuts on a deal like this."

Marion shook his head. "Five grand for four hundred acres of cactus. Good work, George!" sarcastically. "The ten percent is okay, though, because it will be a long time before we net a dime off these claims," he winked at his brother-in-law. "Especially with us keeping the books."

George chewed his lip for a moment, then said, "Well, uh, the contract says ten percent of the gross on all sales off his claims. Hell, I figured we'd be up in the three or four hundred percent profit range like we were on that New Mexico stuff."

Marion was furious. "You idiot! Stick to selling houses will you? You were so Goddamned eager to take me for a ride that you just screwed yourself good. I'll tell you this much, if the Company does come in on a deal here, your friend, Regelstorp, will make a hell of a lot more than you will off these claims. Ten percent of the gross could be all the profit there is depending on what it costs to get the stuff out of the ground. You better hope this is a real big deal or else that we can stake some claims of our own."

"Well look," George explained, "these Canteen claims are staked out in a big cross; five claims in each arm connected to this center one. We are standing in the middle of the cross right now. There's no telling where the real strike is from this little hot spot. There might be ore anywhere around here," he pleaded.

Marion was examining the radioactive sandstone with a magnifying glass. "The analysis showed about a tenth of one percent uranium which is pretty good for this kind of mineralization. Tell you what, I'm going to get a drill rig up here to do some sampling and I got a couple of boys who do some jobs for me down in New Mexico that I'm going to send up here. They work cheap and won't attract attention like a survey and staking crew from the Company would. It won't cost much to stake a big square around this cross of yours and then we'll have her pretty well pinned down." Marion smiled for the first time. "To tell the truth I feel pretty good about this one. We just might have something. One thing, though, you smart bastard. If I get the Company up here and this deal starts producing, we split the profits off these Canteen claims. I'm the only leverage you've got, George, and if you don't play the game my way I'll see to it that you don't play at all."

"Oh hell, you know I meant to cut you in on those claims from the start, Marion. Jesus, blood is thicker than water, you know." Frailey capitulated easily to Marion's position of strength and more forceful personality.

They were both chilled through and glad to get back in the pickup. George opened a steel thermos of steaming coffee and poured into thin red plastic cups, which nested in the screw lid.

"Who owns this Palmer spread in the canyon?" Marion asked. "Is it local or one of these big corporate outfits like Burcott?"

"Fellow by the name of Winston. He's a Goddamn fairy from California who married into the Palmer outfit."

"What is the ranch worth if we just offered to buy it outright?", Marion inquired.

"I'd say about a million," George replied, "but they won't sell jack shit. This is one of the old timers. Palmers been working this canyon since 1870."

"Hmmmm. Maybe we could just get an option for a hundred thousand or so and make Pass Road right-of-way a part of the deal. It would cost near a million to build an all weather road up here if we have to go around this Goddamned fault scarp," Marion mused. "No use getting the cart ahead of the horse. I'll have a drill rig or two up here pretty soon. I'll also make sure Pronto and Shug get started staking more claims next week. You'll have to show 'em what we want, George. Just lay it out so we cover the four quadrants cut by Regelstorp's cross. It'll only be a few hundred bucks to file the claims and we can let them drop if the drill samples don't show anything. These two boys are pretty rough customers so nobody will be in here trying to stake in front of us. Keep them out of town as much as possible and we will save a lot of trouble. The longer we keep this quiet the better chance we have to get the biggest slice of the pie. Now, try to take care of things up here and I'll handle the Company when the time comes. From now on you play straight with me, George, or, by God, you'll be sorry you ever made that telephone call to me in the first place."

"Okay, you can bet things will go smooth on this end. Let's just get the show on the road," George nodded. He started the pickup and gingerly eased into low gear for the rough ride back out to Pass Road.

MILO CASHES A CHECK

With the D-Z Fall roundup only a week away Ballard Crown was keeping Milo Harris busier than spit on a red-hot stove. Ballard always invited half of Galena County out to the roundup and barbecue making it one of the benchmark events of the year. Some guests helped with the last couple of days of gathering strays, herding the cattle into corrals and loading up trucks for shipping. Many invitees only came for the big barbecue after the work was finished but others came early to participate in the dust, grime and excitement of the cowboy's work-a-day world. Milo's job was to command his crews in herding widely scattered cattle towards a central collection point. There was a series of large holding corrals with smaller satellite pens for separating the animals after their long Summer of running wild on the high grazing lands of the Bench. Many cattle had already been collected and sold earlier as Crown attempted to catch a higher beef price. Still, all the cow-calf pairs, about twenty huge old range bulls and remaining two year old steers and heifers had to be brought in; all told, perhaps two thousand animals. After two weeks of hard riding and camping on the Bench, Milo was tired, dirty and badly in need of a hot shower and a few hours rest. Most of the cattle had been pushed down from the high range to within a mile of the holding corrals. Every draw and gully was crowded with milling herds kept in place by the availability of a few muddy water holes and horsemen who were stationed on main trails above the animals. The idea was to contain the cattle for a short calming and resting period followed by several hectic days of hard work to classify and load the animals and transport them off the Bench to market or to feed yards on Winter pastures below the rim. Milo gave his mare free rein and headed down rim trail towards headquarters. The horse was as anxious as Milo to get to the barn.

Ballard Crown had a long list of errands to be run in town and was glad to see his Foreman ride in. He was busy with preparations for the coming fiesta.

"Here's a check for twenty-five hundred dollars. There's enough there for a hundred pounds of red kidney beans, a sack of Walla Walla sweet onions and a sack of them red and green chilies over at the market. You better get some cases of good sour mash whiskey and plenty of beer, too. And listen, I let the county taxes on the ranch go right up to the deadline this summer and now it has got to be paid by tomorrow or I'm late. You get the cash out of the bank and take it over to the Assessor's office in person so it for sure gets paid in time. Now, I know you're goin' to be hangin' around that Bull Run all night but you better be back here by tomorrow afternoon or else have your ticket punched for another soft lay-out somewheres," Crown threatened good-naturedly.

"So you're gonna' make that damn Texas Draino you call chili again this year, huh?" gibed Milo. "You remember last year, Charlie Potter's tongue swoll up 'til he liked to choked?"

"Son, there's no decent folks going to chaw up a steak without they got a plate of beans to go with it. We invite 'em out here; we got to treat 'em right. Now you go get yourself dolled up and looking a little more like a human being and chiva-ree that truck on into town. I'll be seein' you tomorrow."

True to his self-promise, Milo's first stop was the Bull Run Lounge where he consumed two tall draft beers with his ham and egg lunch. The second thing he did was call Ryan Baker at his newly opened office.

"Hello, Rockhound. What you up to this fine day?" Milo inquired.

"Harris?" Ryan questioned, "I thought you were out making love to Ballard's doggies. I'm analyzing a bunch of deep well resistivity logs for Mid-Continental Oil from their field out at Scorpion. Some people work for a living. I can tell by the juke box, you're over at the Bull Run."

"Elementary my dear Sherlock," Milo replied, "but not for long. I got things to do and people to see. How 'bout meeting me over here after supper and I'll show you the finer points of pool shooting? I could also get you a seat at the poker game tonight and really get you educated."

"Shoot, Milo," Ryan declined, "I have to run this report in to Casper when I get finished. Won't be back 'til after 11:00 tonight."

"Well, say hi to Madam Ruby down at the Sand Bar for me. You had your chance; now I got to give my money away to that same old crowd. You comin' out to the D-Z barbecue this weekend?"

"Sure, if you save that old sway back mare for me. I got kind of lonesome for the way she'd roll those big brown eyes at me."

"Good," said Milo, "you'll love Ballard's steak and chili. That stuff is hotter than a two-dollar pistol. Well, see you later, Ol' Ryan. Keep at it."

Milo hung up and set off to make his purchases. First stop was Orville Smith's Wyoming Agricultural Bank to cash Crown's check. Racism was a significant factor in Milo's life, as with many minorities, but overt incidents were relatively rare. There were not many Negroes in Sheila's Tree and Milo was looked upon as an oddity rather than a threat for the most part. He usually went only where he was known and accepted but intolerance was as common in Sheila's Tree as any other community in America.

The teller was a young woman unknown to Milo when he presented the large check made out to cash and signed by Ballard Crown.

"Are you Ballard Crown?" she asked.

"No Ma'am, but I work for Mr. Crown," Milo replied.

"I can't give you twenty-five hundred dollars in cash," she frowned. "Have you got a letter or note signed by Mr. Crown?" The amount of money represented by the check almost equaled her annual salary.

"No I don't, Ma'am, but I have a driver's license and Mr. Smith knows who I am," Milo was patient.

"Mr. Smith is not here today," she snapped. "You must come back later or tell Mr. Crown to come in himself."

"Look, I have errands to run and I need that money. It belongs to Mr. Crown, not you. I guess you mean well but everybody in town knows I work at the D-Z. I'm not moving until I get that money. Call Iris Patton. She will tell you who I am."

By this time there were several people in line and the teller's face was beginning to burn with indignation.

"I won't call anybody except the security guard if you don't go on your way. Do you think I'm going to hand over that kind of money to any colored person who walks in here?" she demanded agitatedly.

Milo glanced around and saw no one that he recognized in the bank. He decided to come back later with someone who could vouch for him.

"Okay," he spoke with some exasperation, "give me that check and I'll come back later."

"You will not take this check," she said icily. "I'm keeping it for evidence."

"Evidence of what, you idiot?" He bit his tongue but it was too late. Milo did not have enough practice at being properly obsequious.

"Guard! Guard!" she shouted, "this man is trying to rob the bank."

Two men in line behind Milo grabbed his arms and pushed him against the counter as a bank security guard ran over with his pistol drawn.

"Cool it, you black son-of-a-bitch, or I'll bust your head," the guard yelled. He fumbled for a pair of handcuffs attached to his belt.

Milo was sure he could easily knock heads of the two men holding his arms but he also felt that the guard might use his pistol. Knowing that the whole encounter was a complete misunderstanding, he decided to stand quietly and wait for an opportunity to explain. Fortunately, it was not long in coming. Juno Castle walked into the bank about the time Milo was presenting his wrists for the iron bracelets.

"Miss Castle," Milo smiled much more calmly than he felt, "could you spare me a moment of your time, please?"

Every employee in the bank recognized Juno Castle. Her accounting firm was employed by the Wyoming State Banking Regulatory Agency to audit all the banks in Galena County. Juno was also appointed by the Governor to serve the regulatory agency as a member of its Board of Directors.

"Milo, what is it?" she exclaimed. "What in the world is going on?"

"This man was trying to rob the bank," the teller was near hysteria. "He insulted me and was insolent and tried to steal money."

"We got the black bastard, Ma'am," the guard almost shouted, "we're just about to call the sheriff."

"What nonsense," Juno asserted. "This man is no criminal. What can you be talking about? He is foreman for Ballard Crown at the D-Z ranch."

"He came in here demanding twenty-five hundred dollars cash in Mr. Crown's name," said the teller. "Look here, Miss Castle." She showed Juno the check.

No one present except Milo knew of Juno's close personal relationship with Ballard Crown and he was just beginning to enjoy the situation.

"I'm going to pick up supplies for the barbecue, Miss Castle. You know how Ballard is about his chili," Milo said.

"This is a legal instrument with Ballard Crown's authentic signature on it, Miss Lane," Juno stated. "Why did you refuse to cash this?"

"He had no note. I don't know this man and he was very insulting," the woman defended self-righteously.

"Do you know me?" Juno demanded.

"Yes, of course, Miss Castle," the Lane woman replied.

"Then give me the money, please," Juno's voice was flat.

After receiving the bills she turned to the guard who had been listening to the conversation. "Are you arresting this man for insulting the teller, or what? I demand to know what went on in here and why Mr. Harris is in handcuffs."

"Well, uh, he was tryin' to cash this check, see," the guard fumbled for an explanation.

"Do you arrest everyone in this bank who attempts to cash checks?" Juno asked sarcastically. The guard was already unlocking the cuffs.

"Don't let me catch you in this bank tryin' to start any more trouble, buddy, or you'll sure as hell find it," the guard muttered as he released Milo.

Milo took the money from Juno. "Thank you, Miss Castle. I appreciate your help." He turned to the teller. "I apologize for calling you an idiot, Miss Lane. Fact is, I have no way of knowing how low your IQ is." Milo turned and strode out of the bank.

STRANGERS AT THE
BULL RUN

Later in the afternoon Milo had the pickup truck loaded down with supplies and groceries for the roundup and barbecue and had tied a heavy canvas tarpaulin cover over the bed. Only the county property tax had to be paid in the morning before driving back out to the D-Z. He returned to the Bull Run Lounge determined to shrug off the unpleasant experience in the bank with some evening recreation.

"Well, if it isn't the D-Z Dude," greeted Iris Patton from behind the bar. "Don't you look like something in that pink shirt with pearl buttons and your snakeskin boots. My, my!"

"Iris, you aint exactly hurtin' my eyes yourself," Milo grinned. "How about settin' me up a nice big pitcher of that draft beer?"

No one at the bar noticed her fingers brush lightly over his hand as she set the pitcher down. Their eyes met in a brief moment of joyful greeting as she asked, "You stayin' for poker tonight or do we have to find some other loser?"

"Oh yeah, I'm on the town tonight. You got a good game lined up?" Milo played at almost every opportunity and nearly always left the table with winnings.

"Sure we got a game lined up," Iris reported. "Some new blood to keep things interesting. Fellow by the name of Tom Regelstorp has been playing for the past couple of weeks." She leaned forward and lowered her voice. "He should have taken a few lessons before he sat down with those pirates. He's lost two or three thousand, mostly to that legal-eagle, Eldring."

"Oh man," Milo lamented, "and me stuck up there on the bench eatin' dust while the buzzards was flocking to the kill. I'll be in the game tonight, though, and I'm going to sit right behind ol' Denton Eldring."

Two men, not recognized by Milo and Iris, walked in and sat down next to Milo. The larger man wore ordinary faded and frayed denim pants and jacket, worn cowboy boots and long shirttail hanging in back. He had a three-day stubble of graying whiskers, pouchy eyes and straggly, thinning hair sticking out under a broad brimmed, soiled straw hat. By contrast, his companion was dressed in cowboy Sunday clothes, clean-shaven, black hair slicked down with redolent applications of hair oil. He was swarthy and compact; filled with nervous fidgety energy. Both men ordered red-eye, which is the cowboy's way of asking for the least expensive straight whiskey available. They sipped and stared straight ahead in silent contemplation, the younger man shredding his paper napkin in long strips.

Milo and Iris continued their conversation.

"You coming to the barbecue this year, Iris?" Milo asked.

"You bet," she replied. "I think I'll come out early and help chase strays. I sure get homesick for sagebrush. Since I been running this outfit I never seem to go riding any more. I used to be one heck of a barrel racer when I was a kid. Could you wrangle me a good cuttin' horse for Saturday morning, Milo?"

Milo started to answer when the slovenly character next to him turned on his barstool and rudely interrupted.

"Say, Boy, you know a fellow 'round here by name of George Frailey?"

Milo froze for a moment, then smiled broadly at Iris and turned towards the newcomer.

"Name's Harris—Milo Harris." He stuck out his hand for a shake. The man looked at the hand; looked Milo in the eye, then slowly extended his own hand. He was stronger than his puffy looks indicated but as Milo continued to smile and apply pressure he began to squint in pain. Milo released his grip after only a few seconds but he was sure the man would not again mistake him for a boy.

"Huh," the man looked a little less grim as Milo let go, "used to milk forty cows a day. Not many can do that to me. Name's Shug. Shug Brown. Brown sugar, get it?"

"Howdy Shug," Milo greeted. "Only George Frailey I know is a Real Estate guy. Has an office here in town."

"Supposed to have a job for us," Shug grunted. "Hey, Pronto, go give him a call we're in town, huh?"

The small, dark man slipped off the barstool, giving Milo an onyx stare as he went to a phone at the end of the bar.

"The Mex and me is partners," Shug said. "His name's Pronto Melindez."

Pronto had George's private office number.

"Frailey? Me an' Shug jus' gets to town. Reinhardt say you gots a job for us. W'at you want?" Pronto was terse.

"Go to the Juniper Motel out on South Main," Frailey replied, remembering Marion's advice to keep the two men out of trouble. "I'll meet you there at 8:00 am tomorrow morning with instructions and some cash. What kind of a rig you driving?"

"We gots Shug's ol' forty-one Desoto. She ain' takin' us out in no sagebrush."

"Okay then, get some supper and go straight to that motel and wait 'til I get there, okay?" Frailey ordered.

Pronto hung up without reply. When he returned to the bar Milo and Shug had gotten up to shoot pool. They were playing eight ball at fifty cents a game. Pronto hated pool because he never had been able to come even close to Shug's considerable skill.

"Gimme shot of red-eye weeth cerveza back," he ordered.

As Iris set the two glasses in front of him, Pronto grabbed her wrist.

"You put out, Chica? Hey, ten bucks for two hours w'en you get off, hokay?"

Iris jerked her arm away. "Listen you little greased pig," she hissed, "if you touch me again or anybody else in this place tonight I'll have both your legs broken. You pay; you drink; you mind your manners. Sabes tu?" She walked to the other end of the bar where Neil Silverstein and Chuck Hardy from the Palmer ranch were nursing their drinks.

Milo and Shug were quietly playing pool and Milo was losing. Shug seemed to have a lot of practice, winning four dollars in an hour of play. Milo, however, felt his touch coming back, having seen his game improve with each attempt. He knew players were assembling in the back room for the nightly poker game and was anxious to choose his seat at just the right location with respect to the other regular players whose habits and idiosyncrasies he often took advantage of.

"Only got time for one more, Shug," Milo said. "How 'bout givin' me a chance to get even?"

Shug was confident. "What you got in mind? Hell, name your poison."

"You let me break, I'll go five dollars."

"Okay Sucker, you called it," Shug said.

Milo made a striped ball on the first shot then dropped three more before missing. He managed to leave Shug in a bad spot up against the cushioned edge of the table where he had little chance to address the cue ball properly for a shot. In attempting a difficult angle, Shug scratched into a corner pocket, giving Milo an opportunity to place the shooter's ball wherever he liked behind the spot marker. It appeared to be an easy chance to run the table as all the striped balls were in accessible positions. Milo carefully prepared to continue play for what should have been an easy win. After the first shot, however, Shug reached over and picked up the cue ball before Milo could continue.

"You spotted that ball in front of the marker," Shug accused. "That's a scratch where I come from, Slick. You' got to spot a ball and it's my turn to shoot."

Milo saw Pronto slide off his stool and walk over to lean in a relaxed pose against a neighboring pool table.

"Well Boys, I reckon you better think this over," Milo said calmly, "because everybody in this place knows I don't cheat. You aren't going to get to first base with this trick. You just forfeited the game when you picked up my cue ball, fat boy, so pull out that five dollar bill."

Shug smiled and walked around the table towards Milo. "Hell, Harris, no shame in losing another game. I never said you cheated—just spotted the ball wrong. 'Course, I don't like bein' called Fat Boy."

He whipped the weighted end of the pool stick at Milo's head in a practiced move almost as good as his table shots. Milo was expecting the attack and his response was much faster than Shug was used to in bar room brawls. Milo ducked below the swinging stick and stepped in with a short right hook beneath the left armpit. The blow did not look like much to spectators but Shug went pale and sagged against the table with all muscular control seemingly lost. Milo spun around and leaped to the side as fast as he could move, barely avoiding Pronto's knife as it snicked past his chest. With the missed strike, the Mexican found himself much too close to an uninjured adversary. He tried to slash backwards at Milo's arm, but like Shug, Pronto underestimated the quickness of the big black man. A clubbing right fist caught Pronto in the back of the head, fortunately high enough to avoid permanent spinal injury, and dropped the smaller man to his knees in a daze. Unlike cowboy fights on Saturday film matinees, this contest was all over after two blows. Milo grabbed Shug by the back of the neck in a stonelike grip of his right hand.

"Hand over the fiver, Fat Boy, or I'll squeeze it out your ears."

Milo was panting more from emotional reaction than exertion. He increased the pressure slightly on Shug's fat neck. Shug groaned and fumbled rapidly for a bill in his shirt pocket, tossing it onto the table with an awkward gesture. Milo gave him a hard shove towards the still kneeling Pronto and both men fell in a tangle on the floor.

"You bastards better behave yourselves from now on or some mean son-of-a-bitch might get after you 'stead of a nice fellow like me," Milo said. "If I ever see that knife again, little brother, I'm going to use it to turn you into a Mexican steer." Milo instinctively came up with the insult most likely to inflict pain on the egotistical Melindez. The two men on the floor could do nothing except glare hatred, however, as Milo turned back to the bar.

Tony Arriaga, Iris' Basque bartender, had just come in for the evening shift.

"Tony, you better watch these two drifters," Milo said. "They act like they like trouble. I'm goin' in back to play poker so keep 'em out of there, okay?"

Tony looked at Iris who was still behind the bar. Seeing her slight nod of assent he smiled agreement with Milo's request. "You bet, Milo. They won't bother anybody else in here tonight. Come on you two, have a beer on the house and settle down." He pushed a couple of glasses across the bar for Shug and Pronto as Milo left for his game.

THE SHOWDOWN

Collie watched long shadows stripe the parking lot behind the courthouse. Having just delivered an enormous draft budget document to Louise Greene for typing, her own desk was clear and there were no more appointments on her calendar. She decided the time had come to confront Del. Collie was anxious to resolve resentment and hostility over his disloyal behavior at the country club. It was not clear how that could be done—certainly the usual mockingly sincere apology was the last thing she wanted from Del. A return to the trust and innocence of their former relationship, so far as her perception of it had been, was forever impossible.

So what does that leave?, she asked herself in perplexity, as if the problem were some Sunday newspaper quiz rather than four years of her life. Maybe Del wants a divorce and I won't have any choice in the matter, she pondered, almost with relief at the thought. But come what may, she thought, I'm going out to the ranch and get it over with. At least he's going to know that I caught him playing humiliating, adolescent games in the bushes with Hand-Me-Down Spielman.

Collie knew that Del would be up on the Bench herding cattle to Palmer loading pens below Garnet Falls. He had decided to sell every young animal on the ranch along with cull breeding stock in order to repay as much as possible to the bank.

Fall smells and color were in the air as Collie drove the county road out of town towards the shadowed dark band of Red Rock Rim, seemingly burdened by the pale orange late afternoon sun. The muted topaz prairie was smudged by a thin sepia haze of dust as grass and cropland slowly retreated into the long dormancy of winter. She passed two large rotary drilling trucks, recumbent masts fluttering red warning flags; "Bruchek Drilling" in black letters across the doors. She wondered idly who might be drilling wells, assuming that the machines were heading towards someone's high rangeland on the Bench. She was always thankful for the year-around water on the Palmer spread provided by bountiful Framboise Creek.

As she expected, the ranch house and grounds were deserted when she arrived. She let herself in, noting dust and disarray of Del's bachelor living. A cleaning woman came every Monday to scrub, dust and wax, so the house was essentially clean, only superficially untidy. She went into the large master bedroom where a chest of drawers full of her clothing and toilet articles were kept, almost duplicating her wardrobe at the townhouse. Collie saw Del's bureau with the top drawer pulled out; papers, letters and personal articles piled high on top, and, for a moment, considered snooping through his things. She flushed at the impulse and conscientiously denied herself even a glance in that direction as she selected a pair of western slacks and cotton shirt from her own closet. She undressed and headed for the shower, pausing for brief self-examination in the full-length mirror of the closet door.

Betty Spielman couldn't stand in my shadow, she thought. I don't look much different than I did four years ago on our wedding night. Delvane must be terribly insecure to need an ego massage from a light weight like her.

She turned with a frown and stepped into the adjoining shower.

I know one thing, she told herself, I'm not going to put up with a woman-chasing boozer and he's going to find that out right away.

It took some time for the gentle flood of hot water to soothe away the frown and ease muscular tension.

An hour later she had venison cutlets, green beans and corn on the cob out of the chest freezer and thawing. She diced three potatoes for hashed browns, spread garlic butter on thick slices of sheepherder bread and was prepared to put everything on the stove the minute Del appeared. She sat in twilight on the flagstone patio sipping a martini as shadows filled the canyon and slowly crept toward the top of the terraced north wall. The murmur of Framboise Creek and moan of the wind in tall trees were a white sound accentuating the stillness of the evening. The yip-yip-yodel of a coyote far up canyon brought a smile to her face. She was much more relaxed, and having faced the worst case for her relationship with Del, she was beginning to entertain a more tolerant and philosophical attitude.

I'm so small, she thought. Our busy lives seem almost inconsequential in a setting like this. Here we are over half way through the twentieth century with airplanes flying faster than the speed of sound, yet this canyon has looked and sounded just as it does tonight for hundreds—no thousands—of years before the first human being ever laid eyes on it. Del and I could fight and scream until the breath left our bodies but this enduring canyon would take no more notice of us than of that coyote singing to the stars. I must remember to keep things in perspective. Somehow our sins and hurts are not so deep and painful up here.

She heard trucks and pickups carrying men and horses and soon Del drove up to park beside her car. He was sweaty, dusty and tired as he walked around to the patio but she rose and kissed his stubbly face with warmth and tenderness. He smelled of horses and manure and leather, which enveloped her in childhood memories of her father and grandfather and evoked feelings of love and security.

"Hi boy." She said. "I had to come up and talk to you."

He smiled gratefully at her friendly tone of voice, having been prepared for a different reception upon seeing her car parked in the drive. Del had been aware of Arctic weather from Collie these past weeks but was not sure of its cause. Deep down he could think of several possibilities though he strove to maintain an air of self-righteousness.

"Good to see you, Honey, though I'm not going to be very entertaining I'm afraid," he said. "Been a long day in the saddle but we got five truckloads on the road. That's about twenty-four thousand dollars for Old Man Smith. I should be able to ship enough to pay off the loan but I can't imagine how we're going to put beans on the table this year." He shook his head wearily and slumped into a patio chair.

"Any more in that pitcher?" he pointed to the martini shaker.

"Yes," she answered, "but no complaints about the vermouth. You would take yours straight out of the square bottle if it were chilled. Go in and take a hot shower. I'll have some food on the table when you're clean and comfortable. Don't be so low! We'll get things straightened out, Del."

For Collie the determination to face up to a frank discussion of their relationship and its value for both of them had already diffused the greater part of her resentment. She was not a deep smolderer but vented inner fires with plenty of fresh air so that emotions burned hot and quick but soon used up the fuel. She was quite a stable and uncomplex person at depth despite her impressive demeanor of self-possession learned by experience at endless city council meetings over the years. She went into the kitchen and quickly put the prepared food on the stove to heat up, setting the table with good appetite for the first time since the country club dance.

Dinner was finished and the table cleared. Collie had eaten well and stuck to conversational gambits not likely to interfere with dining or digestion. Del was quieter, consuming more Burgundy wine than food, it seemed, though he did express appreciation for the venison dish which he particularly liked. Now they were both caught unaware in the awkward presence of their mutual estrangement. The evening was over and it was time for husband and wife to retire but the purpose of Collie's visit to the ranch was unfulfilled and neglect of their conjugal relationship for past months was a wall between them.

"Well my dear," Del smiled somewhat wryly as he tapped cooling ash from his brier pipe, "we can make up for some lost opportunities tonight. Let's go to bed."

"Do you really want to make love to me?" she asked in a low, serious voice.

"Of course I do. It's been a hellish summer. I'm afraid you and I haven't been at the top of my priority list because of these financial worries and everything."

She wanted to demand more about his priorities and why Betty Spielman seemed to rank ahead of her but his eyes were dark with fatigue and he seemed, to her, sad and vulnerable.

A few minutes later they were in bed, both attempting to perform normally while each carried a burden of ill will towards the other which, though invisible, weighed them down emotionally like the cumbersome trappings of a deep sea diver. In nature's arbitrary way it was Del who eventually had to roll away on his own side of the bed and assume functional blame for their inability to communicate physically any better than verbally. Collie was struck also with woman's guilt for her inadequacy in summoning the necessary response.

"You are dead tired, Del. We expect too much of ourselves. We need to be together more and I must help you with the worry and burden of running the ranch. I've been selfishly indulging my own interests in town while you were single-handedly keeping us afloat."

She was propped on an elbow gently rubbing his back as she earnestly resolved to repair their contract.

"Maybe I should drop the office. If I were to forget about reelection next year you and I could have more time to devote to each other."

She could not see his face. Her own needs blinded her to the recognition of his tense reaction to her words. He already felt humiliated and stung with shame at his failure to perform just moments earlier. Years of nearly full-blown alcoholism had eroded tolerance for emotional discomfort. He flung back the light bed covering and swung his legs abruptly to the floor so that he was poised, sitting naked, on the edge of the bed with his rigid back to a surprised Collie.

"You ball crusher! You black widow!," he grated in a shaking voice, "You'd love to come back and take over your precious ranch, wouldn't you? You wear the Goddamned pants and I wear the Goddamned apron and we live happily ever after!" He was shouting hoarsely. "Let me tell you something, Baby, I'm not tired and I'm not worried. I'm just tired of you!"

He stood and jerked angrily at the sliding door of his closet. It jumped perversely off its track and fell awkwardly against the hangered clothing within. Collie's reaction to the outburst propelled her out of bed also. She stood with arms outstretched, palms shielding her from the violent accusations.

"You're talking like an idiot, Del. Weren't you listening? I want to help you—not hurt you." She strove to keep her voice level and controlled.

"Now I'm an idiot! You are a wonderful help." He pulled a pair of pants and shirt from his closet; groped through his dresser for shorts and socks. "You'd help me most by just staying the hell away from me. You're going to help me to death if you don't back off. I'm heading for town."

"No!" She grabbed his arm and tried to turn him towards her. "You can't run off now. We've got to get to the bottom of this one way or another. This is one conversation you are going to finish."

"Bullshit! Bullshit!" He grasped her wrist in his left hand and jerked her forward so they stood chest to chest in a pose of ultimate confrontation. His teeth were bared in a grimace of anger as he drew back his right fist to strike her.

"Go ahead and hit me you—you two-timing coward! You aren't man enough to handle me any other way."

Del was not a wife beater.

"Oh Christ, you're a poor excuse for a woman." He shoved her backwards onto the bed and turned hurriedly to pull on his clothing.

"Dear God, what's happened to us?" she cried in anguish to herself, rolling over to bury her face in the pillow. Delvane left with no further parting word.

Hours later, the risen moon was a mottled silvery seal on the charcoal sky as Collie stood on the flagstone patio shivering slightly in the cool silent air of midnight. It was a sad night and she was pressed down with sullen aftermath of the unhappy evening; however she found her vision clear and mind at ease concerning the future with Delvane Winston. There was no future—only the unraveling of legal and emotional entanglements at the fastest possible rate. Her mind was chiefly preoccupied with thoughts of the immediate future and how her personal troubles would conflict with responsibilities and duties to the city. She thought herself shallow and ineffective, unable to control her most intimate relationships.

Behind her the unexpected burr of the bedroom telephone hardly disturbed the silence of the pallid, night-filled canyon but a thrill of alarm traced her already agitated mind as she turned to answer.

HIGH STAKES POKER

Milo walked into the poker room at the Bull Run still suffused with energy and excitement from the fight with Shug and Pronto.

"You got a five dollar stake, at least, to set down with, Cowboy," grinned Denton Eldring sitting to his right at the felt covered table.

"Hee, hee, hee," cackled Carl Haney. "That Mex' come about the width of a red pussy hair from carvin' his name on your hide."

"Yeah," responded Milo with a mock grimace, "he never got the job done though, an' don't you go putting a big foot in your mouth, either, Doc." Milo's little joke referred to Haney's profession of podiatry and brought a laugh from the others.

Tommy Jutes, owner of the Tiptoe ranch, reminisced, "'Minds me of the time a Californicating big city hunter jumped me in a bar up at Tensleep. I never handled it quite as good as Milo. The son-of-a-bitch liked to beat me to death before the bartender cold-cocked him with a chunk of pipe. It turned out he was a lawman of some kind from Los Angeles and one tough bastard."

"We gonna' play some cards or set here jawin' all night?" complained Babe Roberts who was two years into retirement from the Railroad.

Tom Regelstorp pushed a new deck of cards towards Uncle Ting, an old Chinese gentleman hired by Iris to deal and run the nightly game. Ting never played but took the house cut of twenty-five cents from each pot over five dollars and enforced the rules. Uncle Ting also shuffled and dealt each hand to eliminate cheating and speed play.

The gamblers played cautiously, each aware of the others habits and manner-isms except for Regelstorp who seemed to play in an oblivious trance. Tom appeared to possess an accurate knowledge of cards and the odds for or against the making of a winning hand but he never recognized the personalities of his opponents. For instance, Jutes liked to bluff and bet his hand before it was actu-ally made, while Eldring played conservatively and seldom bet unless he believed he held a winner. Tom played every hand alike, staying or folding his cards depending entirely upon what he himself held with little regard for the possibili-ties of another player's chances. Milo quickly realized that table chatter, cunning glances and fake hesitation which sometimes influenced the play of others was wasted effort on Regelstorp, so he played patiently, conserving his stake for an opportunity which he hoped to see before the evening was over. The game was played for table stakes, that is, a man could bet only the amount of money on the table before him at the beginning of the deal. Milo noticed that Regelstorp never left more than about one hundred dollars on the table, thereby limiting his ability to win or lose any more than that amount on any one hand of play. In the usual course of the game the pots varied from five to ten dollars but occasionally two really good hands or determined players would bump up against each other. These infrequent confrontations were eagerly awaited by each player and often winners or losers were determined by only two or three plays during an entire evening of poker.

Past eleven o'clock, with only a couple of hours left to play, Uncle Ting announced a game of five card stud, which turned out to be the big deal of the night. Milo was encouraged by a pair of fives back to back on the first two cards and decided to call Regelstorp's bet of two dollars on an ace showing. Babe Rob-erts and Carl Haney both folded their hands but Eldring and Jutes called with jack and ten showing respectively. The next card gave Tom a queen to go with his ace, three fives for Milo and each of the other two got a king. There was lots of color on the table but Milo's pair of fives showing got the bet. Figuring that three fives would probably win the hand, Milo bet only five dollars hoping to keep the other players in the game. Regelstorp called the five-dollar bet and raised ten more which notified all concerned that he had aces or queens paired for sure. Only Milo called the raise; Denton and Tommy folding their hands to wait for a better chance. The next deal brought Tom another ace and Milo the case five. Milo knew that Tom's best hand was three aces but thought Tom would have read his four fives as well, otherwise Milo would have folded along with Eldring and Jutes on the previous bet. Milo tossed twenty dollars into the pot expecting Tom to fold immediately. Instead, Regelstorp called the twenty and raised fifty, which was all the remainder of his chips on the table. Milo happily called the bet and sat patiently waiting for the final card to be dealt by Uncle Ting so that he could expose his hand and rake in the pot. Milo was dealt a seven and Tom a queen which gave him two pair showing but an obvious full house with an ace **or** queen in the hole. Milo's four fives were better than Tom's hand of cards no matter what he had in the hole.

"Okay Tom," Milo smiled, "turn 'em over and read 'em and weep." He started to expose his hole card and pull in the modest pile of chips in the center of the green felt table.

"Hold it there!" Regelstorp commanded. "If you aint gonna' bet them three fives I get me a chance, don't I?"

Milo realized with a mental eye-blink that he had badly underestimated Tom's inexperience at the game. "He really thinks that li'l ol' full boat has me beat," Milo told himself.

Feigning a slight frown of puzzlement, Milo said, "Well, Tom, we're playin' table stakes here an' you're all in the pot. You can't go to the well in the middle of a hand."

"Shit, Harris, I don't mind gettin' more money out for this here hand if you don't. Christ, man, you can't take it with you."

Every man at the table felt that Harris was sitting on a sure winner but since he was well liked and played often as opposed to Regelstorp, who was an unknown newcomer and obvious tenderfoot, no one said a word about the house rules.

"Uncle Ting," Milo appealed, "if we both decide to play no limit and we're the only ones in the pot, I guess you wouldn't say nothing contrary would you?" He squinted fiercely at the little Chinese man to try and emphasize the seriousness of his point. Uncle Ting was hardly the inscrutable Oriental.

"Hell fire, you find crazy fool to make crazy bet, Bull Run no care."

Milo glanced uncomfortably at Regelstorp to see if he were intimidated by this sarcasm and was delighted to see pockets being turned out and a greasy wallet being deposited on the table.

"All right, Harris, I got seven hundred, fifty-six dollars right here," Tom challenged. He pushed the bills out on the table with a triumphant shove. "That's what I think of them three fives of yours."

Milo sat in quiet contemplation for a moment wondering just how much money Tom might have in his sock. "You know when you went to your pockets that means we got no limit here, don't you?" Milo asked.

"Sure. That's why I shoved her all out there. You going to call or not?"

"I guess I'm going to call all right. I'm going to write a check and throw in this pot, Tom. Mr. Eldring and Mr. Jutes will both vouch for whatever I bet. I wouldn't bet more than I'm good for."

"Bullshit," Tom responded crisply. "I got green out there an' that's what you better get ponied up if you want to play with me. If these fellers are so damn sure you're good for it you can borrow off them."

"There's no bank open this time of night. I'm tellin' you my check is as good as gold," Milo asserted.

"Put up or shut up, Harris. I'm about ready to pull this pot."

Milo still had over two thousand dollars of Ballard Crown's money in an envelope carefully hidden in his locked pickup truck. The money was required to pay the tax bill and various items of equipment, which Ballard had ordered for the barbecue. Milo knew the money would be needed before his return to the ranch the next day but he also knew his cards were better than Regelstorp's, so there was no risk in adopting a temporary loan from his boss.

"Give me three minutes and I'll get the Goddamned money. I might get more than you think." Milo got up without waiting for a reply and quickly went out the back door to the parking lot. He unlocked the cab and pulled the seat forward, retrieving a cash envelope from within a pile of old burlap sacks. As he turned to go back inside he sighted the slight figure of the newcomer, Pronto, paused beneath a street light on the sidewalk thirty feet away, rolling a cigarette with quick practiced motions. Milo could sense cold black eyes piercing his back as he strode across the parking lot to the waiting drama at the poker table.

"Here's my bet," Milo said tersely, deliberately peeling off twenty, one hundred-dollar bills onto the pile in the middle of the table. "I'll see your seven fifty-six and raise you twelve forty-four, and, by God, I want to see cash."

A raise was the last thing Tom expected. He began to wonder for the first time what Milo was so proud of. He had never considered the possibility that his aces full could be beaten.

"Now that's a pure crock of shit, Harris. You saw me empty my poke. I aint got another cent and you can't just buy the pot out from under me." Tom appealed mutely to the others who merely stared blankly or grinned at his discomfiture.

Uncle Ting said, "Come on, come on. Got to deal cards now."

Regelstorp frowned and glanced almost furtively around the poker table. He opened his dirty canvas windbreaker and unzipped a long inside pocket, withdrawing a fat envelope marked with smudges and coffee stains.

"Just hold your water now," Tom said. "Read this here doc'ament and tell me what you think I'm worth, by God."

Milo unfolded the mining claim royalty contract but quickly became bogged down in the whereas and party of the first part legal phraseology.

"What the hell is this, Denton?" he asked, tossing the paper to the lawyer.

Eldring absently plucked at his thick black eyebrows, rapidly scanning salient points of the contract. The others at the table were, by now, deeply curious about Regelstorp's mysterious assets and sat silently awaiting a pronouncement. Tom, too, was anxious to gage the effect of the contract in raising his status amongst the players. He had felt superior and elevated above the others all along and now his secret was about to become public knowledge with attendant recognition and respect.

"Well Milo, you must be a gambler or you wouldn't be here," said Eldring, tossing the contract onto the considerable pile of chips and cash. "This paper is a contract between our friend, Tom, here, and Mr. George Frailey concerning a bunch of mining claims. Seems Frailey has agreed to pay five thousand cash plus royalties of ten percent of the gross sales on any mineral mined and sold off these Canteen claims."

Tom grinned triumphantly and slapped his palms down in a gesture of triumph and finality as if all questions were now settled. There was speculative silence for a few moments as Milo was trying to figure out if he had missed something.

"What the hell are you getting at, Regelstorp?" demanded Carl Haney. "You got to tell us a story, here, if you expect to get let back into that pot of money."

"It's me you got to deal with," Milo interrupted, leaning across the table, "an' I'll tell you, that piece of paper don't mean jack shit to me."

From the way Tom was acting, however, Milo had a feeling that there might be more to the contract than Eldring's comments had revealed. He knew he had the pot won so the only suspense, so far as he was concerned, was how much more he might be able to squeeze out of Regelstorp. Milo was willing to listen.

"B-Jesus, can't you figure it out?" Regelstorp scoffed. "Mr. Frailey is the biggest shot in this town an' he knows them Canteen claims are hotter than a firecracker. We got tested proof, an' besides, my ol' uranium counter went off like an alarm clock when I set her down on that ore strike. It plumb pegged the needle so I guess that proves what I got. If Frailey believes in it enough to pay me five thousand just to tie up the deal I guess that ought to convince you boys. Harris, let me throw in a' IOU for the twelve forty-four against the royalties off these claims and we'll get this game runnin' again."

"Don't get your balls in an uproar," Milo said calmly. "I wouldn't take an IOU off you if you had ol' Orville Smith's signature tattooed on your butt. Or George Frailey's either for that matter. What you need, my man, is twelve hundred and forty-four dollars in good, hard cash if you want in this pot."

As Tom began to curse and sputter Milo interrupted. "Look here, Tom, you just sign that contract over to me and toss her on that pot and we can turn these cards over. Hell, I know I got you beat anyhow."

"No way, Harris, you son-of-a-bitch. This contract is worth more money than you ever heard of." Tom snatched up the papers and waved them frantically in the air before the players. "I'll buy and sell all you dumb bastards once these claims start producing. You can keep this penny-ante poker game and shove that pot up your black ass!"

Milo could see that poor Regelstorp was on the verge of hysteria. His language was offensive in the extreme and provocative beyond the point where Milo's usual pacific nature could be counted on to control his response to the deadly insults. Gunfights were only historical memories in Sheila's Tree but certain words remained starkly taboo in the code of the West. To call a man a son-of-a-bitch was certain challenge to mortal combat, let alone the offhand reference to illegitimacy of all the assembled witnesses. Milo was forced to respond in the expected fashion, though his youth in the black ghetto of Oakland, California had exposed him to verbal abuse of such descriptive fantasy that the trite, ritual insults of Sheila's Tree always seemed ludicrously innocuous to him. In three unhurried steps Milo was around the table and had Regelstorp pressed firmly against the wall, his throat in the grip of Milo's right hand; the index finger of Milo's left hand pushing Tom's beaklike nose sideways across his face.

"Man, you got diarrhea of the mouth and I'm going to make you eat those words. You take back your filthy names for me and the rest of these boys or your nose is going to get turned inside out. I got your money, I don't need your mouthy bullshit," Milo grated.

Tom could not answer because of the force of Milo's grip on his throat. He was not able to fight back or loosen Milo's hold and only shook his head from side to side in short jerks, turning red and gasping harshly for air. As Milo finally let go and stepped back, Tom slumped against the wall massaging his neck.

"Jesus, I never meant it bad. We talked that way in the Army all the time. I take it back. Leave me the hell alone," Tom wheezed, almost weeping.

"Look man," Milo stated in a conciliatory manner, "we got unfinished business on the table here. I'll take your word for it that these mining claims might be worth something someday if you want to call my bet."

Tom rubbed his throat and glared at Milo. "I got the best poker hand I held all week," Tom declared. "I'm bound to have a winner if you let me in that pot so don't do yourself any big Goddamn favors."

Milo shook his head in disbelief at Tom's blind naiveté. "Mr. Eldring can just write up a paragraph on the bottom of that contract to where you sign over half interest to me; we both sign and I'll call that good enough to call my twelve hundred and forty-four buck raise," Milo proposed.

"Jesus, Milo, you're the biggest sucker I ever seen at a poker table," jeered Babe Roberts.

"Screw you, old man," Tom bellowed. "I'll show you assholes how to play this game. Go ahead and write up something," Tom addressed the Attorney. "The faster we turn these cards over the better I like it."

Denton Eldring grinned and scratched a few lines on the last page of Tom's contract.

"My fee is twenty-five dollars for this, Harris. I don't do legal work for nothing."

He offered the paper for both men's signatures and witness validations from the other three players at the table.

"I'll take this to the office on Monday and have copies typed up for both of you and get the addendum recorded at the courthouse. She'll be completely legal. Now lets quit screwing around and turn over those hole cards," the Attorney said.

No one except Tom Regelstorp was the least bit surprised to see the fourth five when Milo turned over his hidden card. Aces full of queens came in a distant second between the two hands.

With Regelstorp broke and out of the game, interest soon waned and the game broke up. Milo stepped out the side door to the parking lot amid half-insulting congratulations for having gleaned the last of Regelstorp's windfall. He walked out to the old pickup and got in but did not start the motor. The others drove off and soon Uncle Ting came out, locked the door, and walked towards his furnished apartment a block and a half away on Nez Perce Avenue. Milo waited in the still darkness for another five minutes, then quietly emerged from the truck and stepped lightly across the deserted parking lot. On the far side of the old frame building containing the Bull Run bar and restaurant, a wooden staircase offered an exterior entrance to living quarters on the second floor. Milo ascended stealthily and rapped gently on the unlighted door. It swung open immediately, as if someone were waiting for the signal, and Milo stepped inside.

DARK OF NIGHT

Pronto inhaled a hot drag on a loosely constructed roll-your-own cigarette and watched the black man disappear back into the Bull Run poker room. He scowled and gently rubbed a throbbing bruise on the back of his head, thinking with regret of the near miss at knifing Milo in the back.

I'll get another chance at that hijo de putah, he thought. Nex' time I be mas pronto.

Shortly before, with his head aching and a morose depression reinforced by Shug's alternate whine and bluster, he had decided to leave the bar for some fresh air. Pronto liked to walk at night, alone, to watch unobserved and learn secrets. The dark, wide streets of Sheila's Tree, lined with bulky, shadowed buildings, illuminated only by weak interior lights or scattered low wattage street lights, beckoned to Melendez's predatory urges. Cover of darkness had always meant both safety and opportunity to Pronto. He lived by self-indulgence, by thievery, lying, cheating and violence, without mercy or conscience. Since babyhood he had survived in the deadly, competitive environment of the worst barrios and among the lowest levels of poverty and criminality to be found in the Mexican border towns of the southwest. He lived by recognizing easy prey and taking immediate, ruthless advantage. Pronto, and Shug as well, were capable of even more serious deeds of crime and violence than Reinhardt had ever asked of them.

Despite having drunk a fair amount of alcohol during the evening, Pronto moved lightly and alertly through the almost deserted streets. His eyes roved darkened alleys looking automatically for windows ajar or vulnerable parked cars as the crisp early autumn air kept him moving at a rapid pace. He felt invisible and powerful in this new town where he was unknown and unrecognized. With no target of nefarious opportunity presenting itself and his head clearing of smoke and whiskey fumes, he prepared to turn back towards the Bull Run. He found himself in the spacious courthouse parking lot on Second Street and stepped into heavy shrubbery of a median strip to relieve building pressure on his bladder. He stood, kneading his penis in a sexual semi-trance, when the back door of the courthouse, no more than thirty feet away, swung open with a flare of light.

Louise Greene glanced at her watch in the hall light before stepping out into the darkness. After eleven o'clock, but she had finished typing the interminable budget and it would be ready for Collie on Monday. Louise had agreed to finish the job over the weekend but plans for a shopping trip to Casper dictated that she stay late and finish up at once. It had been a long tedious day, leaving her back-sore and weary. She walked around the parking strip and approached her trim blue and white Chevrolet, unaware of the lithe, menacing figure crouched in shadow by the front fender. Pronto had not noticed the car at his back on the other side of the landscaping shrubbery until it became Louise's obvious destination. As she fumbled to insert a key into the car door, the predator needed only two silent steps to attack. His left hand clamped over her mouth as his body pressed her hard against the car door. His right hand held the knife against her throat. He pushed the weapon against her taut skin in a slight sawing motion, causing a shallow scratch, which set aflow a smear of blood. Louise was paralyzed with terror at the suddenness and violence of the assault. The man's weight nearly knocked the breath from her lungs and the bright, burning pain on her neck became the center of sensational awareness. She thought she was being killed.

"Don' make one leettle noise if you wan' to save you' skinny neck," hissed Pronto. "I keel you like a chicken if you make one move or one scream."

He moved the knife shallowly again and another crimson stain flowed down her throat. She mewed a shaking sob against his palm and shrunk away as much as possible towards the car. He took his hand away from her mouth and clutched a handful of shoulder length hair instead, slamming her face against the car top. She gasped in pain but made no sound for fear of the pressing blade. Quickly returning the switchblade to his pocket, Pronto picked up Louise's fallen handbag. With his shoulder leaning into her back, he searched through the purse, removed twelve dollars it contained and stuffed the money into his pocket. He reached around Louise's body, turned the key still dangling from the lock and started to open the car door. The interior light came on with startling brightness and he quickly closed the door with a shove.

"Fock it, lady. You gots not'ing in there I wan' anyhow. There's sometin' else you gonna' do for me before I turn loose you' skinny white ass. You' gonna' like it."

His right hand was under her pink cashmere sweater and she squealed thinly through clinched teeth as he fiercely squeezed her breast.

"Shut up, Goddamn it, if you don' wanna' lose more than a piece of ass. One more yelp an' I gonna' haf to do you fast while you' still warm," Pronto snarled grimly.

It was a brief business to force her ahead of him into the foliage and push her face down on the rough layer of landscaping bark. Quick, cruel hands ripped off black skirt, sweater, shoes and stockings and, finally, underwear, so that she felt icy air and scratching, prickly contact with the cold ground. As her cheek pressed into the bleached wood chips she whispered desperate pleadings.

"Please don't. Oh God, please don't. Please let me go. Oh God, help me! Please help me somebody!"

Her voice began to rise in hysteria as he tore at her clothing and mauled her body. With a cruel jerk, he pulled her head up and stuffed one of the nylon stockings into her mouth. He poked and shoved until she was effectively gagged, then loosely bundled the skirt around her head to further muffle cries and blindfold her eyes. Throughout the attack he had been careful to prevent a full look at his face. Louise had been too frightened and shocked to think of fighting back but she instinctively clawed at the wrapping around her head. He wrenched her arms behind her back, bound her wrists tightly with the remaining stocking, and rolled her onto her back. Pronto was suffused with a sense of euphoria as the totally helpless girl struggled and squirmed beneath him.

What Melindez did to Louise bore little relation to a sexual act, nor was it inspired by normal hormonal urges. He was responding to vicious impulses fostered during a tortured, abusive childhood and criminal adulthood. His temporary control over her physical body was the permissive signal affirming any unspeakable cruelty or humiliation that he could think of. He bit her breasts and buttocks; pinched, struck and intruded every part of her body with probing, hard fingers, until, at last, at the zenith of enraged excitement, he slipped muscular arms between her legs and beneath her knees, doubling her body so that she was spread and exposed for the deepest, fiercest, final penetration. He thrust and plunged furiously within her body, seeking the blast of release that would be the culmination of his terrible assault. Louise felt each jarring strike as lacerating pain. In her contorted position she could barely breathe and her helplessness under the malign intensity of his attack was terrifying. Prevented from crying out by the stifling clothing, only her mind screamed the agony she felt. It seemed an eternity before he slumped over her wounded body in sweating, gasping subsidence.

Louise lay tightly curled, legs clamped together and knees pulled to her breast, as waves of deep, grinding pain pulsed from her groin. The burning torment of scratched, bruised and abraded flesh was nothing compared to the percussive beat of internal injury. It was long minutes before the searing shock began to wear off and sensations other than pain entered her awareness. The monster was gone. Her body began to shake with cold. She wanted to live; to be safe; to hide; and wash herself clean. She tried to sit up, shaking the skirt from her head and laboriously pushing the gag from her mouth. With concentrated effort of mind and body Louise finally managed to pry the elastic loops of nylon from her wrists and was free. As if in a trance, thinking of only one small objective after another, she gathered her scattered clothing, picked up her purse, and, trembling with cold, shock and fatigue, stumbled into the car. She drove home to her small one bedroom rental house and immediately called Collie Winston, the one person in the world who could possibly, it seemed to her, cope with or assist her in coping with the catastrophic horror of the last hour. Having stammered a disjointed and nearly unintelligible plea for help, Louise simply let the receiver of the phone drop and hurried to the bathroom. She stood under the shower blasted by almost unbearably hot water until every drop of heated liquid was used up and the stinging spray began to cool.

Collie dressed hurriedly and broke records in her Studebaker on the trip back to town. As she sped down Second Street, all but deserted at 1:00 am, Ryan Baker was just returning from Casper after a long day of business meetings with the oil company. He was startled as Collie's gray coupe flashed across the intersection in front of him, her face a white blur behind the windshield. Without hesitation he followed her speeding flight for another five blocks and pulled in behind Collie as she parked and hurried up a narrow concrete walk towards Louise's modest front door.

"Collie," he cried, "what is it?"

"Ryan Baker. What are you doing here?" Collie was distracted by his call. "Never mind. Oh Ry, just wait out here until I call. It's Louise Greene—she has been...hurt. I may need you. Just wait—wait." She turned and hurried on, letting herself into the house as Ryan stood beside his car prepared to wait as long as necessary until Collie reappeared.

It was a long and trying night. Collie soothed, calmed and comforted Louise, offering sympathy and support to her distraught and suffering friend. After awhile Louise regained some composure; Collie's apparent acceptance of her violation as a tragic accident led to a calmer perspective on her own part. Shock, rage and grief gave way in reluctant increments to small gains of self-possession that had been destroyed by the humiliating attack. Collie persuaded Louise to be taken to the hospital and to contact the Sheriff's office.

By five o'clock in the morning Ryan and an exhausted Collie sat in his car in the driveway of Collie's townhouse. Louise was sedated and sleeping in a private room at Mercy Hospital.

"My God, Ry, I can't believe the interrogation those Deputies put the poor girl through", Collie deplored angrily. "You would think she had lured that man down to the parking lot on her own, the way they kept hammering at her. That sadist, Wilbur Shliefsanger, made her repeat every disgusting detail at least three times. Doctor Hysett said it was the most brutal attack of that kind that he had ever seen."

"It's a good thing you were there with her", Ryan said.

"You can't believe what was done to her. He has to be caught. Louise said he sounded like a Mexican but she never even saw his face. How can such things happen in Sheila's Tree?" Collie pleaded.

"We live in an insulated world here, I guess. It's hard to accept that a degenerate animal is walking our streets," Ryan responded.

Collie shuddered and shook her head. "This has been the worst night of my life. It seems as if the whole world has turned dark and ugly in ways I never expected. I think I've just about seen the ruination of everything I ever loved or wanted." Turning a pale and tired face towards Ryan, who was watching her with all too easily read emotions of his own, she clasped her arms about herself as if to provide some support that no longer came from inner conviction.

"You're dead tired. Maybe things look worse than they should right now. Louise is a strong, healthy young woman. She can survive this with the support of friends like you and her attacker will certainly be caught. This town is too small for someone to get away with a crime like this." Ryan reached out and put a hand on Collie's shoulder in a tentative gesture of sympathy. Collie's eyes wavered and she bowed her head under Ryan's steadfast gaze.

I have thought about you ever since that ridiculous meeting at the swimming hole, she mused silently. I even let myself imagine what it might be like to be really close to you. I can tell you find something attractive in me; you're almost like a little boy at times, so naive and yet intelligent and understanding. Poor Ryan, you would be appalled to know me as I really am, someone unable to shape and control her own life. I have to find myself and get a handle on things before I can even think of taking more risks.

"I must go in," she murmured, quickly moving over to leave the car.

BARBECUE AND
DIAMOND DRILLS

The D-Z barbecue was a western party of many facets. There were three tables of bridge in the parlor of the big house for some of the elder and more sedentary guests; young children were dashing about the spacious grounds, climbing trees and riding ponies in the meadow below the spring, while most of the adults sat about, pitched horseshoes or strolled in conversational groups. Iced tubs of beer and tables with rows of whiskey bottles were located in convenient abundance.

Meanwhile, the actual fall roundup of cattle was going on atop the Bench and many neighbors and friends were taking part in the activity. Iris Patton and Ryan Baker had ridden up the steep trail early in the morning along with a small group of other sometime cowhands. Upon arrival at the top, guests were sent by Milo Harris, in groups along with one or two of his regular hands, to various locations among the ridges and shallow canyons where cattle were to be found. Their job was to comb animals out of the brush and herd them towards loading corrals from which they would be trucked down to market or to D-Z winter feeding yards. Ryan was assigned to ride up a wide, heavily brushed draw about three miles and then scatter out with Squirrely and Cowboy to search the upper range for strays that might have been missed during the past couple of weeks. Once separated from the group, Ryan decided to ride over to the site of the water tank, which he had examined earlier in the summer. He saw that his careful instructions had been followed in spreading and compacting a thick impervious clay layer over the gravel bottom of the small canyon. A broad earthen dam had been constructed of compacted sandy clay mixed with gravel and built up to a height of about sixteen feet. At one end of the crest of the dam a rock-lined spillway would allow escape of excess water when the small reservoir filled up to overflowing in the spring run-off. From what he could observe, Ryan was sure that his careful drawings had been followed to the letter and that the tank would hold water throughout the dry summer season once melting snows were captured.

Ryan noticed many cow tracks in the recently disturbed earth surrounding the new watering pond and decided to ride on further up the now-dry water course in search of strays. Less than one half mile above the dam, still on the D-Z range, he came upon a high masted rotary drill rig churning and grinding away at the floor of the wash. Drill sampling, of course, was very familiar to Ryan. A tool of the geologist's trade, the drill provides a means of probing unseen depths and recovery of rock samples from far below the surface. He supposed, at first, that this crew was hired by Ballard Crown to drill for water. There were a few wells on the Bench drilled by ranchers to obtain a secure supply of stock water for the dry season. As he watched, the men began to pull sections of drill pipe out of the hole and stack them beside the rig. He noticed wooden racks laid out on the ground containing long cylinders of rock core samples which were being carefully labeled and saved for study. Ryan knew immediately that he was not watching water well construction but mineral sampling on a large scale and in a systematic way. He walked his horse up to the drill truck and assumed the innocent role of a working cowhand, which he hoped he resembled.

"Howdy fellas," Ryan greeted. "Reckon you're gonna hit water down there 'fore long?"

"Why shoot, Slim, we aint drillin' for no water..." one of the driller's helpers began derisively, only to be cut off by a quick command from the leader of the crew.

"Shut your face, Hamm!" A huge, black bearded man at least six feet, four inches in height fixed Ryan with a steely glare. "What the hell you moseyin' around up here on Gov'ment land for, Cowboy? We're tryin' to get somethin' done here and we don't need no Goddamn gawkers. You better just haul it up on that nag and move it outta' here."

"You got it wrong, Mister," Ryan smiled neutrally. "This is D-Z range you're setting on and if Ballard Crown isn't paying for your footage, I'd say you are trespassing. Is your name Bruchek?" Ryan had noticed the name painted on the truck.

"My name is Bruchek, all right, and you can tell your boss any damn thing you want to, only just haul your ass before I kick it. You aint no cowboy." The big man had throttled the diesel engine to an idle and thrown a clamp on the drill string to hold it suspended in the hole. He turned his full attention on Ryan. "What do you know about "footage"? You aint as dumb as you look. Who sent you up here to check us out?" Bruchek was used to the secrecy and subterfuge of mineral exploration and was now convinced that this intruder was an agent of some rival group trying to penetrate New Mexico Mining Company's interest in the area.

Ryan walked over to the racks of core samples and started to bend over for a closer examination. He could see that the rock was mostly sandstone with some of the core broken and missing. Gaps in the core footage, where the strata was too soft and unconsolidated to come out in a solid round bar of material, were filled in with sacks of loose drill cuttings. Ryan made a serious mistake in ignoring the hairy driller. He felt a smashing blow to his left hip as Bruchek's foot connected and sent him flying to the ground. He did not stay down long. Bruchek grabbed his shirt and jerked him erect, then delivered an open handed slap to the jaw with stunning force. The big driller spun Ryan around and hurled him against his horse with a two handed shove.

"Climb in that saddle and get the hell out of here while you can still sit up, Sonny. I aint goin' to say it again."

Ryan grasped the saddle horn to keep from sliding to the ground again and waited a moment for shooting stars to clear his head. He pulled himself into the saddle and started the horse back down towards the roundup. A splash of blood drooled from the corner of his mouth and every jogging step shot pain through his buttocks. Ryan realized that he had stumbled upon a serious and secretive enterprise being expertly carried out by an extremely formidable operator.

WORK AND PLAY AT
THE ROUNDUP

Milo was doing the work of three men. He supervised a swirl of man and animal activity taking place over several acres of holding area, corrals and loading chutes. Cows, calves and yearling steers and heifers were herded down in small groups from the gullies above to three working corrals near a dirt lane with access to Pass Road. Mature animals that already bore the D-Z brand were separated, examined and loaded into waiting cattle trucks. Sound cows that were determined to be good breeding stock were hauled down to pastures below the Bench for wintering and saved to replenish herds next year. Older cows past their prime or those somehow injured during the year on the high summer range were culled for sale and loaded onto another truck bound for the slaughterhouse. Branded two to three year olds of both sexes weighing from six to eight hundred pounds on the hoof were also loaded into market trucks. These sleek and healthy animals provided prime beef to the butcher shops of America and were the principal financial support of the D-Z operation. Most years several hundred young beeves were produced for market. All the traditional cowboy skills were displayed by Milo's experienced 'punchers and many of the roundup guests, as well, who helped cut out and separate the nervous, bawling animals. The scene was a broiling confusion of running horses and cattle; clouds of fine, aromatic dust; smells of hair and hide and sweat. It was a convivial, optimistic time as crews worked together harvesting the annual "crop" produced by careful management of grass, water and animals during the year.

Within a few hours the work routine was pretty well established and Milo had some time to ride about checking on the various phases of the operation. In one draw where a small herd of cattle was waiting its turn to be escorted down to the corrals, he came upon Iris Patton and Corky Noonan cutting out another dozen animals. Iris and her mount flowed through the herd in effortless, economical runs, separating selected animals, bunching them together and moving them off towards the roundup area a quarter of a mile below. She always seemed to know exactly when a skittish calf was ready to break away or dart back to the main bunch. Her horse was there in a few steps, blocking the way and gently forcing the stubborn, range-wild cattle to move in the proper direction.

Corky had no such easy facility. His horse was more skilled than he, though once a few head of stock were separated and moving he was able to trail along and keep them going in the right direction. Unfortunately, Corky had made a major miscalculation about his physical condition and abilities. Three days previously, after months of introspection, extended dialogue with his wife and doctor, reflection on his family of five healthy, active children and more dialogue with his wife, Corky had reluctantly decided to go forward with minor surgery known as a vasectomy. A tiny incision, two quick snips, and the Noonans were no longer concerned about family planning or birth control. Corky was overweight and more at home behind a drafting table or in a pickup truck than atop a horse. Hours of jogging, bouncing and sliding about in the saddle produced unforeseen complications in what was normally an imperceptible and easy healing process. As Milo rode up, a pale and hurting highway engineer swayed forward over the saddle horn.

"Oh sweet Jesus, Milo, help me down off this splay-footed son-of-a-bitch. My Goddamn balls are swoll up like a couple of Bartlett pears!"

Milo and Iris helped the suffering tenderfoot into a cattle truck, administered several aspirin and sent him on the long bumpy ride over to Pass Road and down off the Bench.

"I always knew cowboys had a lot of balls," Iris taunted Milo as they rode back along one of the cow trails.

"Go ahead and laugh. Poor ol' Corky was in downright agony. It's going to be awhile before he can even walk, let alone make any use of his cojones," Milo shuddered in sympathy.

"Well, maybe that won't be as hard on Corky as it would be on you." She laughed and spurred her horse ahead; turned off the trail into a dense stand of luminous yellow quaking aspen and pulled to a stop in a sunny glade against a tall outcrop of tumbled granite boulders. She dismounted ankle deep in freshly fallen leaves and met Milo with open arms as he swung out of the saddle.

They made love slowly, with passion and energy arising from too seldom opportunities to be with each other.

"I never get enough of you, Iris. You're in my thoughts night and day. I feel like a school kid."

"I don't know how we got into this, my darling, but I'm as bad as you are." She rubbed dense curls on his chest with her forehead, filling his nostrils with the pale scent of her chestnut hair. "Sometimes I think we should just run away to Tahiti or somewhere and be together forever."

Iris could not see the squint of pain that her words brought to Milo's eyes. He was very much aware that his view of their relationship was different from hers, but, because of the depth of his feeling, he was hesitant to explore the extent of her fear. Milo was a rare black man whose self-esteem remained relatively untouched and untrammeled by the constant psychic erosion of racial discrimination. Somehow, despite childhood in a black, urban neighborhood where poisonous racial impacts were felt every day of his life, he had managed to develop a rational, healthy self-image. He saw himself as a man, with certain limitations and handicaps to be sure, but with a good mind, superb physical skills and confidence that he could be accepted and valued as an individual rather than a cultural or racial stereotype. Few of his friends or family were able to achieve a comparable level of sanity. Many saw themselves through the eyes of the powerful majority and fulfilled expectations of inferiority with unhealthy acceptance.

"I love you, Milo. I never knew a man could be like you are—as strong and tough as a mountain ram but sweet and gentle as a little baby lamb. I could lay here and fuss over you all morning but Mr. Crown would probably fire you and I know if my ass gets much colder I'll probably just freeze to the ground and be up here all winter."

Milo rolled over in the thick carpet of rustling leaves and held the girl against his body. The sun radiated some warmth but the air carried a sting of cold autumn.

"In the past six months I've made love to you in every hidey-hole in Galena County, woman. The other night in your apartment after the poker game was the only time we've seen a real bed in that whole time. Seems to me you're pretty much at home with leaves all stuck in your hair."

"I know! And one of these days we're goin' to get caught and you'll have more to worry about than a couple of stickers in your underwear. If this hick town knew what you and me was up to we'd both get tarred and feathered. My Daddy, bless his alcohol-pickled soul, would roll over in his grave if he could see me now. I was always kind of independent and wrong headed like a female James Dean and when you came along I just never seemed to notice your sun tan"—she ran her hand along his smooth muscular thigh—"but sometimes I get scared to death when I think about what we're doing."

"There's places where we could live together just like regular folks," Milo suggested softly. "I don't think I can get by any more without you."

She lay in stillness upon his broad chest without the usual wisecrack that often hid her feelings. She kissed him deeply and then jumped up like a boyish nymph and began to dress. They hurried back to the demanding tasks of the roundup, their passion for each other unquenched; her fear and uncertainty unassuaged.

URANIUM RUSH AND POLITICS

That evening, as hot, spicy chili, thick steaks and strong coffee satisfied appetites sharpened by the long day of work and play, news of the uranium discovery began to circulate. For many it was only an item of novel interest, hardly distracting from the main topic for gossip and outraged discussion, which was the violent rape of the Greene girl. For others the significance of a possible new source of wealth in the community posed an arena for speculation and opportunity. Ryan Baker became a center of attention as various groups heard rumors of activity on the Bench or distorted reports of the Bull Run poker game. Ryan's swollen jaw was impressive evidence that somebody was guarding secrets around the drill rigs which had been seen at work over a broad area on the upper ranges of the D-Z and Palmer spreads. The allure of riches in the earth, waiting to be found and exploited, took hold of many imaginations as stories were repeated and embellished. Bill Spielman, the city councilman, told of a cousin in the four-corners country who staked several claims one Sunday afternoon and sold them two weeks later for three hundred thousand dollars. Hector Grubb, a hired hand at the Tiptoe ranch, told how Milo Harris had turned down an offer of fifty thousand dollars for his share of the Canteen claims on the night of the poker game. Dr. Carl Haney was one of those in the group listening to the totally fabricated rumor and he wondered which one of those present at the now famous poker game had been so perceptive of the value of Regelstorp's paper at the time. Someone else had heard that a big Eastern conglomerate was ready to invest millions in the development of a vast open pit mine which would employ hundreds of laborers at astronomical wages. All of a sudden, at the D-Z roundup barbecue, the Wyoming uranium rush put out flourishing shoots and became a vibrant powerful tree of activity. Ryan was handicapped to some degree by his professional knowledge of the rarity and difficulty in development of a profitable commercial mining venture. He thought in terms of investment capital, development costs, ore body exploration and evaluation, marketing, and all the exacting technical details which most of those present had no ability to visualize. As a result, he downplayed the wild rumors both in his own mind and in discussions that swirled through the crowd, citing difficulties and obstacles instead of participating in the expanding excitement and optimism. His trepidation was unshared by the majority. A few dropped everything and drove back to town immediately in order to prepare for prospecting ventures at first light the next day. Many made plans of one kind or another, depending upon their particular business or perspective, to participate in this unique opportunity. Raymond Crown was mentally composing the front page of tomorrow's Galena Journal with lurid headlines and tales of discovered wealth. Orville Smith was visualizing investment possibilities for his bank and so it went, as near hysteria mounted.

Among those relatively disinterested and untouched by the exhilarating ramifications of a possible uranium strike was a subdued Collie Winston. Louise's rape was more, to her, than a terrible crime victimizing a close friend. Mixed up in her mind on that awful night was the last sordid encounter with Del, the growing realization of financial problems, fear and self-doubt about her own ability and objectives, so that the abuse suffered by Louise became a theme of constant, depressing worry. Numbly, she had visited the law office of Liam O'Brian, an old friend of her parents, and started the cold, legal process of divorce. She felt that her life was a tinsel replica of something she had once had, and that her interests and activities were futile and insignificant. Too many stressful and distressing events added up to distracting anxiety and Collie's stoic unawareness of self was working against her. Her unselfconscious personality caused her to overlook the personal effects of these psychic buffets and, instead, blame herself for having somehow allowed it all to happen.

She was toying with her food, deep in thought when an old political mentor, Wyatt Paige, found a moment to sit down beside her. One of Ballard Crown's more notable guests, the senior Senator from Wyoming was greatly interested in the breaking news on everyone's lips at the gathering. He was an ex-professor of economics at the University at Laramie, having taught Juno Castle and many others before turning to national politics, and was a good friend to many ranchers and businessmen in Sheila's Tree. Indeed, to be elected in Wyoming, one had to be on first name acquaintance with a large share of the four hundred thousand residents of the state. The Democratic system of popular vote never worked so well nor took such literal form as in the sparsely populated western states where personal evaluation was the voter's gauge of a candidate's worth. Collie, at age eighteen, had worked as a Congressional Page in Washington DC upon being nominated for the position by a newly elected Senator Paige. Later, in 1947 after completing her Masters in political science at University of California, she was employed by Paige on his personal staff, but the nation's capitol immediately following the war years was a madhouse that Collie hated. After eighteen months of very hard work during which time the only social engagements were "parties" where young female staffers were expected to serve as willing concubines for all levels of military and political brass that flowed through the city on post war assignment, she returned to Sheila's Tree to help her father on the ranch and await the return of Delvane Winston from his military assignment in England. Despite her refusal of the easy practices of many of the Senator's staff, she had remained Paige's friend and supporter and he sought her out at the barbecue.

"Madam Mayor, as beautiful as ever and, I'm sure, a good deal more experienced and tougher than a few years ago. Are we holding the political organization together since the presidential election last year, my dear?"

"Oh yes, Wyatt. General Ike was so strong here that the Grand Old Party actually picked up support. I can't imagine who the Democrats will run against you next time. There isn't a single name in the State that could oppose you at this point," she reassured the Senator.

Senator Paige was well aware of his invulnerability and, after two strong drinks of Ballard's excellent black label whiskey, was expansive and relatively depoliticized. He was never completely off stage, however, and even his most domestic conversation tended to resemble a class lecture.

"What is your opinion of this uranium business, Collie? Everyone here seems to be excited about it. There is a great need to increase our military stockpiles, and with Stalin's death the potential destabilization of the Kremlin makes national security a vital concern, to say nothing of this infernal Korea business. Also, I've seen what these contracts with the Atomic Energy Commission can do for the local economy in some of my colleagues' States to the south."

"I happen to know someone who can keep you perfectly informed, Senator. Mr. Baker is a recent arrival in Sheila's Tree who has opened a geological consulting office. He will make sure you know what is going on here. Things seem to be happening so fast I've not heard the details, myself, as yet."

"Meanwhile," beamed the Senator, "lets avail ourselves of another helping of Ballard's Texas chili. My, that's good stuff."

Collie and the Senator were reseated at a long wooden picnic table beneath a tall butterscotch fragrant ponderosa pine as Ryan diffidently approached and nodded to Collie, his plate heaped with steaming beans and steak.

"Please join us, Ryan. Let me introduce you to Senator Paige. Wyatt, this is our resident geologist and expert on the uranium question, Mr. Ryan Baker."

"Senator Paige it's a pleasure to meet you. I'm new in Wyoming but your statesmanship and reputation have certainly gone a long way beyond the limits of your constituency. I am a great and long time admirer."

"We contribute where we can," the Senator smiled happily. Approval was never better placed than with a politician.

"Ryan! What happened to your face?" Collie exclaimed in alarm as she noticed the swelling on his lower cheek and jaw.

"Oh, it's nothing." Ryan was embarrassed. "I ran into a big roughhouse on the upper range who didn't care for my looks. I zigged when I should have zagged, I guess." He gently touched his swollen face and, seeing their obvious interest, continued. "Well, it was one of those drill rigs pulling core samples for somebody or other. Funny thing, it was on Ballard's place and when I reported to him, Mr. Crown knew nothing of it. The big guy, Bruchek, is an experienced man and he wasn't about to tolerate a stranger around that drill site."

"If the man is trespassing, Ballard could have the Sheriff up there with a warrant in no time," Collie declared.

"They'll be long gone before anybody could get there," Ryan observed. "It only takes an hour or so to pull the drill string and move on. He was down only a couple hundred feet, though. That's much shallower than I would expect if they're really looking for Uranium."

"Do you put any credence in the rumored strike, Mr. Baker?", the Senator asked.

"Until today, I was as skeptical as anyone in Sheila's Tree but given this welt on my chin, I have to start thinking somebody has a lot to hide," Ryan answered. "It could be that this Regelstorp fellow really did stumble onto something. I've seen and heard about such things happening time after time in this crazy mining business. I'll tell you, Senator Paige, it seems to me this whole thing deserves some serious consideration."

"We are talking about a material that is not only vital to the national defense of the United States but extremely rare and valuable as well," the Senator stated. "As Chairman of the Agricultural Committee I would be very interested in the development of this resource. On the recommendation of Mrs. Palmer...er...Winston, I would like to ask you to serve as my local staff liaison on this matter. Any hard information you obtain could be of great use to me in assessing the value of these developments on the national scene, Mr. Baker."

"Well, of course, Senator, I would be proud to be of service. I could do a quick investigation and report within a couple of days but if something is actually out there it will require some considerable work to get the details."

"Call my Aide, Paolo Riscotti, on Monday to settle the details and consider yourself under contract. I shall expect to be well informed on all mining and geological activities taking place out here in my home state, Mr. Baker."

"Please call me Ryan, Senator Paige. I appreciate Collie's kind recommendation." He smiled at Collie and shook hands with the Senator. "I think I can provide what you need, Sir."

As the chill deepened with early evening shadows, the barbecue festivities began to break up. Collie and Ryan found themselves seated alone at one of the rustic picnic tables under a thick-limbed old cottonwood tree that shed fitful drifts of golden leaves at the slightest stir of breeze. Over the weeks of their acquaintance they had acknowledged interest in each other without direct words, but, nevertheless, in a fashion that both understood. Ryan would never embarrass Collie with his attentions so long as she remained married, but his admiration became more focused as the friendship developed. They often found each other almost by accident and were content to explore growing confidence and mutuality. Collie's mild depression over Louise's rape and the impending divorce stood between them and made even more remote any impulse on Ryan's part to promote the relationship.

"I met that Phil Stover guy from National Ammunition over by the horseshoe pits this afternoon. He said you were close to a deal on issuing permits for a cartridge manufacturing site down by the railroad?" queried Ryan.

"Yes," she answered, "I think it's going to work out. We'll have to give them a five-year moratorium on property taxes and cut the building permit fees in half, but they expect to employ over forty people by this time next year. The building project alone will bring over $300,000 worth of business into town."

"Sheila's Tree is growing...changing fast, Collie. Now that this uranium business is heating up, it seems like Galena County is at the boiling point. I suppose people see it as an economic boom." Ryan ventured.

"That's the name of the game as far as the City Council is concerned. We've sat out here in the backwater long enough according to them," Collie said. "I'm proud of bringing more prosperity and a better living standard to our city. Everything has a price tag, and I suppose some degree of innocence lost is a part of progress. But, what a horror, to think that Louise is suffering so because of these despicable criminals that seem to be a shameful part of the process. Danger of that kind was unthinkable here before we started seeing all these strange faces in town. Now I sound like some kind of neurotic Xenophobe but it's true anyway."

"Do you know that Jake Walker has abandoned Louise since the attack?," Collie continued. "I guess she is lucky to be rid of the soulless creature, but she must feel terrible. She keeps saying that she feels guilty in some way for what happened and Jake is just reinforcing that by his rejection. I wonder what love and trust mean to a person like Jake? How could you possibly hurt someone who has been through an experience like that?" Collie's thoughts seldom strayed far from that desolate night of stress and pain.

"Don't dwell on it," Ryan suggested sympathetically, "Let's think about her recovery. Say, Collie, I caught a ride out here with Iris Patton and haven't seen her for hours. Could you give me a lift back to town?"

They said thankyous and goodbyes and joined the caravan of vehicles on the washboarded, dusty road to Sheila's Tree. A glaucus full moon rose slowly in the southeastern sky and hung as a giant shadowy globe above the silhouetted horizon.

"Take the next right at Warner Road," Ryan pointed, "and go up on top of Horsecollar Butte."

The low hill was five miles from town but its weathered crown provided a good view of patterned residential lights and moonshine on Chopstick reservoir, beyond.

"How lovely," commented Collie. "I've never been up here in a car before. I used to ride horseback around the base of the hill on outings with the Girl Scouts when I was a kid."

"I found this lookout last summer when I was driving around getting acquainted with the countryside," Ryan said. "It's about the only high spot except for the Bench, of course."

They sat in silence for a short while as the car engine creaked and cooled in the night air.

"I heard you went to see Mr. O'Brian. It's all over town already, Collie. I can tell you are very sad."

Collie was not surprised that her marital troubles were common currency. Sheila's Tree was not a place where secrets of that kind could be kept.

"It's a failure of the worst sort." She turned towards Ryan who was clearly visible in the bright moonlight. "I'm sorry it happened, but there doesn't seem to be any choice. There's nothing worthwhile left for Del and me to share."

"You seem to be—you are—so competent and...and alive. I can't imagine how any man could be fool enough to let you go." Ryan felt there was risk in his impulse to take her in his arms, and yet he was irresistibly drawn. "I have held you twice before in moments when you were terribly upset. Can I hold you now—just for comfort and...and...?"

He did not wait for an answer but pulled her close. Their first kiss was deeply satisfying like the quenching of a prolonged thirst. They held each other in silence, her head on his shoulder, her fingers gently tracing the outline of his bruised jaw. Collie's nagging burden of restlessness and disquiet faded slightly and a sort of inner calmness, almost fulfillment, eased into her consciousness. In only a moment, each felt a quickening tide of physical need and stroking caresses became more urgent. Collie could feel a whole new world in Ryan's embrace, an excitement and mystery and challenge which her younger self had never fully experienced. The emotional swirling depths almost swept her away.

"No," she murmured, "not yet. It's too soon, Ryan. I can't deny what you have already felt and seen in me, but I'm off balance and out of step with myself. If you and I are going to mean something more to each other it has to be real and, somehow, earned. Do you understand?"

Collie was afraid to express her inner concern and confusion. Her feelings for Ryan were clear enough; a feeling of safety and comfortable belonging mixed with anticipation and taut sexual excitement, to say nothing of her admiration for his keen mind and generous nature, but the failure of her relationship with Del remained strongly in her mind. She was amazed at Ryan's intuitive empathy and felt the strength of his physical attraction towards her. Even though her body responded strongly to Ryan's advances, her imagination and memory of the emotionally devastating breakup with Del held her back. For Ryan, his love for Collie, once expressed, became a living, driving, shaping force that buried forever the reticence and insecurities of his youth.

TROUBLE ON THE
BENCH

The day following the D-Z barbecue, every Palmer gate on Pass road was cut and flung aside as streams of vehicles sped towards the Bench. Casper Cedalius, an old prospector who had tramped with little success over many a Wyoming mountain range in search of gold, and Toby Swanhunter, the Arapaho rancher, formed a partnership and were among the first wave of amateur prospectors to begin a minute and exhaustive, though unsystematic, exploration of the Big Horn foothills. Although it was barely light, they were not the first on Pass road. Only a quarter mile from Palmer headquarters they came upon Corvey Hansen sitting spraddle-legged in the frosty road, his blood soaked shirt steaming in the cold air. Casper and Toby quickly returned Corvey to the Palmer bunkhouse.

"I jest told 'em to hold their horses whilst I opened the gate," Corvey whispered. "The son-of-a-bitch jumped out of the pickup and smacked me with a jack handle 'fore I could even turn around. I never see'd a man drive right through a stock fence like that in all my days."

The following weeks and months, as Casper and Toby staked claims and grubbed rock samples up and down the ridges and hills of the Bench they observed contentious and sometimes violent scenes. There were adventurers and opportunists scrambling for advantage, real or perceived, and the usual constraints of law and custom were thin and easily forgotten or transgressed. Fights broke out; claim sites were contested, sometimes with fists or even guns; property and supplies were stolen or destroyed. The Bench was a mean and dangerous place.

The hard, cold hand of winter made a fist. Ground blizzards shrieked low and opaque across the naked prairie. Frigid, silent days with temperatures twenty degrees below zero or lower followed frequent storms. Plants and animals sought natural shelter in dormancy or hibernation. Only men, driven by greed and ambition, prowled over the Bench during breaks in the terrifying cold.

Shug and Pronto were hiding out in an abandoned cook shack on the old Cielo Grande silver mine property not far west of the Palmer ranch. They had completed their work of staking the additional Canteen mining claims as instructed by Reinhardt and Frailey just in time before the rush got started. With no further immediate assignments they were told to remain in hiding until called upon. Shug happily spent his days playing solitaire or reading western paperback novels and consuming the plentiful provisions brought in on weekly visits by Frailey. Pronto was not so content. The frigid temperature cut like icy metal through the bones of his spare frame and drove him to huddle by the glowing hot wood stove. Inactivity was making him crazy and his mood was poisonously irascible.

"I gots to haf a womans up here Goddamn quick. That fockin' Frailey better bring a fockin' whore up here nex' trip or I goin' cut his cojones off," he cursed. "Why we fockin' aroun' out here in the boondocks, anyways? We ain' even cash that fockin' Reinhardt's check yet." The pair had been paid one thousand dollars each for the claim-staking job. "Come on, Shug, you lazy asshole, lets go to town now. Get off you' fat butt."

"Will you just shut up? After what you did to that woman you know damn well we can't go back into that hick town. They'd have you strung up from the nearest light pole on sight. Shit, I'll help 'em if you don't quit bitchin' about everything."

Pronto spit on the glowing iron stove top. "I should haf cut her Goddamn t'roat w'en I had a chance," he growled. The unceasing wind pressed with shrieks and moans around the eaves and warped shake roof of the old shack and the blinding silver winter persisted.

YELLOW CAKE AND PASS ROAD

It was a winter of hard work for Ryan. His investigations for Senator Paige quickly uncovered existing and newly recorded mining claims, including the Canteen claims filed in August. Guided by location information written as part of the notice of discovery, Ryan searched out the central monument of Canteen One and quickly found Regelstorp's radioactive lode. Ryan did some sampling of his own. Analysis confirmed the low level uranium content and the immediate possibility that an economically justifiable mining district might very well be developed on the Bench. While analyzing the impacts of this discovery in his reports to Washington DC, Ryan saw that a missing element in Galena County was the ability to mill the raw ore and extract the complex sodium di-uranate concentrate, called yellowcake, for sale to the United States Atomic Energy Commission. By Federal law, the AEC was the only legal buyer of the politically sensitive product. Sales contracts for yellowcake were carefully negotiated and approved by the United States Congress. Financial incentives provided by the Federal government promoted aggressive development of even borderline ore deposits. Uranium was a key ingredient of atomic weapons development as the cold war with the Soviet Union rapidly assumed its historical dimensions.

The right to mill and process uranium ore was also contracted by the Atomic Energy Commission and authorization to build a mill in a given mining district was a prize of great value to the company receiving a permit from the Government. Usually, for reasons of economy and security, only one mill was allowed to be constructed in a particular area, requiring all mining operations in the region to deliver ore into the steel jaws of the chosen facility's rock crusher. The mill owner was granted a monopoly that reaped a steady and substantial tariff from each ton of ore processed.

Once these facts became clear to Ryan he immediately began to make plans to obtain milling rights for the central Wyoming mining area. Paolo Riscotti, Senator Paige's aide, was a source of information and political contacts most useful to Ryan as he danced the bureaucratic pavane of Government regulation and permitting process. Collie's influence with Senator Paige, who made a number of personal telephone calls to various key bureau chiefs, coupled with Ryan's tireless interviews, report writing, and personal supplications before House and Senate Committees, finally resulted in his interests being seriously considered for the milling contract. By mid-winter of 1953, Ryan had formed a company, which he incorporated under the name of Wyo Nucleonics, and obtained an option on a mill site parcel a ways north of town next to the railroad siding. Financial assets of the company were limited to his own three thousand dollar savings account and, since the estimated construction cost of the proposed mill was more than three million dollars, lack of investment capital was a crucial sticking point with the AEC in awarding the contract. Ryan was in need of financial backing to ensure approval of his milling application.

New Mexico Mining Company was also a candidate for milling rights acquisition. Marion Reinhardt had not expected any problem at all in obtaining Atomic Energy Commission approval for his company to become the ore processor for the Canteen District as the new mining region came to be known. NMMC was experienced in the uranium industry, had great capital reserves and prominent connections in Washington DC. A few routine inquiries by Reinhardt, however, were rather coolly received. The preoccupation with setting up offices in Sheila's Tree, relocating personnel and equipment and pushing the mineral exploration team to endless hours of mapping, surveying, and calculating orebody economics and locations, had diverted Reinhardt's attention from the ore milling contract.

Marion was on the phone with Alvin Waterson, Vice President in charge of open pit mining operations for New Mexico Mining Corporation, at the Company headquarters office in Seattle, Washington.

"By God, Al, we've got a hell of an orebody here. The drill records practically design the pits for you. We're talking less than two hundred feet of waste overburden and thousands of tons of half-percent uranium ore. The geology is pretty obscure so it's hard to predict where you're going to find the stuff. We are pattern drilling on a grid and finding streaks and beds of ore in what looks like random deposits at about the same depth all over the place. I have been very careful to guard these confidential geology reports but I think the word is starting to get out. You can't keep our people from talking once they get to plotting these rich ore intercepts on our cross section maps. It beats the hell out of anything I ever saw up to now."

"That's only part of it, Marion," Waterson's voice carried a strident note. "I've been hearing that there are some other problems that you haven't taken care of yet. Where are you planning to process all this rich ore? My last Washington report says that some Wyoming corporation is going to get the mill contract for your Canteen district. And another thing, we don't have any final ore haul costs in your economic analysis. We need some answers, Marion. This project isn't moving along the way the Board likes to see it. I want you down in Gallup next Tuesday at the regional Board meeting with some answers or we may send Ed Cholick up there to straighten things out."

"Don't threaten me, Waterson. The Canteen ore body is going to be the biggest thing this company ever got hold of and I found it all on my own. The Board isn't as dumb as you seem to think they are. As for Cholick, the ignorant son-of-a-bitch isn't even a good accountant, let alone a mine manager. My answers will come in the form of cash flow starting in a few months from now. If you don't want to look like a damn fool you better start boosting this project to the Board instead of bad mouthing me. I don't put up with bullshit, Waterson, especially from a pencil pushing kiss-ass like you."

Al Waterson was not used to confrontation in such a direct and earthy manner. His position with the Company was earned through skillful financial operations and aided by marriage to the daughter of a major stockholder in the corporation. In his five years with NMMC no one had ever spoken to him as Reinhardt just did.

"See here, Reinhardt, you needn't talk to me like a sailor. You clean up the details on this operation and get a complete project report in by next Tuesday's Board meeting or I'll recommend your immediate replacement. Is that clear?"

Waterson did not wait for an answer but slammed the phone receiver down to conclude the call. His fingers drummed nervously as he read the Board agenda packet, thinking of the impact to be made by a report of huge estimated profits from the Wyoming uranium strike. Nevertheless, he felt that some useful pressure had been applied by his conversation with the difficult Mr. Reinhardt.

Delvane Winston was spending increasing amounts of time in town since the divorce papers were filed. He felt that the Palmer ranch and Collie's interference in his management was the whole source of his problems and further struggle was no longer of any importance to him. He knew that he had little legal claim to any ownership in Collie's inheritance and the prospect of financial hardship was less difficult for him than the loss of face and status in the small town. He usually drank at the Longhorn Saloon on a back street near the railroad station where few of his previous acquaintances were likely to be encountered. He conversed occasionally with railroad crews, cowhands, driller's helpers and others who visited the place on days when the weather was too bad for outdoor work. He drank steadily all day but never to the point of uncontrolled drunkenness. Few former friends, not even Collie, were aware of his descent into acute alcoholism.

George Frailey, however, was keeping informed on every detail of Del's activities. He and Reinhardt had renewed their discussion of Pass Road as the only viable ore haul route into Sheila's Tree and George sensed that Winston's personal problems might provide some opening for obtaining a right of way. Since the Waterson phone call, Reinhardt was obsessed with finding a quick solution to the haul road problem. He was furious that control of the uranium-processing mill was apparently lost to NMMC and the raw ore would have to be trucked more than thirty miles to the Wyo Nucleonics site. Marion asked his brother-in-law to explore any possible means of getting permission to use the Pass Road.

The musty reek of tobacco and spilled beer thickened the tenebrous atmosphere of the Longhorn Saloon as Frailey entered from the bright frosty street. After a brief period of iris aperture adjustment he spotted Delvane seated alone at a small table apparently staring intently at the wall mounted bust of a long eared jackrabbit whose head was adorned with a miniature pair of forked antlers.

"Well, Delvane Winston," George approached the table in the hearty manner of a stockbroker making a cold call, "haven't seen you in a coon's age. How are things going in the cattle business?"

Del looked up dully and brushed his stubbled chin with a left-handed swipe. "Screw off, Frailey."

"Look, Winston, we need to talk business. I think I can offer you a hell of a financial deal if you're interested," George said as he seated himself, ignoring Del's greeting.

"Not innerested. Shove off, Frailey."

"Pass Road, Winston, Pass Road. How would you like to see a nice two lane paved highway with right-of-way fences all the way through the canyon and up onto the Bench?"

"Itsa private road—part of the ranch. All these damn trespassers are gonna be pros'cuted. Almost killed poor ol' Corvey. Since the silver mine shut down nobody has any right on that road 'cept the Palmer outfit. Keep the hell away from me, Frailey," Del spoke none too clearly.

"Who the hell built that road in the first place?" Frailey asked. "How come the Palmer outfit thinks they own it?"

Del shook his head in irritation. "I already looked it up at the courthouse right after me and Collie took over the ranch. The road was built back in 1895 by the silver mine and ol' E.L. let 'em go through the place. The road belongs to the ranch but Cielo Grande got a haul wagon easement for their use while the mine operated. That's all there is to it, Frailey."

"You got a copy of that easement somewheres so a fella could take a look at it?" queried Frailey.

"From 1895? Oh hell yes, I carry it around with me all the time. Jesus, Frailey, get outta my sight will you?"

"It's worth some money to the New Mexico Mining Company to get ahold of that road. I got contacts over with them as you know, Winston, and I might work you a pretty sweet deal," Frailey proposed smoothly. "They'ld probably buy the road and give the Palmer spread a perpetual easement. Might be worth forty—fifty thousand bucks." Frailey knew almost exactly how much the Winstons had borrowed from the bank.

Del no longer had any great interest in the operation of the Palmer ranch. Upon receipt of the legal notice of divorce he had withdrawn both physically and emotionally from the affairs of Sheila's Tree and his role at the ranch. All of his insecurities and self-doubt had risen in a dark tide to sweep away the shallow pretensions of his public façade. Rejection by Collie, though he knew that his own actions were the cause, removed the last prop from his precarious self-esteem. His deepest regret and pain came from the loss of Collie. Delvane consciously loved her more in his loss than he ever thought he had during their marriage. He was sinking deeper each day into depression and alcoholic stupor.

"No deal for me. I make no more deals. Just shove off, Frailey. Leave me alone, Goddamn it." He turned his back to George and fixed his attention once more on whatever inner thoughts were born of his failures.

George Frailey left in disgust and drove over to the NMMC town office to renew conversations with Marion Reinhardt. It seemed as if options were narrowing in the search for a way to move ore off the Bench but Frailey was confident that there were still more ways than one to resolve the problem.

BACK AT THE RANCH

Neil Silverstein entered Collie's Mayoral office with his beat up old black Stetson in hand and an inquiring look on his rugged sunburnt face.

"Miz Winston, I'm real sorry to have to come to you with this but the boys out at the ranch don't rightly know what to do next," he stated diffidently. "Mr. Winston, he's up and left the place as you prob'ly know. Not that it's much of my business, but I was kind of Foreman under Mr. Winston and I feel like I got to get some sort of go-ahead from you on how we should be handling things."

"Of course, Neil," Collie smiled in an attempt to set the man at ease, "so no one is left in charge of the ranch, then?" she queried.

Neil's answer was only an eloquent shrug of his broad shoulders.

"I am so sorry to have left you in this position," she said. "I had no idea Del would simply go off with no word or explanation. He hasn't stayed in touch with me. How long ago?"

"Well, just a few days since the last time he showed up out there, though we've seen little of him for the past several weeks. He told ol' Corvey that he wasn't coming back this time. He took a bunch of his stuff and the new Dodge pickup so we don't figure to see no more of him." Neil was embarrassed to be discussing intimate personal business with Collie though he could not see any alternative. "We never got our checks last payday, neither," he explained, "an some of the boys are kind of worried."

"Oh dear," she exclaimed, "I'll take care of this immediately. Please don't worry about your pay and tell the rest of the men that loyalty will be rewarded. I don't intend to let anyone go. There is plenty to do to get that ranch in shape and

I'll need good men to do it. Will you stay on as Ramrod, Neil? I'll see that you get the going wage for the job and I'll throw in a bonus after fall roundup if you sign on."

Neil smiled for the first time in the interview. "You bet, Miz Winston. I can run that outfit fine if you just back me up."

"I hope you aren't concerned about taking direction from a woman, Neil," she looked directly into his eyes but in as non-threatening a manner as possible, "because I will be giving you quite specific orders and I will expect them to be carried out."

"Why, I reckon I been taking orders from somebody or other all my life, Miz Winston. No reason it should be different now, but I know how to give 'em, too."

"We'll get along just fine then," Collie smiled, "and we can get started right away. I'm going to call Juno Castle to set up bookkeeping and payroll for the ranch. You can take this note pad and write out the names of all our hands and their monthly pay rate if you know it. If there is anyone you would prefer to let go just tell me. Give me a list of everything you think should be done over the next few weeks and any problems that have come up so we can go over it together. Then make a list of all the supplies you need to keep things rolling. You can work at that table over there. Let me know when you're done and we'll see about getting things sorted out. And one last thing," she smiled again to make sure he was at ease with her, "I have taken back my maiden name since the separation. You can call me Miss Palmer if you like."

Collie got Silverstein set up at the table and returned to her work. She could see that life was going to get more complicated very quickly. Collie resolved to accompany her new Foreman back out to the ranch and see how Del had left things. She felt a guilty lift of pleasurable anticipation at the thought of being actively involved in the ranch again.

POLITICS

Months spent in Washington DC taught Ryan hard lessons about politics, the real value of money and human behavior. He nearly lost his bid for the uranium mill authorization because he had no immediate capital backing for the project. Personal or corporate wealth was the first consideration taken into account by the power figures in government and the second thing was who your friends were or who spoke in favor of your appeal. Senator Paige wielded his broad power base and found support for Ryan's cause from many influential sources including Senate and Congressional committees, military spokespersons, individual lawmakers and, finally, with telling effect, from the Executive Branch itself in the form of a letter of recommendation signed by the Secretary of Interior, Douglas McKay. As these developments were slowly unfolding Ryan was looking for money. Pete Riscotti and Ryan had managed to locate and apply for a funding source offered under a National Defense appropriation through a classified experimental weapons development program. An Air Force Committee offered a grant up to one third the total investment required for approved proposals. Qualifications for the entitlement were very narrow and rigid but neatly fit the purpose and timing of the uranium mill project because of its obvious impact on military preparedness. With approval of this grant on the books, Ryan at last had something concrete to bring to the table in discussions with other possible sources of funding and the reality of his project was beginning to take form. The problem remained for Ryan to raise the balancing two thirds of financing in less than six months or New Mexico Mining Corporation might yet be chosen to construct and operate the mill.

Ryan learned that the latest advances in ore milling and separation technology were being developed in South Africa where the newest and most effective methods were in use to coax complex uranium compounds out of the rocks and sediments containing them. Through one of his former professors at Colorado School of Mines Ryan established contact with a young Engineer, Sean Mochery, working in Bloemfontein, South Africa and began, by correspondence, serious discussions of the design and construction of the uranium processing mill.

Collie and Ryan were developing a disturbing and uneven, though much more than friendly, relationship that both felt held the potential for a closer and, perhaps, lasting commitment. Ryan could not figure out why Collie, honest and straight forward in most things, seemed inhibited and uncommunicative about their possible future together. They seldom got to enjoy one another's company because both were so busy. Letters were exchanged regularly while Ryan was in Washington or elsewhere away from Sheila's Tree, as they both attempted to maintain contact and involvement in their lives. Ryan remained unaware of the extent of Collie's struggle for inner control and the return of her previous optimism.

Time passed quickly during which a flood of miners, engineers, truck drivers, equipment salesmen, mechanics and a whole diversity of service and trades people moved into Sheila's Tree. The city boomed economically as housing and support infrastructure of all kinds was rapidly built. Collie managed to secure the location of Philip Stover's National Ammunition factory in Sheila's Tree and this, in turn, led to further inquiries by other small industries in search of inexpensive land and growth potential. As Mayor and chief administrator of the rapidly growing city, Collie's reputation and recognition soared around the state. She was an excellent organizer and conducted business with efficiency and fairness. She surrounded herself with competent, honest and loyal staff. Her own intelligence, common sense and a thorough understanding of Wyoming culture and politics enabled her to take carefully considered positions and make good decisions, bringing consensus to a sometimes ill-focused City Council. The flow of money from taxes, permits, licenses and development fees brought support for Collie's dream of a new City Hall separate from the Galena County Courthouse that had heretofore leased space to the municipal government. Engaging an architectural firm and planning the new building was a time consuming but interesting and gratifying project.

A great sorrow was the fact that Louise Greene was never able to return to work. The horror of her experience, followed by Jake Walker's brutal rejection, caused damage that neither counseling nor medication could repair. As an only child whose parents had passed away, Louise had no family support and her reclusiveness and despondency soon discouraged overtures from her small circle of friends. One Saturday just before Christmas Collie stopped by to encourage Louise to join her on a shopping expedition. Though lights were on and a radio was playing inside the little house there was no answer to repeated knocking at the front and back door. With breaking heart Collie followed a hastily summoned City Police Chief, Bertie Larson, into the bedroom where Louise lay dead from a potent mixture of aspirin and alcohol. Pronto Melindez had taken everything of value from Louise in the short minutes of the parking lot rape. When only hurt, inappropriate guilt and hopeless dejection remained Louise gave up her seemingly ruined life. Collie vowed never to relent in the search for the vicious attacker. She remembered every word that Louise had repeated for the Sheriffs Department interrogation.

ALL KINDS OF NEW DEVELOPMENTS

By early June the heavenly scent of blooming lilac signaled a new spring. In Wyoming, the burgeoning season is announced by the appearance of green grass on prairie ranch lands where cattle are turned out to forage and roam freely across the range. The warming weather this year also allowed the great rumbling earth-moving machines of NMMC to begin the task of stripping away overburden from the rich uranium ore lying several hundred feet below the surface. The first small open pit mine under development, called Canteen I, was located close to the original discovery monument staked by Regelstorp.

Ken Bruchek and his crews were becoming familiar faces among the new arrivals in Sheila's Tree. Bruchek began contracting with other mining companies besides NMMC as the regional search for uranium expanded rapidly. His drillers used a method of freezing cores below the water table by circulating super-cooled oil through the doughnut shaped diamond encrusted drill bit in order to extract solid frozen cylindrical samples from the friable gravel beds that often contained uranium deposits. In this way the sediment samples were recovered totally intact just as the layers of unconsolidated gravel had lain under the surface for millions of years. Geologists could obtain a precise view of the minerals and their insitu environment. This technological advantage put Bruchek's rigs in high demand despite premium charges in comparison with other conventional drillers.

Iris Patton was a benefactor from the increased business activity and rapid population growth. Two poker games were run simultaneously most nights at the

Bull Run to accommodate the recreational needs of the highly paid industrial workers. Friction arose early between the leisurely local cowboys and the aggressive newcomers who neither knew nor cared about traditional Wyoming folkways and rustic gentility. The poker games became hotly contested affairs that were much more difficult to control than in the old days. Uncle Ting had given up the job as houseman, being unable to keep the game running smoothly and speedily under the raucous demands of the new breed of players. Tony Arriaga, the loyal bartender, and his brother Alonzo, even larger and more physically imposing than Tony, were put in charge of gaming. Even so, violence in the form of screaming arguments and occasional fistfights became all too common at the Bull Run. On weekends young prostitutes from Casper drove over to Sheila's Tree and found great demand for their services.

The passage of months wrought changes in the routines of Sheila's Tree and its inhabitants. People and events were moving faster, lights seemed brighter and social and economic pressures mounted for Wyoming natives and newcomers alike.

Brilliant stars gleamed fitfully through the rustling branches of fully leafed summer cottonwoods. Cool, dry air soothed the naked bodies of Iris and Milo as they lay on a picnic quilt in a secluded glen not far from Chopstick reservoir. They had spent a rare day together fishing, swimming and eating specially prepared goodies from Iris' kitchen in a remote area on the south end of the reservoir. The day was done and they rested languidly after another stolen session of lovemaking. Milo found soul-filling contentment with Iris as he never had experienced before in his life.

"Iris, you pull me in like a whirlpool. I love you so much I think I'll just melt down and puddle up like a scoop of ice-cream left out in the sun," Milo whispered. "We have to make some plans, girl. I can't go on about my business anymore like you were some kind of a special bonus for weekends and holidays."

"You know I feel the same about you," she smiled tenderly, then shifted subtly away so that their bodies did not quite touch. Her voice quavered slightly. "Milo, how can we come out in the open with me white as a toadstool and you brown as coffee? There's nobody ready for that kind of thing around here—including me, I guess. I just can't picture us married and going to parties and stuff like married folks do. Who would our friends be?"

"We have friends," Milo replied gravely. "Wyoming isn't like Oakland or some other big place. I don't feel the hate and fear out here like I used to back in California. Not so bad, anyway," he qualified. "We could get us a ranch and have our own outfit. I'd be happy with you anyplace. We can't let other folks tell us how to do with our lives, Iris."

"I'm just plain scared. I don't know how I fell for you and I can't figure out what to do about it. When I'm not with you I almost hope you'll never show up again and then when you come waltzing in I feel like I'm going to explode if I can't feel your hands on me." Voicing her apprehension in his presence brought out all the long held back emotion and fear. She began to sob in bitter heaves and turned her back. "I—I just can't go on, Milo. It's not you—it's me—I just can't keep on doing what we've been doing." She cried hoarsely and raggedly as if the unhappiness of her inner feelings were being torn from the depths of her body. She was not accustomed to weeping.

For one of the few times in his life Milo felt helpless in the face of something so important and vital to himself that he could not conceive of existence without it. He wanted to shake her or pry her mind open with his bare fingers. And then the real fear of losing her washed over him in a wave of anxiety.

"Iris, Honey, I'm just black. I don't have some loathsome disease or horrible secret. Please don't be like all those others who can't understand how people are. Don't make up some big deal that we can't overcome. You and me can do anything we want to. Can't you just love me and trust me to make it all come out good?" Milo's voice, though calm and strong, held a pleading note.

"It is a big deal," she sobbed, "and I know you can't fix it no matter how strong you are. I've thought and thought about what might happen and I know just what every single person who ever saw us together would think. They'd think that I was some kind of whore to go off with a Nigger—that's what they'd think." She turned and crumpled in his arms letting tears fall on his chest as he gently rocked her shaking form.

The drive back to Sheila's Tree was a sad, lonely trip for both of them. Milo wearily acknowledged to himself that bigotry comes in many forms and the bruising reality that some aspects of his racial heritage were a burden in this American culture that he would carry to the grave. He was, however, both determined and patient. Milo resolved not to lose Iris without trying everything in his power to prevent it.

HIGH FINANCE AND COUNTER CURRENT DECANTATION

With help from Senator Paige, Ryan finally worked out a solution to finance the Wyo Nucleonics mill construction. Paolo Riscotti wrote up an amendment to an important omnibus Senate Bill sponsored in part by his boss that completely clinched the deal for Ryan. The net result of the amendment was to provide a United States government guarantee on the financial success of the mill project. With this assurance the Crown brothers, Ray and Ballard, gave personal guarantees on Ryan's bank loans, which, in conjunction with the Air Force grant, began to feed cash into the design and construction pipeline. The deal had been easy to sell once all aspects of the government-backed contracts were fully explained and understood. The total estimated cost of the uranium mill was $2.7 million dollars, of which $900,000 was provided by the grant. Paige's amendment, tacked onto a military appropriation section of the carrier bill and touted as a national defense necessity, underwrote the unfunded portion of mill construction cost. The legislation specified that independent collateral must be provided for the remaining $1.8 million not directly funded by the government, however, with the special provision that failure of the project within ten years due to any reason other than criminal malfeasance would result in Uncle Sam paying off the whole of the debt. It was essentially a free ride with a huge potential payoff going to the financiers whose only participation was the requirement to file acceptable financial statements. Not a dime of actual cash or debt payment was asked of the Crown brothers. Orville Smith's Wyoming Agricultural Bank jumped at the chance to provide the $1.8 million at a low interest rate because of the Government guaranteed fail-safe provisions.

The first thing Ryan did was hire Sean Mochery to come from South Africa and take over as Design Engineer for the project. The young man was brilliant and focused on his work; proud of the innovations and science that he and others were pioneering in South Africa. He leased an old building that had once housed a roller skating rink during the World War II era and refit it with working cubicles for engineers and draftsmen. With a deadline of only a few months to get the plant built, tested, and functional, the headquarters for Wyo Nucleonics became a center of frenetic activity. Ryan and all the others on the team were working long hours.

"Only a small fraction of the material fed into the mill is uranium. The concept is to reduce the ore to a condition that allows for maximum interaction with the extraction chemicals in the most economical fashion," Mochery discoursed. "We have to grind the raw ore to a particle size about equal to talcum powder and use an acid solution to selectively leach out the uranium compounds from all the residual waste material. Then the uranium solute goes to a separation step which we developed recently in South Africa, utilizing a series of large wooden vessels called counter current decantation tanks to collect the uranium charged liquid into an enriched feed for the later stages of the process. The concentration and purification of the decanted liquor is accomplished by ion exchange towers very similar to an oversized home water softener. Finally, we remove a few residual contaminants, filter and dry the final product, called yellow cake because of its brilliant lemon color, and ship it in barrels to the Atomic Energy Commission's weighing and sampling plant at Grand Junction, Colorado."

"This is the first mill built using all these new processes, isn't it?" Ryan asked.

"This is absolutely the best technology available," answered Mochery. "Believe me, I've been planning this for years. I am sure we can get the mill finished under budget and in time to begin taking ore as soon as NMMC or any of the other startups are ready for delivery. You Yanks have a knack for getting supplies and materials to the jobsite and Bristol-McCready is as good a construction contractor as I've ever worked with."

"How about radioactivity?" Ryan posed. "Are the mill workers and communities in the area safe from exposure to this material?"

"There will be dust blowing off the ore haul trucks, evaporation ponds for the waste liquid from the milling process and, perhaps, other by-products which may be sources of very low level radioactivity. None of it has ever been shown to be hazardous to human health by casual contact," Mochery answered. "Every human activity carries some risk, you know, and the payoff in development of this natural resource is worth it. We should let the health and medical experts worry about this aspect. We know the Bureau of Mines people are not going to permit any dangerous activity. They have approved every plan we've submitted so far."

Ryan was not completely reassured but the project proceeded as fast as Mochery could push forward the complex mix of planning, design, deliveries, manpower and construction. The engineer seemed to be on the job twenty-four hours a day and everywhere at once.

THE HAUL ROAD

Marion Reinhardt was getting desperate for a solution to his ore haul problem. The Canteen I pit was nearly stripped of waste overburden and almost ready to start producing truckload after truckload of rich ore to be processed at Ryan Baker's mill, still under construction, next to the Great Northern railroad siding a short distance outside of Sheila's Tree. The NMMC Vice President, Alvin Waterson, had proven to be a stronger adversary than Marion had supposed. His accusations of poor management against Reinhardt were beginning to gain a hearing within the company and Marion knew that the only acceptable response was an efficient way to transport ore off the Bench. Red Rock Rim still imposed its impassable face exactly as it had since the first human being stood in wonder before the natural wall of rock.

"Damn it, Marion, I told you what Winston told me months ago about Pass Road," George Frailey exclaimed. "We know the old silver mine hauled ore through that canyon. Look, I even brought a mimeographed copy of the original contract that ol' E.L. Palmer signed back in 1895."

"Where the hell did you get this?" Marion asked. He took the dark, smeared copy of the easement document and held it to the window light as he attempted to read the tightly penned words. The old fashioned hand wrought script was clear enough with straight, even spaces between lines.

"I got it from the record stacks over in the courthouse basement. John Steen, the County Recorder over there, lets me work around the place on my own," George answered. "I go over there all the time to record deeds and look up land surveys and stuff. I know where most everything is in those big files at the County."

"Hmm," Reinhardt muttered, "that means this is a legal document and binding on the Palmer ranch just like any other contract. Too bad it just allows passage for the Cielo Grande bunch. Look here, George," Marion pointed to a certain sentence in the document that described the right-of-way for the silver mine haul wagons, "couldn't we just add a phrase in here, something like, 'or any other future mineral producer' right in this spot after this sentence? This is a handwritten document from clear back in 1895 and there sure as hell aren't likely to be any copies around. If we were real careful we could fix this up and then use it to prove we had a right-of-way just like Cielo Grande."

"Boy, I don't know Marion. We'd sure have to do it right. Where you gonna get the right kind of ink and copy that handwriting and everything? What if Winston or the Mayor has an original copy stowed someplace dating from clear back then?"

"Listen, George, this is the first thing I've seen that has half a chance to work out for us," Reinhardt said excitedly. "It's almost too easy. Christ, for the kind of money we're talking about here I can get the best forger in the United States. There's plenty of guys around who know how to do this stuff if the price is right."

"Well, you still got to get ahold of the original paper from where it's filed over in the Courthouse. How are you going to do that without Steen knowing about it?" George questioned.

"We can't go off half-cocked and screw this operation up," Marion replied. "Lets get down to business and start figuring things out. You can learn a lot more from that drunk, Winston, if you work it right."

Marion and George talked and planned for several hours working out the details of their criminal scheme. Even though Shug and Pronto had left their silver mine hideout months ago and returned to their haunts near the Mexican border, the two roughnecks figured largely in the whispered plot.

ALTERING HISTORY

The cranky old DeSoto, even more beat up and decrepit than on the previous trip, rolled back into Wyoming with Shug and Pronto disheveled and tired from the long drive up from El Paso, Texas. They always came when called by Reinhardt because he paid well and took care of them when necessary. They could count on a payday and usually small danger compared to the perilous activities they often pursued when on their own resources. They drove straight out to the NMMC Company mining camp at the Canteen mine site and were immediately put on the payroll with spurious titles and job descriptions. They were assigned a small but comfortable room in the newly constructed men's dormitory and spent their time playing pool or rolling dice in the rec room with other laborers who happened to be between shifts. No one ever seemed to notice that the two men seldom left the building and never reported to work.

It was not long before Marion called them in to Frailey's real estate office in Sheila's Tree and explained in detail what was required to obtain the Cielo Grande easement document from the County Courthouse. Frailey told them exactly where the records were located in the courthouse basement and even drew a sketch map for assured clarity. He also explained how to open the big dusty record books and find the exact page where the desired document was located. The books were titled by year and all recorded documents were registered and filed in chronological order. The cracked and desiccated leather bound deed volume for the year 1895 rested on a top shelf where it had lain mostly undisturbed for well over half a century.

On a moonless night a few days later the two criminals quietly broke a low basement window and entered the darkened courthouse. Referring to their diagram of the premises they soon located the 1895 deed volume and extracted the Pass Road easement document drawn up by E.L. and Cielo Grande Silver Company so many years before. Shug carefully inserted the brittle page between two cardboard covers and secured it with several rubber bands. In order to cover the theft of the one document of interest, they systematically went through many of the other shelved volumes tearing out pages, ripping apart books and strewing the floor with torn and damaged documents both new and old. Pronto was particularly efficient and accomplished at the destruction of decades of legal record keeping and historical data that preserved much of the history of Galena county and its development over the years. Only Shug's intervention prevented him from starting a fire in the mess of loose papers and broken volumes littering the floor.

"Come on, damn you. We got what we came for and you sure done enough to throw the stupid bastards off the trail," Shug ordered. "Let's get the hell out of here."

George Frailey was an occasional volunteer at John Steen's call for community assistance in cleaning up and repairing the damage to the courthouse records. The inexplicable crime of vandalism was an outrageous puzzlement to County and City officials, however, police investigations neither discovered a motive nor pointed to any perpetrator. Frailey's familiarity with the record system and location of many tracts and his frequent visits to the records room prior to the crime enabled him to assist with the repair and reconstruction of documents as few other than regular County employees could have done. George became a familiar sight in and around the courthouse cleanup.

The careful alteration of the stolen document was crafted by a skilled artisan who normally made his living in San Francisco, California by forging documents for military draft evaders anxious not to take part in the United Nations police action in Korea. His long waiting list of youthful customers was put on hold for several days as the forger undertook Marion Reinhardt's job for a cash payment of two thousand dollars. Chemical analysis and physical tests were performed on both the ink and paper to determine composition, density, reflective index and absorption characteristics. Once a counterfeit ink was developed to match the existing document it was a simple matter to imitate the writing on the old manuscript. When Reinhardt at last was shown the finished product with the changes and additions in wording, he was confident the forgery would never be detected. The closest examination under powerful magnification showed no differences in calligraphy, color, or style from the original hand written text. He even exposed the work to ultraviolet light and found that the new ink fluoresced in exactly the same color and brightness as the old. George Frailey had no trouble finding an opportunity to reinsert the altered page in the 1895 volume and replace it in its old location on the top shelf of the stacks along with all the other tomes being repaired, sorted and restored as nearly as possible to their original state. Within days NMMC, at Marion Reinhardt's direction, had filed a Galena County District Court motion of entry to use Pass Road, declaring it a public domain open for public use.

I'LL SEE YOU IN
COURT

Collie hired Denton Eldring, a childhood acquaintance, to defend Palmer ranch and maintain ownership and control over the roadway.

"I'm afraid I don't understand how this mining company can claim our roadway," Collie stated. "We have always maintained a fence—actually, about six fences—across that road and closed it down completely during fall hunting season. It has only been the last year that we've been unable to stop people from trespassing. At first we tried to be neighborly about it but soon enough we started to really suffer from gates left open, garbage dumped on our property and so much traffic that the live stock was getting hit by vehicles all the time. Sheer numbers of these uranium people have just overwhelmed our ranch hands."

"You say there is an easement document, however, dating from the last century and signed by E. L.?" asked the Attorney.

Collie explained the details, as she recalled them, of the Cielo Grande agreement. Collie had to admit that she had never actually seen the document but only heard about it from her Grandfather.

"There definitely is a contract concerning the road on file at the County Courthouse," Collie assured the lawyer, "Del told me he looked it up one time long before the break-in over at the courthouse upset everything."

"Well, you have been served with an injunction asking the court to open the road to NMMC haul trucks based on an existing easement and also citing the economic necessity for them to get their mine product down to Baker's processing mill."

Eldring thoughtfully reread the papers served on Collie. "It would seem that the key element here is that Cielo Grande easement. If it gives you ownership, then we will have a pretty good argument. If it doesn't, we still have some collateral arguments concerning the potential injury to the ranching business. After all, even if they prove a right to use the road they can't keep on damaging your spread. We will see what we can do, Collie," Denton smiled reassuringly.

"By the way, Leah Anne is hosting our usual dinner and bridge party this month and, since John and Naomi Delaney are out of town, she wants to know if you would care to come. She has asked Judge Kirby and needs a partner for him if you would like to play." Collie and Del had often substituted when a member couple was forced to miss the perennial group's bridge night.

"I would love to, thank you. Nobody would miss an invitation to Leah Anne's cooking by choice." Collie replied, "I'm assuming since the Judge is old enough to be my father that this is not some attempt to marry me off since the divorce?" Collie laughed. "It does seem a little early for match making, even for your Leah Anne."

"Oh no, I would guess that there aren't many matches for you around here. And besides, you can probably take care of that department for yourself. We just need a fourth for bridge, that's all," the lawyer smiled.

Collie was gratified that there seemed to be no rumors concerning a relationship of any kind between herself and Ryan Baker. She was unsure for her own part if there was indeed a relationship and, if so, just what kind. She felt better having put the Pass Road matter in Denton Eldring's hands. She had considered going to her divorce lawyer, old Liam O'Brian, but decided in the end to hire the dynamic Eldring who was developing a sharp reputation as a winning advocate for his diversified clientele all over the state.

MILO'S MISERY

Milo could not stay away from the Bull Run. He was frustrated and desperately unhappy in a situation over which he exercised little control and had few options for change. Iris was steadfastly ignoring him. Indecisive and hurt herself, in emotional turbulence that precluded a rational view of her deep attachment for Milo, Iris avoided him whenever possible. When he came into the bar she would hastily withdraw to the restaurant or retire to her living quarters upstairs. The fun and excitement of their old masquerade was outgrown and the shared bond of their love offered only pain and loneliness because of Iris' ingrained fear of their racial differences. A strongly implanted childhood bias impacted her unconscious life view more forcefully than her actual experience with Milo as a loving, kind and intelligent man. Their almost negligible genetic differences, easily detected by socially trained observation of superficial physical details, provided the excuse for an emotional barrier that she was unable to overcome.

Milo often ended up at the poker tables despite the fact that his skills suffered from a despondent state of mind. He played too aggressively and was not as observant as before. As a consequence he usually lost his stake early and had to leave the game. On one such evening after dropping over forty dollars in a few hands to players whom he once would have considered easy pickings, Milo wandered back into the bar and put in a telephone call to Ryan Baker.

"Hey, Baker, you been working too hard. Come on down to the Bull Run and hoist a cool one with me. I'll even pay for God's sakes," he begged.

"I haven't heard from you in weeks, man. I thought maybe Ballard finally wised up and ran you off," Ryan gibed.

"You're the one that's been out of circulation," Milo objected. "Take a break from your damn politicking and have a drink with a friend in need."

Something in Milo's tone caught Ryan's attention. "The politics are over but I have been working like a dog on getting this mill project going. Maybe I will come over and take a little break. God knows you cowboys sure know how to relax."

When Ryan entered the bar he found it a very different environment from the quiet recreational lounge of months earlier. A three piece western band was attempting Ferlan Husky's, Wings of a Pure White Dove, vocalized by an overweight middle-aged singer who was a pale shadow of Mr. Husky's talent. The place was noisy and crowded with working men and a sprinkling of women with their husbands or boyfriends. There were several provocatively dressed young women who seemed to be unattached and on the lookout for fun. Ryan located Milo seated at a tiny round table almost lost in a far corner of the room. The formerly popular pool tables had been removed and replaced with more bar tables and a slightly enlarged dance floor.

"Say, Bud, you look like somebody pulled you the wrong way through a knot hole," Ryan greeted his friend. "What's got you down?"

The racial aspect of his troubles was an impediment to easy discussion, however, Milo was comfortable with Ryan and knew that their relationship had become close enough so that both were very nearly color blind with regard to their friendship. The two friends found their common interests in work and sport more than in mutual acquaintances or intimate knowledge of each other's private lives. Ryan, in common with everyone else in Sheila's Tree, was unaware of Milo's true relationship with Iris Patton.

"What else gets a healthy, handsome young man like myself down in the dumps?" Milo smiled somewhat wryly, "It's a woman, naturally."

"Well, that's better than money problems," Ryan smiled sympathetically. "From what Denton Eldring told me the other day about your lousy poker playing I thought maybe you wanted to tap me for a loan. He says you are losing your ass lately at your favorite game."

"Yeah, I have been a mite distracted an' that's not so funny." Milo dropped the humorous cover and looked as concerned as he actually felt. "I'm nuts about a girl that feels the same way about me only she's afraid to show it. I can't figure out which way to go. I hoped maybe you could give me a little advice."

"Oh man, Milo, you are probably asking the least savvy guy in the state a question about how to get along with girls," Ryan shook his head thinking of his perplexing relationship with Collie Palmer. "What do you mean, she's afraid to show it?"

"Her name is Iris Patton," Milo watched Ryan's eyes carefully as he spoke the words, looking for a facial reaction that would be easily recognizable.

Ryan was silent for several moments as the information sunk in and the various ramifications of the simple statement evolved in his mind.

"Did I pass the test?" Ryan asked with a smile, noting Milo's intent look. "I can see why she might have a few reservations about a relationship with you. Guys like you are still getting knocked around, or worse, in some places for being seen in the company of a white girl. I would hope folks around Sheila's Tree might have a different attitude, but realistically I can understand her misgivings. What does Iris want to do?" he asked.

"I guess she can imagine a life without me in it," Milo answered, "which is more than I can imagine about her. She has admitted to loving me, but is just too ashamed or scared to be yoked up with a black man. She is looking at things through somebody else's eyes and it's going to kill our chances for happiness together. You're the only person who knows about me and Iris, Ryan. Maybe you could talk to her about it—give her a chance to get her feelings out in the open. Could you do that?"

"Damn, Milo, that's really a tough deal," Ryan shook his head worriedly. "I'm not that well acquainted with Iris, though I certainly think highly of her, but this is about as sensitive a topic of conversation as you could dream up. Why would she listen to me if she can't even look at her own feelings honestly? I'm afraid I might just screw things up worse."

"Yeah, I guess maybe...Milo paused as a bulky figure hovered over their small table.

"Say, I thought I recognized you," Ken Bruchek pushed his large crew cut head into Ryan's face. "Damned if you ain't the guy snoopin' around my drill rig last year. I know you,—you're building the uranium mill out north of town. Did you enjoy that little boost to the rear end that I gave you, smart guy?" he sneered.

"Yes, I was snooping," Ryan replied calmly. "I apologize for that and I guess I had it coming to me for lying at the time.

"You've got some guts to admit it," the tall man grunted. "I eat little shits like you for breakfast. I ought to slap you around some more just for fun."

He caught a handful of Ryan's flannel shirt and jerked him out of his seat as if to follow words with action. Adrenaline flooding his system, Ryan braced his feet and smashed a right fist into Bruchek's midsection with all the force he could muster. It felt as if he had taken a swing at a tree trunk. His knuckles encountered iron hard abdominal muscles that did not yield a centimeter to the considerable force of his blow.

"Ha! The little piss-ant needs to get stomped on," Bruchek grimaced and held Ryan almost off the floor.

Milo was on his feet and grasped Bruchek's wrist before he could deliver a blow. He forced his body between Ryan and his adversary. Bruchek let go of Ryan and stepped back a pace in surprise.

"Hey, you Goddamn Jig, get your hands off me," he snarled, twisting his wrist free in a quick jerk.

The two men stood face to face, poised for battle, sizing each other up with quick assessments of potential strength or weakness. Bruchek was two inches taller and thirty pounds heavier than Milo's compact two hundred twenty pound, six foot, two inch frame. Both were experienced hand to hand fighters, each realizing that he was faced by an unusually capable foe. In the moment of hesitation before the first blow was struck Jake Walker, dressed in civilian clothes but still bearing the aura of state police authority, pushed the two men apart.

"Knock it off, you two. People are trying to have a good time here, not get messed up in a bar fight," he shouted loudly. "I swear to God I'll arrest you both if you don't back off right now!"

Ryan was standing beside Milo by this time and quickly spoke up.

"You bet, Jake. You're absolutely right. Mr. Harris and I were just leaving. No offense intended or taken—we're on our way." He took Milo's arm and pulled him towards the door. "We are leaving right now, see?" Ryan was hustling Milo along as he spoke.

"You two chicken shits haven't heard the last of me, yet," Bruchek called tauntingly as they went out the door.

WINTER OF
HARDSHIP

Winter again closed down almost all outdoor activities as Wyoming experienced one of the coldest years on record. Immense snow drifts buried roads and fences and made hard going for the animals, both wild and domestic, suffering from loss of food sources and open water for drinking. Mine stripping stopped almost completely and Ryan was able only sporadically to continue construction of the mill. The Canteen pit, now deepened to an elevation well below the shallow water table, became an icy wonderland of icicles, frozen waterfalls, benches and shelves of crystal as ground water continually seeped out of the pit walls and froze upon exposure to the frigid air. Forced inactivity and loss of progress was an insufferable frustration for many of the newcomers, both laborers and business owners or managers, who lost paychecks or watched investment debt accumulate interest without useful production. Wyoming old-timers, on the other hand, were used to the rhythms of nature and the natural pace of the four distinct seasons during a normal year. There were several murders and suicides in the state that winter, bearing witness to the fact that new and unknown stresses were at work among Wyoming's small and often isolated population.

Marion Reinhardt was one of those seriously effected by pessimism and doubt about the eventual success of his mining operation despite the known richness of the uranium deposit. He had seldom faced so many severe obstacles in the development of a mining property and the hard winter added to his frustration. The ground water problem was particularly unexpected and vexing. There was so much of it that, even in good weather, stripping became a race between the ability of the great rubber tired scrapers to remove the waste material covering the ore body and the ability of the high volume ground water pumps to drain off the pit and keep it open for business. With the onset of freezing conditions it became impossible for the dewatering pumps to function and the ice got deeper and thicker each day, filling the void of the now silent mining pit.

In addition, the court trial date for NMMC's law suit against Palmer ranch for the right to use Pass Road was only a few months off and the Corporation's chief Attorney, Harold Perlmutter, seemed none too sure of himself.

"The last time I met with Eldring to talk about a possible financial settlement out of court he was as cocky as Yankee Doodle," Perlmutter frowned as he reported to Reinhardt. "He practically sneered when I showed him a copy of the Cielo Grande document."

"The right-of-way is clear enough in that paper, signed by E. L. Palmer and accepted by all parties for over fifty years, Harold. What in the hell do you need to win a case for God's sake?" Marion ranted. "Did you get your law degree in a Cracker Jack box?"

"Nothing in the law is that cut and dried, Marion, and this guy is no backwater Podunk shyster. I'm telling you he has some other angle on this and I'm damned if I can figure out what it might be. He ought to be holding his hat and begging us to pay a token road usage fee but he acts like he's running the show. Is the Judge on the case his brother-in-law or something?"

A chilling stab of sudden fear clutched at Marion's heart. He was afraid he knew the reason for the opposing lawyer's defiant attitude. Was there another copy of the old agreement besides the one in the courthouse? Reinhardt's mental toughness came to the fore.

"You're being paid to win these cases for us, Harold," Marion stared at him coldly. "If you can't beat this small town bum, we'll have to get a firm we can depend on. Maybe you better get out of here and start figuring things out. Anyway, I got work to do whether you have or not." He peremptorily dismissed the Attorney and immediately called George Frailey.

"There's only one thing I can figure for this Eldring guy's attitude, George," Marion was earnestly going over the latest information from Perlmutter with his brother-in-law, "and that must be some idea that the Cielo Grande document isn't on the up-and-up. I don't see how anybody could be on to anything but maybe you can talk to Delvane Winston again and get something out of him."

"That drunk is so far gone I don't think you could get a hiccup out of him, let alone any reasonable explanations," George replied.

"Well, George, you're not going to sit around with your cock in your hand while this deal goes to hell on us," Marion snarled intensely. "Use some imagination! Get over there to the Longbranch where he hangs out and see if you can pry something out of him. Find out if there was ever another copy of that old easement paper. Jesus, man, do something instead of telling me what won't work." Marion's verbal abuse was the product of his growing concern and fear but George was getting tired of his brother-in-law's outbursts.

"Screw you, Marion," George declared, "I'll take care of my end of this business. Don't worry about it!" He slammed the telephone receiver down with a crash.

The passage of more than a year and a half since the divorce had worked much evil on Delvane Winston. Collie had tried more than once to create some pathway of communication or help her ex-husband in some way after becoming aware of his alcoholic illness. He was too proud to accept any advice or aid from her and refused to contact his family in California as well. Collie found out that Del had opened a small personal checking account in Smith's bank shortly after the divorce and she deposited funds periodically to keep him in spending money. Delvane was so removed from reality after a few months that he never even questioned the fact that the account always seemed to have a positive balance. He didn't know or care where the money came from, only that he was able to pay his tab at the Longbranch often enough to satisfy management and retain his place at the bar. He managed, somehow, to keep up appearances in personal hygiene and appropriate clothing but his mental state deteriorated to the point of paranoid withdrawal bordering on catatonia. All he did was sit and drink all day while staring at the wall. Sometimes he ate half a sandwich or a salad placed before him by the bartender. George Frailey tried to engage Del in conversation in order to pump more information, however, he never got a meaningful reply to his probing questions.

"Come on Winston," he wheedled, "think back on that Cielo Grande easement. When was the last time you saw it?"

"Go ask Toby Swanhunter, you pig!" Delvane was in a nasty mood.

"Has your wife got a copy of that easement?" insisted Frailey. "You know she's sleeping with that Ryan Baker guy, don't you? I'll bet you never knew they went home together from that country club dedication bash, did you? I saw 'em leave together. I bet he got a piece of your woman that night, Winston. Why do you think she dumped your sorry ass?"

"You don't know anything you fat bastard. Get out of here and leave me alone," Delvane stated coldly.

Frailey tried a few more conversational gambits with no result. Delvane slipped away into the distorted world of his mental interior and gave no further response.

FRUSTRATION AND WORSE

The trouble between Milo Harris and Ken Bruchek was a source of intriguing gossip and speculation among the crowd of miners and cowboys who frequently patronized the Bull Run. Ryan's part in the original argument was overlooked and dismissed because the obvious match, if it came to a showdown, was between Milo and Bruchek. The situation rapidly developed into an almost legendary contention with Milo the favorite of the local crowd and Ken Bruchek supported by the new wave of mine workers. While neither man was particularly angry or grudging of any action of the other, as talk of the confrontation spread and increased around town they both began to feel some pressure to perform. There seemed to be a certain honor at stake and avoidance was, for all practical purposes, almost a social impossibility for either man. They were equally confident in their abilities and each felt no doubt that he could whip the other simply because neither man had ever lost a meaningful fight since childhood. Within a few weeks the prosecution of the inevitable battle became only a matter of when the two would meet at an appropriate time and location for the event. Any thought of a reason for the unpleasantness was beyond consideration and the public perception of the two men's eventual meeting evolved into a game-like atmosphere similar to a baseball world series or an Olympic event. Speculation was the rage at every gathering of men in the County and many bets were laid. Not surprisingly, given the disparity in size and weight between the two, Bruchek was the odds-on favorite.

As the year 1955 progressed in its short reign, the frigid weather gradually let up and signs of a distant spring could be felt and sensed. Snowdrifts shrunk and the glacial deposit of frozen ground water in the Canteen pit began to soften and melt. The flow of Framboise creek increased in volume day by day carrying detritus and waste the like of which was never before seen in Palmer canyon. After eighteen months of frenzied activity on the Bench by prospectors and miners intent on exploring, drilling or digging up every acre of the plateau, the annual thaw and runoff brought more than a volume of fresh snow melt as in past years. Rather than a clear icy flood in its upper reaches, Framboise creek's rushing torrent was an ominous yellowish brown, thick and turbid, loaded with eroded earth from fine silt to coarse gravel and even small boulders that scoured the streambed bare. Moss, water plants, insects, snails, crayfish, worms and larva of all kinds that provided food for the trout population and other denizens of the canyon were scrubbed out of their hiding places and flushed down the creek. Where the water velocity lessened, huge sand and gravel bars were deposited that diverted the flow and eroded new courses into the edges of the Palmer ranch pastures. The catch basin at the foot of Garnet Falls filled with rocks and gravel which built up in just a few weeks during the heavy spring snow melt to form a water saturated mound upon which the cascading waters poured. It was a completely different scene than the one enjoyed by Milo and Ryan only months earlier. A kind of death was overtaking Framboise creek. Already, there were cans and bottles, packaging, garbage of all sorts from the busy camps of workers located across the mining district spreading odious debris throughout the Bench and the canyon.

Collie was furious. Feelings of impotence and inevitability about the rapid deterioration of her ranch and the surrounding region made it difficult for her to fight back. Too many people, organizations and even government agencies were conspiring to uphold and encourage the forces that were despoiling the countryside. There was a huge financial incentive for almost everyone in the state to keep the uranium boom going without legal or civil hindrance. Also, a real and undeniable need existed for the radioactive metal as a keystone weapons building ingredient in the United States national defense system. It was the next thing to pro-Communism to object, at any level, to the mining operations in Wyoming and elsewhere. Senator Joseph McCarthy of Wisconsin, a friend and colleague of Senator Paige, was at the height of popularity and public approval in his search and exposure of anti-American sentiment in the country. Collie was too good a politician not to recognize that public opposition to the mining ventures on the Bench would be impossible to sell to her constituents in Sheila's Tree or to anyone else considering the existing opinions and popular positions held by most people. She and her Attorney, Denton Eldring, were working out a strategy.

"We have to keep pounding away at New Mexico Mining Corporation as the primary culprit here," Collie stated. "You have to show that their excessive use of Pass Road is putting an unlawful and damaging strain on the ranch. Personalize it! Although other companies are in the startup mode, nobody else is using the road for ore haul as yet. Is there any way to tie the deterioration of Framboise creek to the NMMC operation? There are laws against destroying other people's property even if Marion Reinhardt's right to use my road is upheld."

"You are right, of course," Eldring said, "but they have a lot of arguments at their disposal to counter our claim, or, at the least, spread the blame around on others who also use the road on a daily basis. Our best bet is to represent you as a small operator struggling to make the ranch go in the face of huge corporate insensitivity and harassment. Their ace in the hole is that damned right-of-way document to Cielo Grande back in 1895. Without that it would be a simple case of trespass. How could your Grandfather have been so—umm—so obtuse as to grant that easement to any future mining company that happened to come along for no compensation? I don't understand it. I've tried to cover up my concern to Perlmutter but he's way too smart not to shove that document right down my throat."

Collie's frown of puzzlement and frustration was his only answer.

GOSSIP

Hamm Stensgaard, one of Ken Bruchek's most experienced drillers, was the center of attention as the crew sat around a tall masted rotary rig eating lunch.

"Well, I hope Kenny beats the crap out of that Coon, myself. Hell, I've seen ol' Ken take on three like him at once and put 'em all in the hospital," Hamm boasted. "You know, I seen that fuckin' Nigger last summer up on Chopstick reservoir with that smart-ass white woman from the Bull Run—you know—that Iris or Rose or whatever her name is? He sure as shit needs his uppity ass kicked good and hard."

"No shit, Hamm, you really seen them two together?" asked one of the younger men.

"God damn it, I said so, didn't I? I was up there lookin' for a deer stand a few weeks 'fore season started and I happen' to catch 'em in the binoc'lars. They were rollin' around on a blanket out there in the woods and really steamin' up the place. He banged her lights out about three times." Hamm grinned lasciviously, "She sure got a nice pair of knockers on her."

"Well, Jesus, man! What did ya do, just get your rocks off watchin'? You stood there and watched that black goat take a white woman? What the hell is wrong with you, Hamm?"

"It's none a your business, Mickie, what I was doin'," Hamm responded vehemently. "It sure as shit wasn't no rape—she was lovin' it. Besides, at the time, I never knowed either one of 'em from Adam. I got nuthin' against any man gettin' a little ass once in awhile."

"I'll tell the world ol' Bruchek won't take it so light. You know how he feels about the Jigs, an' when he hears this here story it's gonna give him somethin' to think about. I bet he breaks a few extra Nigger bones just for the hell of it after he hears this."

The year 1956 was the real coming of age for the uranium boom. All the exploration, preparation and development was brought to fruition as ton after ton of rich ore was mined, transported and processed in Ryan Baker's modern mill. By far the largest producer in the region was NMMC from the Canteen pits, however, other ore locations were discovered and numerous companies, large and small, were opening mines also. Soon the mill was operating at full capacity for three shifts seven days each week and allocations were made to the various companies on a tonnage basis for the processing of ore. Sean Mochery was fine tuning every step in the milling process and quickly found the most efficient level of production for uranium recovery and mill cost efficiency. Producers were required to blend their raw ore so that the uranium content of the average mill feed was within a narrow range which best fit the capabilities of the mill. Soon there were huge mountains of ore, sorted by richness of uranium content, stored in proximity to the mill. Several tons of yellowcake were produced and shipped to Grand Junction every day. Ryan was, at first, stunned by the amount of money rolling in each month. Despite the huge costs for manpower, chemicals, energy and all the rest of it, there was still more profit than the most optimistic projections had foreseen. All of the construction debt was paid off in the first six months of operation. Ryan was soon wealthy beyond his most exuberant expectations. He became a millionaire so fast that it was difficult for him to assimilate what was happening. His life style was slow to change and few of his friends or acquaintances, except for participating insiders, realized how financially successful the milling monopoly was. The Crown brothers also prospered out of all proportion to their slender investment in the project.

Not everyone in Sheila's Tree was experiencing such good fortune. Iris Patton was making plenty of money from the Bull Run restaurant and bar, however, rumors were surfacing everywhere about her affair with Milo Harris. The very thing she feared most was coming to pass. No one offered any first hand proof or made overt accusations but the scornful glances, snickering laughter that stopped abruptly when she appeared, and snubs from some former good customers in the restaurant all served to verify what her guilty conscience already felt. She no longer made the rounds of the dining tables or joked with patrons in the lounge. She stayed in the kitchen or, often enough, failed to show up for work at all and remained almost a prisoner in her apartment. The worst part of her alienation and despondency was the loss of Milo. She ached for his touch, for his companionship, for his good-humored presence, and yet could not bear to face him. Finally, after long indecision and in a state of growing depression, she made up her mind to sell the Bull Run and leave Sheila's Tree. Within two weeks she had closed a deal with Juno Castle at a price below the actual worth of the thriving business and moved away from her home town in search of a new start—somewhere.

REVELATIONS AND CHALLENGE

Milo, for many of the same reasons as Iris, changed his normal gregarious habits and began sticking close to the D-Z. There was no longer any attraction in going into town for recreation. He was unconsciously avoiding a showdown with Ken Bruchek, not from fear, but simply because he was unable to generate any personal interest in the hostilities. As the weeks passed he put more and more effort into the ranch and the constant battle to maintain the herd and keep order on the high pastures in the face of continuing trespass and environmental disturbances, though the D-Z was much less severely impacted than the Palmer ranch. It was several weeks after Iris had sold the Bull Run and left the community before Milo heard the full story.

"Damn, it seems mighty funny to see Miz Castle lording it over the Bull Run 'stead of Miz Patton," Squirrely observed at breakfast one morning after a week-end trip to town.

"What are you talking about, Squirrely?" Milo demanded. "What was Juno Castle doing in the Bull Run?"

"Why, Miz Castle done bought the place up, lock, stock and barrel, a few weeks back. She's the new owner, Milo. I thought everybody knew about that already."

Milo never said a word but quickly excused himself and made straight for the ranch house.

"Mornin' Ballard. How's the rheumatism coming along?" Milo addressed his boss.

"Ah, hell, Milo, I can't hardly get around with these knees. I'm sure glad you got things scrut'nized out there. I don't see how I'd get the job done without you on top of it." Ballard was still in a bathrobe drinking his morning coffee. "Bessie takes mighty good care of me but I ain't much up to spendin' ten hours in the saddle no more."

Bessie Taylor was a longtime housekeeper at the D-Z and had taken care of Ballard's domestic needs for the past twenty years.

"Ballard, I just heard something out in the bunkhouse that's got me wondering. Has Juno said anything to you about buying the Bull Run?" Milo asked directly.

Crown was aware that Milo and pretty near everyone else knew of his long-term relationship with Juno Castle. In fact, it was general knowledge around Sheila's Tree.

"Why sure, son, we talked it over some before she jumped in." Ballard looked questioningly at Milo. It was rare for anything like personal topics to come up in their conversations.

"Umm—well, I—I," Milo was uncharacteristically tongue tied as he sought to find out the particulars behind Iris' sudden decision to sell. "Damn it, Ballard, why would Miss Patton want to sell out just when the place is doing so good?" Milo finally burst through his unease.

Crown immediately got the drift of Milo's outburst and, having heard some of the town gossip, could clearly perceive his discomfort with the topic.

"Now Milo," Ballard said kindly, "I reckon Iris Patton must have been upset at all the ol' hen cluckin' goin' on around town. She never said as much to Juno but the lady was clearly all lathered up about this mush that some of those drillers was spreadin' about. Maybe you ain't heard the partic'lers?" he questioned.

"I haven't heard anything," Milo grated. "What kind of gossip are you talking about?"

"Well, yore bound to hear the worst sometime. From what Juno told me folks are mentionin' yore name and her name in the same sentence." Seeing the look of astonishment and apparent hurt on Milo's face, Ballard quickly added, "Son, I don't know nor want to know, nuthin' about yore business. This here town is a pretty small pond and the frogs don't mind their own Ps and Qs much."

Milo was almost choking with cryptic emotion. "Who is doing all the talking, Ballard? Why would anybody say bad things about Iris Patton? Did you say drillers?" he almost spat the words.

"I understand you and that Brahma bull of a man, Bruchek, had a little set-to some time back and a lot of folks is taking it up. I'd heard all that quite a spell ago but then, they tell me, he come roarin' into the Bull Run one night and says he's goin' to teach somebody a lesson about leavin' white women alone. He made no bones about who he was talkin' of. Then that whole bunch of his started tellin' all manner of nasty gossip and the pore gal was made a butt of ever' small minded Righteous Rachel in town."

"Ah, my God, I should have known. Ballard, I swear to you Iris and I have done nothing to be ashamed of or hide. I'd marry her in a minute if she wasn't so scared of what people would say—are saying right now, I guess. We never made this messed up world but I can tell you, color don't make a man different. This was Iris' worst fear and now these slimy tongued bastards are making it all come true. By God, I'm going to find Bruchek and we'll see who the teacher might be."

Milo was beside himself with pain and anger as he turned to go looking for the driller. There was a terrible need to ease the pressure of his frustrating circumstances with all-out fury and action. Milo was ready to fight.

"Now ease up a mite, son," Ballard's voice rose in volume. "You aint goin' to have the most popular position in this thing, whether it's right or wrong. There's many out there who would side with Bruchek as you well know. You can't beat the vinegar out of all of 'em."

Milo stopped for a moment in the door, then turned to face his boss. Though his face was grim, a fleeting half smile passed over his visage.

"I may not beat 'em all but Bruchek is a good place to start." He strode purposefully toward the old D-Z pickup truck.

It was close to eight o'clock in the morning when Milo pulled into the parking lot of Ryan Baker's modest office building adjacent to the uranium mill north of town. There was a layer of fine dust covering every exposed surface of the mill complex and the huge rumbling ore trucks already were coming in a constant dinosaurian parade of noisy fuming turbulence to be weighed, sampled and emptied onto designated ore piles. The growing tailings pond where acidulous liquid and waste solids from the milling process was expelled for collection and evaporation glittered festucine yellow in the morning light. Ryan's huge new black Buick was already parked in its reserved spot by the side entrance.

"Ryan, my man, once again I humbly come before you requesting aid," Milo stated with a sardonic sweeping bow, hat in hand.

"Well, this time I hope I can actually do something for you. I heard Iri town and I felt like a dirty dog for not having said something when you as' to." Ryan pushed aside the sheaf of milling reports that had occupied his attention before Milo entered.

"Oh hell, I doubt you could have made any difference as it turns out. I guess you heard all the ugly bullshit going around?"

"It's a small town, Milo."

"I'm going after them, Ryan. These bastards have no right to even mention Iris' name, let alone talk all that dirt about her." Milo was shaken with emotion but Ryan could see the annealed resolve in his narrowed eyes and rigid facial muscles.

"Listen, Milo, this battle between you and Bruchek isn't funny anymore. Your feelings are too much involved and any fight now might well lead further than you want to go. What if one of you gets seriously injured? You or Bruchek, or maybe both, could end up in jail."

"How do you know how far I want it to go?" Milo's voice was flat and hard. "I'm going to teach that big white son-of-a bitch a lesson he'll never forget."

"Listen to yourself. You're acting as much a bigot as he is. I'm warning you, Milo, this is going to end badly and you won't help either Iris or yourself."

"You're warning me?" Milo grimaced with no humor at all. "I came here to ask if you knew where to find the slimy bastard. I guess I'll find him myself, thanks."

He spun about and left abruptly, sliding the pickup sideways in loose gravel as he accelerated out of the parking lot. Milo knew that Bruchek Drilling headquarters was located on the site of the NMMC Canteen mines with office in an old trailer house parked out in the sagebrush. There was a spacious lot behind the makeshift office with rows of open sided machinery sheds where the drill rigs, grease trucks and pickup fleet were parked when not working at a drill site. Milo decided that home base was probably the best place to look for his man and so he drove out towards Pass Road and the Bench. Milo was fleetingly sorry for the stiff words with Ryan Baker, recognizing that his friend only expressed interest in his well being, but his mind was absorbed with the approaching confrontation and thoughts of how best to deal with Bruchek physically. There was no doubt that a fight was going to take place and he wanted to be the winner.

Milo walked up the gravel pathway lined with colorful sedimentary boulders and stepped upon the rough wooden stair to the mobile home office entrance. He pulled the flimsy door open and was met with a ham-sized fist slamming accurately and powerfully into his right cheekbone. Milo flew backwards off the small porch and landed on his back in the middle of the path, strange lights flashing and winking on his retina. He rolled to his knees and felt a crushing blow to the ribs, this time delivered with all the strength of Bruchek's right leg and boot.

"I been kind of watching for you, Harris. I was starting to think you were too yellow to come around. Come on, get up—you're making this too easy for me." Bruchek laughed heavily and stepped back for a moment while Milo struggled to catch his wind and get to his feet. His thoughts raced as he tried to assess the situation and regain some control over events. He felt stupid for having been caught off-guard in such an obvious way. Milo saw that Bruchek was much too sure of himself and over-confident because of his easy opening blows. I wonder, thought Milo, how long it has been since this guy actually had anybody put up a fight? Maybe I can get him on the receiving end for a change.

Milo had come prepared for speed and movement. He was wearing sneakers instead of his usual cowboy boots and a pair of soft leather roping gloves on his hands. He got to his feet and reeled unsteadily as if practically unconscious. Bruchek came pawing in with his left extended, right fist cocked for another big blow. Milo delivered three quick straight head-rattling jabs to the face and a right cross to the jaw over the drooping left hand of his opponent before Bruchek could blink an eye. Stepping closer, inside Bruchek's swing radius, Milo beat a hard series of lefts and rights to the stomach. Next a right uppercut smashed into Bruchek's jaw and he staggered back with a surprised expression as blood flushed from his broken nose. Milo was in front of him like a shadow, driving blow after blow to the head and midsection with all the power of his long muscular frame. Bruchek roared in pain and anger, realizing that this adversary was in a category far different from the brawlers and bar fighters against whom he had built his reputation. Neither Milo nor Bruchek were formally trained boxers though both were hard and fit from their physical work. Milo soon asserted himself as the better athlete; quicker, better conditioned, and smarter in conducting the fight. Bruchek charged in with his head down, swinging widely, trying to use his weight and strength, but seldom finding a target. He could never prepare solidly for a punch or move rapidly enough to evade Milo's accurately repeated shots. Milo jabbed and punched with deadly cumulative effect until the big driller was dazed and nearly blinded by swelling flesh around his eyes. Bruchek was tough and unwilling to quit but rapidly losing strength. His ability to remain conscious and functional dwindled with each new round of blows from the smaller man. Milo's offense began to change as Bruchek became more and more debilitated. He too' longer swings with his feet planted further apart so that each punch was m' powerful and damaging than the last. Finally, Bruchek sank down slowly t' knee and then toppled forward completely unconscious.

Milo was gasping for breath as he strove to repair the oxygen debt run up by the extraordinary exertion expended in the battle. He felt drained and sorrowful rather than exhilarated as he had expected. There was no satisfaction in having beaten his man and the basic problem of the loss of Iris was, of course, still unresolved. Milo started to turn away when he realized that a small group of Bruchek's men had gathered during the course of the fight and were standing in a menacing semi-circle between him and his pickup truck. Several had oaken pick handles or iron jack handles in their hands. The fistfight was over but Milo realized that his troubles had just begun. No man said a word or gave any signal but suddenly three men at once stepped in swinging their weapons. Milo felt an explosive concussion to the ribs that fractured bone and tore muscle. At the same instant a sweeping blow to the outside of his left knee brought him down with a crunch of bone and tissue. He tried to roll and cover up but the rain of blows came furiously at every exposed part including his head. The silent men labored on for several minutes flailing and kicking at his prostrate form until he lay, twitching spasmodically and gasping in hoarse liquid gurgles. At last they picked up his inert body and flung him, like a bag of garbage, into the back of the D-Z pickup.

"Drive 'im down along the haul road towards town and park his junker off in the brush. I'll come pick you up right now. Hurry!"

Two trucks swirled out of the driveway in a spray of gravel as the men hurried to cover evidence of their vicious attack. Mercifully, Milo Harris was deeply unconscious, hovering at the edge of a final release into long silent darkness where pain and human concerns, good or bad, were of no further importance. Shallow sputters of bloody foam puffed from his mouth as the pickup truck bumped along the washboarded dirt road towards a spot where it could be handily abandoned.

RESCUE

Ryan Baker continued to work through the mill production figures for several minutes after Milo walked out of his office. He was slightly irritated at Milo's huffy attitude towards his seemingly conservative advice about a showdown with Bruchek and yet there was a nibble of conscience at letting his friend go out alone looking for trouble.

"Damn, I should never have let him out of here without me. He probably figured I would volunteer, at least, to be his second in this goofy fight. I better go find that cowboy before he gets his head torn off," he muttered to himself.

As Ryan drove through town towards the County road to Palmer Ranch and Pass road, he saw an unfamiliar figure stalking stiffly along Main Street. Ryan quickly recognized Delvane Winston whom he had not seen for months since Collie's divorce.

Wonder where he's been hiding?, he thought idly. I never knew he was still in town. Thought he went back to California. He looks kind of funny some way...and his thoughts returned to the immediate search for Milo Harris. Everyone knew that Bruchek's headquarters office was located out at the NMMC Canteen pits.

Ryan realized that he needed to step on it if he expected to get there before the fireworks. He pushed down on the accelerator of the heavy Buick.

Forty-five minutes later and just a few miles from the New Mexico Mining Company's Canteen complex, Ryan saw the D-Z pickup parked thirty feet c the road surrounded by waist-high sage brush and partially hidden by an ero outcrop of sandstone. Had he been traveling in the opposite direction, the p˙

would have been completely hidden from sight. As it was, the midmorning sun glinted off the windshield at just the right angle to catch his eye and he quickly brought the Buick to a stop on the soft sandy shoulder of the haul road. He could see fresh tire tracks where the pickup had run off the road and through the brush to its partially concealed resting-place. He approached the truck cautiously, wondering what Milo was doing in such an unlikely location. He quickly spotted smears of blood darkening the sideboards, then Milo's limp and broken body sprawled in the bed of the pickup.

Oh my God, what have they done to him? Ryan could see that his friend was desperately injured and wondered if he dared to move him. I can't leave him here, though, so that means I have to get him in the car.

Ryan ran back and drove his powerful car through the loose sand and brush to a point as close as possible to the pickup. Milo outweighed Ryan by more than forty pounds but adrenaline and fear lent strength. Being as careful as possible, Ryan slid Milo out of the pickup, carried him cradled in his arms and placed him in a semi-reclining position on the back seat of the car. Ryan could see there were broken bones and a terrible slash across the scalp above Milo's right ear. Blood oozed from many of the wounds and this gave Ryan hope that his friend might still be alive. There were few other indications that any vitality lingered in the torn and battered form. The thirty-mile trip down Pass Road and into Sheila's tree was never made in less time. Ryan drove recklessly around ore trucks and other sparse traffic at speed far greater than the dirt road was meant to be traveled. He pulled up directly to the ambulance entrance of the Mercy hospital and delivered his friend's limp body into the competent hands of the emergency room crew.

DARK DREAMS

George Frailey's spiteful words at their last meeting in the Longbranch saloon had a far greater impact on Delvane Winston than Frailey intended or could have imagined. The idea behind the malicious goading was to anger Del and get him to respond in some way to George's questions concerning the Cielo Grande right-of-way document, but the suggestion that Ryan Baker, or any other man, could have any sort of relationship with Collie was more than Delvane's alcoholic reason could tolerate. He sat for days drinking and brooding, imagining alternate outcomes to his various life projects and finding blame for his failures in the acts of others. His pride and self-image were damaged most by Collie's contemptuous rejection. In Frailey's scathing words he found a scapegoat and focus for his losses and degradation and surrogate suicide in the bottle. Ryan Baker gradually became the symbol and substance, in his mind, for all the wrongs and ruin that plagued his benumbed brain. Eventually, on the verge of a complete paranoiac breakdown, he began planning an action which, as contemplated in his disabled mind, would culminate in victory and revision of his fall from grace. In the ebony lacework of his delusion Delvane imagined that the only honorable course for righting the failures, redeeming his honor and proving his manhood to Collie was to end his unhappy existence in a sensational public self immolation, made true and perfect by taking Ryan Baker to Hell with him. Concentrated purpose glittered in eyes squinted against the bright September sun as Del left his bar room refuge during daylight hours for the first time in many weeks. In the pocket of his tweed jacket he carried a small .22 caliber semi-automatic "snake gun" that he gripped tightly with a sweaty hand, his index finger applying spasmodic pressure to the trigger guard.

DEATH WATCH

Ryan called Ballard Crown from the admitting desk of the hospital. An hour later they sat in the coffee shop of the Cielo Grande hotel quietly waiting for word from a duty nurse who had promised to call Ryan there as soon as the Doctors offered any opinion on Milo's condition and prognosis.

"I know he has family in California," Ryan offered, "but I have no idea how to get in touch with anyone out there."

"He gets letters ever' so often from his Ma. I reckon we could look in his quarters and see about a return address, mebbe."

"Umm—I don't suppose you know much about his private affairs," Ryan glanced sideways at Ballard, "like, anybody else we should be calling, for instance?"

Ballard stirred his coffee absently then smiled faintly and bent his weather-beaten head towards Ryan. "I reckon you must be a pretty good friend of his, that so?"

"Well, yes, I guess so. He shared some fairly personal things in his life with me at times."

"We might as well stop beatin' around the bush. He was real shook up about Miz Patton sellin' off the Bull Run. They had some kind of understanding between 'em, or misunderstanding as the case may be, but I do believe he would want her to know about this misfortune of his."

"No question in my mind about that," Ryan sighed in relief at Ballard's shared knowledge. "Do you know where she is or where to get in touch with her?"

"Juno Castle might have an idee, but mebbe not, too. Miz Patton was some upset when she pulled out of here and was pretty much lookin' to get lost and stay lost."

"Well, I failed Milo once by not talking to her when he asked me. I don't propose to make the same mistake again. I intend to find Iris Patton if I have to get every private investigator in the country on it."

A tall, rangy man rather uncomfortably dressed up in expensive lizard skin boots, sharply pressed pinks held up by a handtooled belt decorated with a huge silver and turquoise buckle, tailored silk shirt and a fancy widebrim Stetson hat rose from his stool at the coffee counter and walked up to the table.

"You two would be Mr. Crown and Mr. Baker?" the stranger queried. "I b'lieve I rec'nized you both from seein' you around town before. I overheerd you mention Milo Harris an' I done seen him with both of you different times. You happen to know where he's at right now?"

"Say, I think I know you too," Ryan took a long look at the stranger. "You must be the famous Tom Regelstorp who made the original strike on the Canteen District. Milo Harris has told me a bit about you and told me the story of the notorious poker game in some detail as well."

"Yes. And I 'member seein' you, Harris, Mayor Winston and another lady up on Pass Road on that same day I made the find. I bet you never had no idee what I had in that ol' backpack that day," Tom grinned a crooked tooth smile. "She all turned out about as good as I was hopin' at the time."

"Speakin' of Milo Harris, son, he come a real cropper this mornin'." Ballard was taking in Tom's drugstore cowboy attire with a rather disparaging regard. "He met up with a passel of hard luck from somebody up on the Bench. I reckon they was real hard cases because he's over at the hospital in pretty bad shape. What's your interest in Milo's whereabouts, if I might ask?"

"Why sure," Tom frowned, "I am right sorry to hear about it. What the hell happened to 'im? I heard he was having a run-in with that driller fella, Bruchek. Maybe Harris finally ran up on somebody a little more hombre than himself." Tom remembered the ease with which Milo had physically overwhelmed him the night of the poker game. "I never had nothin' against Harris. He won that poker game fair and square."

"Well," said Ryan, "the fact is, Milo is in pretty grave shape. He got beat up in a very brutal way and is unconscious at present. We're waiting for word from the emergency room right now. From the looks of things I would say it's about a sure bet that he was facing more that one person this morning."

"Damn. You mean he may not pull through?"

Neither Ryan nor Ballard wanted to answer that question.

"Oh man! There ain't no justice in this world," Tom fretted. "Why, Milo Harris sure picked a bad time to get hisself banged up. His half of the royalties offen them Canteen claims of mine are stackin' up over at the bank in a trust account bein' held by the mining company. I found out they never made no try to get ahold of Harris. You can't trust them bastards no way. Ol' man Smith, hisself, was the one tol' me that Harris has got a regular fortune over there waitin' for 'im to claim it."

The waitress beckoned Ryan over to the cash register and handed him the telephone.

"Mr. Baker is that you?" the duty nurse inquired. "The patient is recuperating now in post-op after extensive surgery to remove pressure on the right side of his brain and set broken bones. He had a collapsed lung from a rib puncture and internal bruising of liver and kidneys, as well. Even if everything else goes very well it may be a long time before he can walk again because of the damage to his left knee. The Doctor has done all he could to repair the injuries but the outcome for Mr. Harris is by no means assured. Doctor said he had lost a great deal of blood and was very close to the edge by the time you got him in here. He has not regained consciousness as yet. You better come on over and talk to Doctor Hysett for the full story."

"Thank you, Doris, I appreciate your call and I will see Dr. Hysett right away." He hung up the phone with the appalling feeling of being caught in a flow of events that he was helpless to alter or stop. There was a sense of impending grief and calamity transcending even the immediate concern for Milo Harris. It was not a rational feeling.

When he turned back to tell Ballard and Tom the grim news he was surprised to see Collie standing by the table. Ryan experienced a distinct physical reaction to her unexpected presence. His feeling for her welled up in a tumultuous surge of emotion. His eyes misted and his stomach stirred with a giddy swooping sensation.

To have her suddenly show up just when I felt the bottom dropping out—to see her standing so calmly and beautifully composed. I never want to face another crises or sorrow or difficulty without this woman by my side, Ryan thought, though only his expression spoke.

Collie read the depth of feeling in his face and expressive hazel eyes but, along with Ballard, interpreted it to be concern for Milo. She touched his hand as he returned to the small group.

"Oh, Ryan, I'm so sorry. I heard part of the story from Sean Mochery. What happened to your friend, Milo?"

"Collie, I'm sure glad you're here. Milo got beaten nearly to death by some-body up on the bench this morning. He went up there looking for Bruchek and apparently found him," Ryan spoke quietly. "I don't believe those injuries were caused by any kind of fair fight. Milo was knocked around with clubs or weapons of some sort."

"My Granddad, E.L., used to say that trouble is as constant as the wind in Wyoming," Collie quoted, "and you have to be ready for a blow at all times. I thought all the talk around town about Milo and Bruchek would end badly. The only thing is, I figured you would be the one in trouble after I heard you threw the first punch at Bruchek." Collie regarded Ryan with an amused half smile despite the gravity of their concern for Milo.

Tom Regelstorp was still standing with the group. "Ol' Milo's sure as hell got a lot of good reasons to pull through. I reckon he don't even have an idee 'bout all that money settin' in the bank waitin' for 'im."

There was little more that Ryan or anyone else in the group could do. The long day ended with Milo remaining in the intensive care unit without regaining consciousness. No one knew the circumstances surrounding Milo's injury or whether a crime had been committed, nor had anyone from Bruchek's drilling company come down from the Bench. Ryan found an opportunity to inform Collie of Milo's real motive for seeking out Bruchek and of his own inadequate role in the misadventure. Only Regelstorp's news of Milo's new wealth, despite its ironic timing, lent any positive aspect to the day. After checking with Dr. Hysett at the hospital and determining that Milo's condition was unchanged and still speculative at best, Ryan and Collie parted with no further conversation or reference to their own relationship. Ryan knew that he could never consider a future without Collie but, despite his earnest intent, the old obstacles still per-sisted and kept him at a distance. Ryan found it difficult to move the relationship on to a more intimate level. He lacked both the skill and the will to flirt or pre-tend indifference or engage in other shallow dramatics. Ryan was not a game player.

Both Ryan and Doctor Hysett were at the hospital early the next morning as the long shadows of dawn slowly began to shorten and crisp autumn air gently warmed to the watery sun. Ryan was on his second cup of bitter hospital coffee when the Doctor finally stopped by the waiting room to report on Milo's condi-tion.

"My concern is for swelling of brain tissue within the cranium at this point. I have removed clotted blood and released the pressure to the best of my ability but there is still a possibility of increasing pressure from swelling or edema."

"What are his chances? Is he going to come out of this?"

"We'll know in a matter of hours. I wish I could be more specific," the Doctor extended his hands palm upward indicating that he exercised limited control.

Ryan could only wait nervously for events to run their course. He was deeply curious to know what had taken place on the Bench but could think of no easy way to find out. He expected Milo to have quite a story to relate when, and if, he regained consciousness. Ryan was determined to see that justice was done if criminal acts were involved. He remembered to start the search for Iris Patton, wishing that she could be here to share his anxiety and bolster Milo's morale if he returned to an aware state. He made a long distance call to Washington DC.

"Hud, this is Ryan Baker. How about meeting me for a beer at Ozzie's Palace?"

"Ryan, you rock shuffler, are you in town again looking for more taxpayers money? I haven't been drunk since the last time I was shooting the bull with you and Riscotti. What's going on?"

Private investigator Hudson Pavel worked out of Washington DC and was frequently in the employ of Senator Paige when information became a critical commodity in the flow of political exigency. He, Ryan and Paolo Riscotti had met often for a cold beer during the Washington days to discuss strategies, tell tall stories and relax from the high tension of their various jobs. Ryan remembered the succession of beautiful young women who served briefly as receptionists and secretaries in Hud's crowded little office. Their tenures were always quite short due to Pavel's spirited and impulsive personality. He was continually screaming for faster, better, more accurate work or else importuning for sexual favors. Neither tactic was received with much enthusiasm by most of the young ladies, though one or two exceptions were the subject of the private detective's best bar room anecdotes.

"Pavel, I need you to find somebody for me. It is real important to a good friend of mine. Hell, I might even pay your exorbitant fee if you get off the dime and do a quick job. It'll probably help if I tell you your quarry is a good looking young lady."

"Damn right then. Give me all the information you have and I'll do my usual magic."

Ryan produced a description, her previous home and business address, information on her bank, social security number, obtained from public records of the sale of the Bull Run, and everything else that he had uncovered or could remember about Iris. He gave Pavel the phone numbers of Juno Castle and Tony Arriaga for further inquiries.

"This should be a walk in the park, Baker. You'll be hearing from me in short order I expect." Hudson Pavel went to work.

An hour later Ryan was reading the Galena Daily Journal with far more detail than usual though not much concentration. He saw Collie approaching from the nursing desk.

"I thought I would find you here. Do you mind some company? The ICU nurse told me how it is with Milo."

"Oh Collie, I can't tell you how much it means to me to have you here. I am so worried about Milo—I feel halfway responsible for the beating he took. I should have been with him but I didn't take it serious enough. If he doesn't make it…," Ryan's voice trailed off in despair.

"I'll wait with you. Have you had breakfast?"

They went down to the antiseptic chrome and Formica hospital cafeteria and struggled with helpings of plastic unsalted scrambled eggs and over-crisped bacon strips. The hours passed slowly but immeasurably more comfortable and pleasant for Ryan because of Collie's presence. They talked of the activities and changes taking place in Sheila's Tree, of their friends, old and new, and possible future trends. They reminisced about Milo's problems and discussed possibilities for his future affairs due to the new affluence. Ryan, after asking for her discretion, shared with Collie the story of Milo's love. He also told her the true details of the poker game story, as related to him by Milo, whereby Harris won partial possession of the Canteen mining claims. The story had become a mythological epic since it had circulated through and through the gossip networks of the community and beyond.

"You say he had a fight with a couple of saddle bums in the bar before the poker game?" Collie asked. "And one of those men was a Mexican with a knife? You know what night that was don't you? It was the same night Louise got attacked. It has to be the same man, Ryan!"

"My God. Milo said those two yahoos asked directions somewhere or how to contact somebody—I can't remember. He must know their names, too."

Doctor Hysett finally returned with news of his patient.

"Milo is going to recover. He is conscious and responding to questions and completely in command of his senses. We are treating him for pain and can only wait for his natural recuperative powers to start repairing the bruised liver and kidneys. The danger of brain swelling or brain damage seems to be past. We must keep him in ICU for another day and then he will be back in his room where he will welcome visitors, I'm sure."

Ryan and Collie exchanged an intimate look of relief and happiness.

"Thank you, Doctor, for all you have done. We can't wait for tomorrow and the chance to talk to Milo."

As they left the hospital Collie was already making plans for an afternoon meeting with Denton Eldring.

THE SHOOT-OUT
AND AFTER EFFECTS

A letter arrived for Ryan from the office of Private Investigator, Hudson Pavel. It was short and to the point.

October 30, 1956
Mr. Ryan Baker
177 North Development Drive
Sheila's Tree, Wyoming
RE: Location, address and phone number of Subject, Iris Patton

Dear Mr. Baker;

Per your instruction in the instant case please find the following information:

Iris Patton
46 Whittlesea Street
Midlothian, Georgia
Phone: DAV-3748

Thank you for your remittance in the amount of $300. It was a pleasure to serve you.

Your Humble Servant,
Hudson K. Pavel, PI

Ryan read the letter in his office and laughed at the formal tone of the missive. This letter was obviously an impersonal form document sent out by one of Pavel's office girls. Ryan decided to drive out to the D-Z to tell Milo in person the news of Iris' whereabouts. It had been a day or two since Ryan had been free to check on his friend though he was confident that the cook, Heidi, and house-keeper, Bessie Taylor, were taking excellent care of the convalescent since his discharge from the hospital two weeks earlier. Milo's wounds had very nearly killed him, however, following a difficult recovery from the concussion and internal organ damage, his good health and vitality encouraged rapid soft tissue healing. The broken bones and damaged tendons required more time to mend and kept Milo inactive and restricted to his quarters.

Besides the letter from Pavel, another large check from the United States Government also arrived in the morning mail. Ryan stopped off at the Wyoming Agricultural Bank to make a deposit in the Wyo Nucleonics Corporation account. After completing the transaction Ryan turned to leave the bank and continue his trip to the D-Z ranch. He waved genially in passing the middle-aged security guard standing at his usual post near the bank entrance and emerged into the autumn sunlight. As the heavy glass door swung shut behind him Ryan heard a series of loud pops and the whine of bullets ricocheting off the concrete step and smacking noisily against the bank doorway. Ryan reacted automatically though not very effectively. He crouched down and made a panicked survey of the scene in an attempt to locate the source of the firing or find some way of escape to safety. He saw a figure standing no more than twenty-five feet away in the middle of Second street with a gun held in both hands at arms length pointed directly at Ryan. After the first barrage of five shots the man stopped firing but held his menacing pose. He seemed to be wavering slightly on somewhat unsteady legs however his finger remained on the trigger. Ryan recognized Delvane Winston from his distinctive riding habit and tweed jacket but the man seemed gaunt and sickly. His hair was long and uncombed and dark eyes were deeply sunken in his haggard face. There seemed to be a frozen moment as Delvane held the smoking gun and Ryan was crouched immobile upon the concrete step of the bank entrance. The bank guard flung open the star-fractured glass doors behind Ryan and charged out of the bank. He was in the act of drawing his pistol from its leather holster on his belt when the firearm discharged in his excited grasp and sent a lead pellet smashing into the shin bone of his own right leg. The guard went down with a scream of pain and rolled past Ryan down the single step and onto the sidewalk.

"I'm hit, I'm hit! Oh God it hurts. I'm hit." The guard was rolling on the concrete and clutching his lower leg in both hands. The pistol lay where he dropped it within a few feet of Ryan's still frozen position.

Ryan stared in dreamlike paralysis at the grotesque figure of Delvane as he slowly turned the gun in his hands and placed the barrel in his own mouth. Ryan and other spectators watched in horror as Delvane pulled the trigger again one last time. The report was a muffled squelch as if someone had dropped a water filled toy balloon on the street.

Ryan immediately turned back into the bank where several tellers and loan officers were gaping in shocked silence in the aftermath of the sudden action.

"You," Ryan pointed at a young lady teller, "call an ambulance, the County Sheriff and the City police. Right now!" he shouted. She looked startled but ran back around the cages and picked up a telephone.

Ryan returned to the now silent, white-faced security guard still lying on the sidewalk clutching at his injured leg. Ryan quickly folded his jacket into a pillow and got the man to lay his head down while he elevated the legs by placing them carefully on the concrete step entrance to the bank.

"I know it hurts but the ambulance will be here in short order," Ryan told the man soothingly. "Just lie still and take it easy. You aren't hurt too badly and everything is all over now. Hell, you're going to be the hero of this shoot-out, the way you came charging out to save me."

After asking one of the bank officers to sit with the wounded guard and take care of him until the ambulance arrived, Ryan ventured out to the middle of the street where Delvane's body lay contorted in death. It was clear that the head injury was fatal. As he gazed at the thin and obviously neglected body, Ryan wondered if he, himself, were actually the target of the attack, as it seemed, or only an innocent bystander caught up in the moment of a man's madness. Since Delvane had never spoken to anyone of his intentions nor revealed his purpose, it was a question that would never find a definitive answer. Not being sure what to do, Ryan simply stood guard over the body without touching anything until three police cars arrived in a dust-up of howling sirens and flashing lights.

Once the long interviews were over and the witnesses released, Ryan's thoughts turned urgently to Collie. He felt he had to be the one to tell her the terrible news and try to offer explanations and comfort. He went straight to the new city hall building and hurried up to the Mayor's office.

Collie's office was spacious and tastefully furnished and decorated. Her walnut desk had plenty of working space and a small, but impressive, Remington bronze. A built-in book shelf along one wall contained a complete set of leather bound City Council minutes covering meetings since the city was incorporated in 1912 and a number of consultants reports and studies commissioned over the years. Original oil paintings of Native American tribal leaders, painted by a well-known local artist, were hung on the wood paneled walls, including one of Usho, the ringleader in the Sheila Fuller story. A familiar carry-over from the old cramped quarters in the Galena County Courthouse was the now healthy and grown large dieffenbachia plant. Ryan was admitted by Collie's secretary, Helen Johnson, and seated in a comfortable padded leather chair.

"Ryan, you hardly ever come up here," Collie smiled in welcome, "how nice of you to come by. Helen said it was important."

"I am so sorry. I have to tell you bad news." Ryan stood and braced his hands on Collie's desk as he bent towards her.

Collie was warned by Ryan's grim expression that the message was ominous and she prepared for some kind of uncomfortable revelation.

"Delvane is dead."

Ryan could see that Collie was deeply effected but stoic and prepared to hear the facts. He explained the strange attack as best he could and answered all of Collie's anxious, troubled questions except those concerning poor Delvane's motive. There were no answers in that area.

"I can't believe Delvane would do these things. You know he had started drinking more and more heavily ever since the divorce? I knew before I finally left him that he was a very weak man. Oh, Ryan, what could I have done?" She began to sob quietly and he came around the desk, placing his hands on her shoulders with gentle sympathetic strokes.

"It's not your fault, Collie. You can't take personal responsibility for the fallibility of others in this world. We're lucky to be able to control our own destiny part of the time without assuming we can always rescue anyone else. You have done what you could to help Del in his troubles and I doubt that anyone could have done more. He was bent on his own destruction one way or another."

"I suppose so. It's just that so many disturbing things are going on. Ever since Louise's attack there has been one disaster after another to the people and ideas that my compass used to turn upon and I can't seem to set things right."

Ryan returned to his chair as Collie composed herself. He was prepared to listen in sympathy and offer any advice or assistance at his command because he could not bear to see her in such confusion. She sensed this and continued to express her feelings and fears so long held within. Collie was at ease with Ryan, feeling his emotional support and interest. She already knew from their conversation in the hospital waiting room that she would never suffer betrayal from this man.

"I haven't really been able to talk things out with anyone." She looked imploringly at Ryan and saw compassion and complete assent in his expression.

"It seems like it started with troubles at the ranch which were the result of my inability to work smoothly with Delvane. Right from the beginning of our marriage he seemed—how should I phrase it?—rather fragile. He was a war hero, he had been a student leader for the months that I knew him in college and yet, despite outward appearances, he lacked confidence. I was used to men who showed determination and strength in their convictions without being aggressive about it but just as a way of life. It never occurred to me until after several upsetting disagreements that he must have seen me as a threat to his control of things. Anyway, I finally had to back off and leave total control of the ranch to Del and he didn't do a very good job of it. Just before the divorce he finally managed to pull us out of debt by selling off most all the livestock but I have almost no resources to continue to run the cattle business. That was such a worry. But, of course, the real reason I finally left him was because of unfaithfulness. You probably guessed that at the country club dedication three years ago when I acted so foolishly."

"In the midst of my own difficulties that horrible attack on Louise and then her suicide just left me devastated." Collie's thoughts turned to that fateful night when she had finally confronted Delvane at the most primitive level. She was not entirely comfortable even yet in discussing her fears and feelings with Ryan. She still felt that she should have been able to find a way to bolster Delvane and, through her strength and understanding, make him the man that she had supposed him to be.

Ryan hoped that he was being a therapeutic listener. He was no psychologist but it was clear that Collie needed to unburden herself of the depressing events that threatened to take command of her normally cheerful and outgoing personality. He constantly perceived her as the powerful and beautiful Helen of Troy who had saved him from drowning, though her present vulnerability, exposing the depth of her human feelings, was also appealing in its own way.

Helen Johnson, Collie's new secretary, knocked and put her head in the door. "I'm going on home if you don't need anything more?" she questioned. "I heard about that awful shooting over at the bank. Is there anything I can take care of for you?"

"For goodness sake, it's after five o'clock," Collie glanced at her watch. "No, no, go on home. I'll see you tomorrow. Thank you, Helen. I'm feeling sad but OK."

"Thanks for coming over, Ryan," she continued after Helen withdrew. "I think you have probably heard all the weeping and wailing you need to from me."

"Not a chance," he replied honestly. "Let me take you someplace to dinner where we can both wind down and talk things out. We always seem to see each other under the most stressful circumstances," he paused and then continued with obvious emotion, "I love you"—He looked at her so straightforwardly and openly that her heart almost turned over—"and that fact has not been getting enough consideration from either one of us over the last few months. When the bullets were flying today I could think of just one thing—the possibility that I might die without having told you clearly and completely how much I love you and need you in my life."

Collie understood and fully appreciated the tension and drive that brought Ryan to her. She felt the power of his passion flowing towards her; enveloping her life and ambitions and pushing them both towards a so-far unvoiced commitment. Collie, sensing the strength of emotional current surging beneath her own conventional reticence and trusting her feelings towards Ryan, welcomed the opportunity to explore this perilous new abyss of vulnerability and exposure. She invited him to her townhouse residence on the bluff.

They enjoyed a relaxing drink on the wooden deck overlooking the back yard while watching an ever-darkening fiery orange sunset paint brilliant gold linings on lenticular clouds arrayed across Chopstick reservoir; the not too distant Big Horn peaks forming a spectacular backdrop. They spoke little at first, simply enjoying quiet companionship and an occasional gentle touch of hands or intimate eye contact. Ryan opened the sliding patio door into the modern kitchen so that cooling evening air could circulate in the house. Collie quickly heated leftover homemade lasagna, whipped up and baked some premixed dinner biscuits, quartered a head of iceberg lettuce with green onions and carrot sticks and uncorked a bottle of Chianti from the wine cupboard. Dinner was ready in a few minutes and they sat down with good appetite despite the trying experiences of the day. Following dinner and disregarding earlier self-admonitions to let go of current emotional troubles, Collie continued to be preoccupied by more practical worries. She could not prevent herself from expressing this discomfort to Ryan's sympathetic ear.

"I'm sick at heart over what is happening to Framboise creek and all the upper rangeland because of the mining. I am really wary of discussing this with you because I know how involved you are in the uranium business, of course." She regarded Ryan frankly.

"No. I'll be honest with you—I'm as critical as you are of the damage I see every day," Ryan returned, "and it is getting worse all the time. Mochery assured me that the mill would be safe and clean and offer no inconvenience, let alone danger, to the community. I know he didn't intentionally mislead but anyone can see the buildup of yellow uranium oxides on the millponds. It looks like a lake of sulfur. Last week somebody put up a big sign in front of the mill that lampooned the radio toothpaste ad: *'You'll wonder where the yellow went when you brush your teeth with yellow cake'*. My crew all got a laugh out of it but I didn't think it was funny. I don't know whether or not there is enough radioactivity there to do any damage over the long run. So far, we are well within all the legal and administrative guidelines."

"Then you see it, too," Collie was relieved. "They are ruining my ranch, Ryan. The Mining Company has killed every fish in Framboise creek and a lot of the vegetation and wildlife in the canyon as well. The whole area is ravaged from all the earthmoving, chemicals, dust, hard traffic and garbage dumping. The high country is too fragile to take this kind of usage. Isn't there any way to get the uranium out without destroying the land in the process?"

Ryan was unable to find a positive response. "We do need the uranium," he shrugged, much in the fashion of Pontius Pilate discussing the trial.

Collie could see his discomfort but, far from wishing to put him at ease, she pressed on with her passionate criticism of the industry.

"I've been both an observer and victim of this abuse of our whole region and I've come to some fairly obvious conclusions," she stated with determination. "No responsible group of investors or Board of Directors or whatever are going to vote against the financial benefit of their own business or stockholders. You simply couldn't expect businessmen to do that. And since that is true, there has to be some outside source of control or regulation to prevent the kind of thing we are seeing here in Wyoming. Like the governor on a steam engine that prevents destructive over-acceleration, so the Federal government has to be responsible to control unabated acceleration of these big industries that cause environmental damage and loss of resources for ourselves and future generations. We are not a pioneer society any longer. Sustained use is the only logical behavior that will work in this overcrowded world from now on. I have been a Republican for my whole life and worked hard for the party because it stands for freedom of business choice and support of the basic conservative strengths of this country, but now I feel the need for new principles and ideas to maintain our national health. This is a huge decision for me, Ryan. I'm seriously considering jumping over to the Democrats and running for a Senate seat against Wyatt in 1958."

Ryan was surprised by this revelation. "You would—will—make one hell of a Senator and I certainly agree with your sentiments. There has to be some middle ground that will demand corporate responsibility but still get the job done by good old American capitalism. I have to tell you something quite personal, Collie, about my own situation," Ryan was almost comically apologetic for his financial success. "You may not be aware that I am making a fortune from the mill contract. In less than two years of operation I'm already at seven figures in the bank. It's almost obscene the way the money rolls in," he said guiltily. "I never had any idea how lucrative it would be when I started out."

"That is wonderful," she reach out and grasped his hand impetuously. "I know how hard you worked to get that contract. Risk deserves to be rewarded and you certainly risked everything you had to build the mill. My goodness, you surely don't look or act like a rich man," she laughed good-naturedly.

"Well, I guess I haven't got the hang of it just yet," he smiled self-consciously, glancing at his wrinkled canvas pants and scuffed cowboy boots.

For only the second time, Ryan and Collie spent hours in intimate conversation, sharing hopes, dreams and fears as never before. Ryan became aware of the complexities of Collie's life and some of the burdens she carried as a result of her strong feelings of responsibility for others. Collie once again renewed her respect for Ryan's unsophisticated candor and honesty as well as his strength of will and purpose. He was the sort of man she had fantasized about as a schoolgirl based on the model of her father, her grandfather and other Western men of her acquaintance like Ballard Crown. They had long abandoned the dinner table and moved to a comfortable sofa in the living room before a small aromatic juniper wood fire. Ryan held Collie's hand gently as their talk became more intimate.

"It is one o'clock in the morning already," Ryan exclaimed. "I feel so close to you." The fire had gently reduced itself to glowing embers that cast a shadowy light on his earnest features. "Somehow, despite today's troubles, we seem to have stepped up to a new level between us. I love you, Collie, and nothing is going to change that or make it go away. We can have a wonderful life together." He held her hands and looked into her face with hope and determination. "Please say you will marry me."

She returned his gaze openly and searched his eyes as if looking for some undefined affirmation that she still needed.

"Oh Ryan, you are the man I should have found the first time. I do love you—but life can be so complicated. Could we just agree to be seriously committed and in love with each other for a time and see what the future holds? I keep having this odd feeling of unfinished business or impending troubles of some mysterious kind. I really can't explain why I'm not making more sense."

Ryan paused in his disappointment, then took her in a warm embrace of trust and deference. This time the kiss was different. They had passed a milestone of some kind and their emotions and feelings were more honest and open than the other occasion atop Horsecollar Butte. Ryan was not an experienced lover but he approached lovemaking with the same curiosity, tenderness and generosity that was always his way. Collie did not think of her fears or mental reservations but responded frankly, without restraint as he began to explore a new physical relationship between them. After moments of mutual stroking, kissing and fumbling with garments Ryan stopped.

"There's only one first time, Collie. We have both been through a lot today but I want things to be as close to perfect for us as we can make it. Lets get in the shower and pretend we're young, impetuous and mad about each other. Hell, that's exactly how I really feel. I want to explore every square inch of you and memorize every last curve and shadow. Besides I've always wanted a wench to soap me up and perform the ritual ablutions."

"Ritual ablutions!," Collie laughed, "what kind of medieval quackery are you planning, anyway."

She soon found out. After the exciting intimacies of a shared bath, their warm flushed bodies inflamed with gentle exploratory caresses, Collie's quite limited experience was surpassed in ways that she had never dreamed of. Ryan was inventive, funny, serious, and deeply concerned for Collie's responses. His lovemaking was tender and careful when needful and energetic and venturesome at other times. Collie's true natural responses were unimpeded. Surprised, at first, by some of the creative things that Ryan did, she soon perceived that he was experimenting and learning as he went along. She joined in the exciting spirit of loving adventure and exercised some erotic imagination of her own. They spent passionate hours that night, the memory of which both were to cherish and treasure forever. Any fear Collie had that there might be some aspect of their relationship that would not fit in the melding of their two formidable personalities was buried in the lush give and take of their physical union. Ryan did not bring up the subject of marriage again but both knew and understood that they would never willingly be parted in the future.

RECOVERY AND
HOPE

A few days following the bank shooting Ryan found himself free to drive out to the D-Z ranch. Milo was sitting up in an old kitchen chair which had been placed near a wood rail fence about one hundred yards from his cabin domicile. He had a Remington .22 rifle resting across the fence and was shooting ground squirrels in the empty horse pasture. The pesky little creatures multiplied at times in great numbers so that they consumed appreciable quantities of grass forage and their holes sometimes became hazardous leg breaking traps for running horses. Usually hawks, ferrets and coyotes kept the squirrel population in check but they survived in adequate numbers to offer an unlimited opportunity for recreational target practice. Ryan parked his car and walked over to the shooter. A pair of crutches leaned against the fence.

"You starting to get around already or did you have Heidi haul you down here piggyback?"

"Howdy, Ry." Milo lined up the iron sights on another little furry target without looking up. The rifle cracked and the distant squirrel flopped over. "See that? I'm gettin' so I can knock 'em over at a hundred and fifty yards."

"I brought you some of those skinny little black cigars you favor. I was going to bring out some doughnuts and stuff but Heidi says you're getting fat sitting on your butt all day."

"Yeah, well she got nobody to blame but herself," Milo grinned. "She feeds me pretty good."

Milo reached for his crutches and gingerly stood up. "Bring that gun along if you would, and we'll go on up to the cabin to talk."

Milo's injured knee was no longer in a cast but a stiff hinged support was belted to the leg and he hobbled slowly and carefully over the uneven terrain. Sweat popped out on his forehead as he lurched unsteadily over a low obstacle at one point. Seeing Ryan's grimace of sympathy, Milo shook his head and grinned, "She only hurts when I'm asleep or awake. Otherwise it don't bother me at all."

They finally reached the cabin and Milo dropped thankfully into his battered pseudo-leather recliner; raising his feet on the extended shelf; the hurt knee supported by a large pillow. Ryan went to the small avocado colored refrigerator and withdrew a couple of beers.

"You are looking better but I guess there's still a ways to go."

"Oh, there's no comparison to how I was just last week. I'm healing up real fast now—no dizziness or anything. Doc says this leg will be almost good as new if I just keep going on it and don't get lazy."

"Milo, I got to tell you something," Ryan looked serious as he pulled Pavel's letter from his pocket and handed it over. "Read this." Ryan was not sure what Milo's reaction would be.

"Midlothian, Georgia. Damn if she didn't get about as far away as she could. How come you to do this, man?" Milo lay the letter carefully on a small lamp table by his chair rather than handing it back to Ryan.

"Well, when you were hurt so bad I figured she would want to know. This only came a few days ago. I haven't tried to call her or anything."

Milo was painfully silent for several moments. "I don't guess things have changed much since she left. I'm still black and she's still white so I don't reckon Iris would see it much different."

"She was too shook up to even tell you goodbye when she pulled out. Maybe if you called her up and had a talk she might reconsider her feelings. You told me she loved you. Maybe she's just waiting for you to go after her."

"I'll give it some thought," Milo frowned pensively. "I'm not a man who gives up easy but she kind of took things into her own hands. Do you see anything wrong with me and her getting together?"

"Milo, I swear to you, you're the only black guy I ever had much to do with because I never was around Negro people. But since I got to know you I can't see that you're different from me in any meaningful way. If Iris really felt deeply about you and was ready to make love with you and all," he hesitated awkwardly, "then, anyhow, I just can't see how she could still see your relationship as something to fear or avoid. She must have had it trained into her so deeply that it isn't even a rationally thought out position. I'll bet her mind is so divided at this point that she's about to go crazy. To give you a direct answer to your question—no, I don't think there's anything at all wrong with interracial marriage. In fact, it may be the last hope for justice and humanity in this world. As long as people look, or act, or talk different there will be an excuse for bigotry and hatred, I guess."

"Thank you for that, Ryan," Milo spoke with gratitude. "If Iris feels half as bad about splitting up as I do then I pity the girl. She is so honest and kind of pure hearted and fun loving, I can't believe she could be so racist and prejudiced against me," Milo commented sadly.

"Soon as you get so you can run down to that rail fence and back without those crutches we could take a little trip to Georgia. How about it?"

Milo smiled, "It'll give me something to shoot for, anyhow. You might as well start booking tickets. Now I got to figure out whether to call her long distance first and let her know I'm coming."

They finished their beers and the talk went on to other less emotional but no less interesting developments in their lives.

"Can you believe how close I came to throwing Regelstorp and his mining claims out of the Bull Run that night? I'm telling you, Ry, I can't believe how much money they are putting in my account down at that bank."

"I can empathize better than you might think," Ryan laughed. "It takes awhile to get used to and then you still don't feel like it's real for a long time. You know that Sean Mochery and I are planning a safari trip to South Africa? He claims he can show me stuff no tourists ever get to see. We are even going down in a diamond mine."

"There's no way I want to go to South Africa. The first thing I did was send my Mama a big certified check so she can go out and buy herself a nice house if she wants to. By the way, I sure thank you and Ballard for letting her know when I was in the hospital. Doctor Hysett talked to her on the phone and made her feel real good about it 'til I got so I could talk to her myself."

They both mused silently for some moments on their improbable good fortune. Great wealth had not been a major goal for either one of these men as they pursued their way in life but the sudden attainment of abundant financial resources was opening doors and providing opportunities that they had never expected or planned for. The possibilities were just beginning to emerge from fantasy and dreams into reality.

"Say Milo," Ryan opened a new topic, "do you think that Melindez character could be the one who raped the Greene girl?"

"I'd say it's a good possibility. He was a mean little punk. Iris told me he made a pass at her that night at the Bull Run, too. I should have figured it out myself a long time ago."

"Collie Palmer sure thinks he's the one since you remembered the telephone call they made that evening. She has already contacted the Sheriff's office and has Eldring looking for some connection between George Frailey and those two men."

"What happened up there on the Bench, Milo?" Ryan changed the subject again. "You feel like telling me the whole story?"

"You can guess it wasn't so pretty," Milo stated glumly. He went ahead and described the whole episode from start to finish as well as he could remember the details. Of course, he had no recall of being dumped into the pickup and driven to the spot where Ryan had fortuitously found him. "I never told it like that to those Deputies, though," he said. "I licked Bruchek fair and square and he never had nothing to do with me getting beat up later. I told the police I couldn't remember nothing. I'm not like Don Quixote in that book Ballard gave me to read last year. My wars are going to be chosen carefully from now on and, to tell you the truth, I think my fist fighting days are over. I won't identify any of those men who attacked me, though I know most of 'em are working for Bruchek, and as far as I'm concerned this fight is over. Whatever happens between me and Iris from now on—well, we'll just have to work it out as it goes. It wasn't the damn gossip that made the mischief, it was her and me going against what some folks believe in that put Iris on the spot. I feel like I can handle that now. I just don't give a damn anymore about what some people think or say."

PANIC AND POOR JUDGMENT

Marion Reinhardt was desperately afraid that Denton Eldring had somehow become suspicious of the Cielo Grande right-of-way document and he could think of only one possible source for that knowledge. Eldring's attitude in pretrial hearings, motions, depositions and discovery meetings had always projected a feeling of confidence and near arrogance that both confused and alarmed Attorney Perlmutter. The corporate journeyman was used to a more staid and predictable legal process where judicial rulings, Attorney behavior and court procedures were factors of law and precedent rather than the poker face psychological ploys of Eldring. Perlmutter had no knowledge of the document tampering carried out by his client but he definitely sensed some confusing counter-currents in the tide of issues cresting about Pass Road. The flurry of subpoenas for mine business documents including payroll records, ore reserve figures, ore production and shipping records and, in particular, any documents or correspondence with John Does one and two, also known as Brown and Melindez, were served on the mining company. The demands seemed excessive and over-zealous to Perlmutter. He questioned Reinhardt about the opposition requests and succeeded in passing along his anxiety to the mine manager who, as usual, took a more proactive course than most other responsible persons would do.

"The Goddamn Palmer outfit is being too stubborn and they know too much," Marion shouted at his brother-in-law. "How could they know anything about Shug and Pronto? That woman must have a copy of the damn contract around somewhere. Old man Palmer probably wouldn't have cut a deal with Cielo Grande without filing a copy of it in his stuff, would he? But why would anyone else even think about that paper since the silver mine shut down years ago? They would surely have tipped their hand by now if they knew we messed around with that right-of-way agreement."

"Winston never said a word about another copy of the right of way," Frailey remembered. "He told me he just went and looked at it over at the courthouse same as I did when the topic first come up".

"We better be pretty goddamn sure before we get in that courthouse in front of a Judge. There's only one chance in hell for them to keep us off that road. If Denton Eldring has a copy of the original easement in his files or if there's a file cabinet or strongbox in that townhouse of the Mayor's or, more likely, still out at the old ranch house in the canyon, we would be in deep shit. I wouldn't be surprised if a copy of the Cielo Grande right-of-way is lying someplace just where old E. L. Palmer stashed it sixty years ago. If it comes out that we doctored up the courthouse file then we can figure on doing about ten years in the state pen."

"You son-of-a-bitch," yelled Frailey, "don't try to suck me in on this deal. You were the one figured out this whole flimflam."

"Who drew up the diagram so the boys could find that piece of paper? Who put it back in the records volume after we got it fixed up? Christ, George, you're in this up to your fat neck."

George Frailey stopped cold and felt a shiver of apprehension down his well-padded spine. He had always felt protected by his brother-in-law's bluster and apparent self-confidence as well as Marion's position of importance in the powerful mining company. Now he was starting to realize that they had gone quite far down the unmaintained byway towards crime and possible punishment as they worked their scheme to obtain a free haul road. Whether or not the Palmer ranch people currently suspected that something was wrong with the Cielo Grande right-of-way document, the very possibility that an untampered copy might surface at some time in the future was now perceived by both Marion and George as a terrible risk. The passage of time since the old Pass Road contract was originated had seemed to guarantee its obscurity and insure that the forgery would go undetected. Suddenly faced with the pressure of confident resistance by the opposing attorney and an imminent court date, both men were coming to believe that their illegal manipulation might have been a fatal mistake.

"Wha—what are you gonna do, Marion?" Frailey stammered, "We can't let nobody catch us out on this thing. I can't get tangled up with the law on this."

The two men eyed each other in silence for several seconds, then began an earnest discussion of whatever options might lessen the probability of their exposure and promote their own interests. Each consideration seemed to flow from previous actions and neither man was capable of, or even cared to think of less dangerous or risky methods to accomplish their goals. Ideas of fairness or legality played no part in their thoughts or plans. Their only preoccupation was the required result of obtaining free passage for NMMC ore trucks through Palmer canyon without revealing their criminal actions.

"Well," Marion eyed his brother-in-law, "in for a dime, in for a dollar. We got no choice at this point but to make sure there's no evidence of that forgery."

"You don't even know if there is a copy of that easement, let alone where it might be. How the devil are you going to take care of it?"

"There's only three places where it could possibly be. At the ranch house out in the canyon, at the town house where the Mayor lives or at Eldring's office. Shug and Pronto are going to take 'em one at a time until they find it or else we're sure there isn't a copy. I don't give a shit if we have to burn down all three places, those boys are going to go through 'em 'til I'm satisfied. And for God's sake keep those two bastards out of sight and under cover while they are up here. We can't afford any connection with them and their damn criminal records from down south. I don't see how they could be tied to us at this point and we need them for this job. Take care of business for a change, George."

COLLIE'S REVOLT

Collie made overtures to certain people in Cheyenne for the purpose of setting up a strategy meeting with a group of political activists who had always been stern foes in the past. It was a precarious and risky business. Her first meeting was with an old friend, Patrick McCall, currently employed as a lobbyist representing the Association of Wyoming Municipalities at the state capitol. He was an energetic, dark haired, well-tanned man in his mid-forties, fashionably dressed in a midnight pinstripe, highly polished shoes and quiet narrow necktie. They were talking in his plainly furnished inexpensive office located close to the State capital building.

"Right now it's important to try and reduce the harmful results of this mining activity. The erosion of Framboise creek, water quality degradation in the creek and the Powder river, killing off of the fish, the prairie chickens, antelope and other game must be stopped and then we can try to put the region back the way it was in so far as possible," Collie stated.

"It isn't a lost cause," Patrick observed. "There is plenty of precedent around the country for laws and regulations to protect public and private lands from exploitation. Many universities are starting to offer courses and even degrees in environmental studies of all kinds. I kind of like your pragmatic approach to the issues."

"I don't intend to become some sort of radical gadfly without credibility," Collie remarked thoughtfully. "I really want to bring a new awareness and political clout to the preservation of nature and the uncontaminated free sort of life that we have traditionally enjoyed here and all around the U.S. for that matter.

No one wants to see all the trees cut down or all the wild game sacrificed or all the rivers and streams polluted but the public simply isn't aware of these things going on at such a rapid rate. The biggest step is educating people and building a consensus for change. We need new laws. That is why you have to help me, Pat. I won't find much tolerance for these views in the Republican Party so I am thinking seriously of jumping party affiliation and running for the United States Senate as a Democrat. Do you think such a move is possible in this state?

McCall was stunned. "Colorado, you have been a Republican all your life. Can't you support these views within your own party? You used to work for Wyatt on his staff didn't you?"

Collie simply nodded patiently and waited for the idea to sink in and take hold. She was not too surprised at Patrick's reaction. He stammered a few more incredulous phrases then paused and studied Collie quietly for several moments. At last he smiled.

"How the hell did you know I am a Democrat? My party affiliation has never been made public with the kind of work I do."

"We have been friends for a long time. You aren't as deep and opaque as you would like to think. I've always known you were a bleeding heart liberal at bottom but I forgave you because I could see you were intelligent enough to do it right. Now, events have led me down the same path and I need a campaign manager and Chief of Staff if I win. How much am I going to have to pay to get you away from the cities?"

"I'm just a poor ol' backwoods boy from over at Wheatland but I may have some dreams of my own. They happen to involve the Wyoming state house, however, not Washington DC. I'll admit you sure have got my attention, though." He drummed his fingers on the desk and stared at a picture of Thomas Jefferson in place on his office wall.

"Colorado, you are the brightest star this state has seen since Wyatt himself came along over twenty years ago. I can't wait to help you with this campaign and there is no reason you can't win it all. Your name comes up at political meetings all over the state and I'll bet your speaking engagement calendar shows it. I happen to know the Democrats are scared to death of you. Colin Gervais, the Democratic Party chairman, will break into tears of joy when he hears you may jump the fence. I wouldn't miss the chance to work for you even if it didn't mean taking a shot at that pompous hot air balloon who currently represents this state. I would rather have a part in beating Wyatt Paige than make love to Brigitte Bardot—and believe me it doesn't get any better than that in my book."

Collie laughed with relief at his comments. "I probably have about the same chance to beat Wyatt as you have to meet B.B."

The two sketched the future and made plans through the afternoon. When Collie finally left there were definite commitments made and responsibilities assigned. A new door was opening and a long uncertain adventure stretched ahead.

BREAK-IN

Neil Silverstein continued to maintain the flowerbeds and expanse of lawn surrounding the now seldom used Palmer ranch house in the same manicured condition that Delvane had favored. He also required the cowhands to tend the business of an active ranching venture more thoroughly and efficiently than had his predecessor. During the nearly three years since Collie had appointed him Foreman, Silverstein brought the ranch back to a condition approaching its peak productive ability. The herd of purebred short horned Herefords was flourishing at last despite the environmental damage to some of the canyon pastureland and high range summer forage. Neil and Collie worked closely and comfortably together in planning and carrying out the various tasks and decisions that moved the ranch slowly back towards profitability. Collie had eventually been forced to place a small first mortgage on the property in order to acquire operating capital for the year following the divorce. Neil was made aware of every aspect of the operation, including financing, and his optimistic assurances to Collie that the mortgage would be paid off comfortably within five years if average beef prices held up, seemed destined to come true. The environmental damage wrought by the increased sediment loading and higher spring and summer water levels in Framboise creek was held in check as much as possible. Little could be done about the dust and noise in the canyon due to road traffic or the loss of livestock due to accidents and poaching.

One cold Tuesday morning in mid-October Neil noticed the patio door into the master bedroom at the back of the ranch house was partly open. He knew that Collie had not visited the ranch for several days and, in fact, he had already instructed a man to prepare the building for winter conditions by turning off water and electricity, mulching flower beds around the foundation and sealing up all the windows and doors against the freezing temperatures and blizzards of winter. He got a flashlight and entered the back bedroom to find a complete disaster of ripped, scattered, broken furniture and fixtures throughout the house. Someone had gone from room to room systematically vandalizing every article of decoration or furnishing. Every desk, file cabinet, cupboard and drawer in the house was turned inside out with contents smashed or scattered on the floor. The marauders were unbelievably thorough.

"Miz Wins—uh—Palmer, I done reported to the County Sheriff already but I reckon you better come on out and have a look-see for yourself," Neil spoke on the telephone. "You aint goin' to believe what they done to the place. I sure hope you got insurance paid up. The whole inside is just wrecked."

By the time Collie arrived from town there were two County Sheriff black and white sedans parked in the driveway. Neil Silverstein and the lean-faced Wilbur Shliefsanger were standing on the lawn in conversation as two other Deputies looked on.

"So you never saw nothin', never heard nothin' an' you aint touched nothin'? Damn if you aint a big help," Shliefsanger stated indignantly. "At least get some dang lights turned on in there so's we can see somethin'.'"

Neil turned with a mildly intolerant look and engaged the circuit breakers in the domestic fuse box near at hand. He saw Collie drive up and hurried over to meet her.

"It sure is a mess in there, Ma'am. I can't figure out why anybody would tear a place up like that."

"Hello, Neil. Thank you for calling." Collie watched as two of the Deputies entered the house while the third stood post at the bedroom patio door. After several minutes the two emerged and Wilbur Shliefsanger approached Collie.

"Mornin', Mayor," Shliefsanger tipped his hat, "would you mind goin' through the place and tell me what's missin'? Last time I saw a mess like this was over at the County Courthouse over two years ago. Fact is, now that I think about it, looks like a very similar operation here. Wreckin' stuff just for the hell of it, apparently."

Collie was aghast at the damage to her home. Beautiful statuary, pottery, furniture and wall hangings were shattered and ripped. Things that her mother had collected or brought from her maternal grandparents' home in Denver and which could never be replaced were casualties of the senseless destruction. Family photographs and recorded music that Collie had collected during her highschool years were torn, broken and thrown on the floor. Tears of sorrow and anger brimmed in her eyes as she gingerly made her way through the house. Every room was the same and yet she could spot nothing missing. Even the collection of guns which had been displayed in cabinets and mounted on the walls of the living room were not stolen, only smashed and thrown about.

"I can't imagine what motivated this," Collie stated as the Deputy Sheriff took notes. "I can't see that anything is missing. Why would anyone come all the way out here and attack me like this?"

"Looks to me like they must of snuck in here in the middle of the night last night. We got no prints or clues that I can see, Ma'am."

A more thorough and careful inspection of the crime scene uncovered nothing. The incident was recorded and kept open for investigation but there seemed to be no leads in establishing a motive or discovering who did it. Collie was finally allowed to clean up the place and even recovered and restored some of her treasured possessions. An insurance claim was filed and eventually paid but the impotent anger and hurt of the home invasion was slow to heal.

SEARCH AND RESCUE

Iris Patton never felt at home in the deep South. The folks were sweetly friendly and polite but, somehow, after weeks had passed in the rural fruit and vegetable growing town of Midlothian she still had not gotten further than the "Good mawnin' Shugah, nice day aint it?" stage. Midlothian was a rustic little village just a couple of miles off state highway 23 on the Big Satilla river in Jeff Davis county not far from Denton and Hazelhurst. After flying into Atlanta, Iris purchased a low mileage 1950 Dodge sedan for the one hundred and eighty-mile drive down to Midlothian. Her old maid Aunt, Willa Grollier Patton, had made her welcome in a tiny eight foot by eighteen-foot mobile home but, for obvious reasons of comfort and utility, the cramped quarters were only offered on a very temporary time frame. Within a few days Iris had found a weather-beaten but fairly clean two bedroom furnished rental house on the outskirts of town satisfactory for her needs. Iris was depressed and lonely following the abrupt departure from Sheila's Tree where she had lived from the age of six. She felt that every friend and acquaintance was lost to her and because of the cruel gossip there could be no going back. She found very little in Midlothian to divert her. Miss Grollier Patton taught twelve grade school children in a one room Quonset hut every weekday and so was usually unavailable to Iris. People had their own lives to lead and, while not unfriendly, found it hard to work a new and rather alien figure into their social routine. Iris drove around the county and observed the farms, orchards and hamlets as they had existed nearly unchanged in the ninety years following the end of the civil war. Or War of Secession as it was commonly called in Jeff Davis County. There had been a slow recovery of economics and political identity over the years with rural electrification, postal service and telephone service becoming common as in most areas of the United States. She visited courthouses, schools, film theaters, public parks and libraries to get a feel for and empathy towards the community and surrounding area. Iris never got a job or made a close friend during the five months that she lived in Georgia. She learned a lot.

Ryan and Milo parked a long silver motorhome that they had rented in Atlanta on the unpaved though pretentiously named Whittlesea Street in front of Iris' house. After only a short stroll through the Atlanta airport they had quickly realized the difficulty of traveling together. In most cases they could not stay in the same hotel or eat in the same restaurant or even use the same sanitary facilities. The motorhome was the best compromise they could think of to accommodate the road trip down state to Midlothian. When they rang her doorbell on a warm, humid September afternoon, Iris was nearly overcome.

"Oh Milo, Milo, you came all this way." Tears flowed without restraint down her freckled cheeks as she flung herself into his arms. "My God, I've missed you so much. I thought I'd never see you again. Oh, I love you, I love you."

Ryan quickly pushed the distraught couple into the house and firmly closed the door behind them.

"Take it easy Iris," Ryan cautioned, "that big ol' motorhome attracted quite a bit of attention down at the service station. Folks will be watching to see what we're doing in town."

"Iris you shook the stuffing out of me," Milo finally caught his breath. "I pictured about ever kind of action in the book for when I finally walked in on you but none of 'em was anything like this. It's like there's a different light in your eyes that I never saw before."

"These eyes have seen things I can't hardly believe. Oh, I read about segregation and racial discrimination but I never imagined how it really is. Do you know they might throw you in jail just for kissing me like you just did? I've visited with some Negro families around here and talked to a lot of people and watched what they do. My old feelings seem so immature and babyish to me now. You know, I never really saw you as a man on your own, Milo, but more like your skin color somehow made you different or basically outside of my real life. It didn't make sense then and it makes even less sense now. I been thinking of all those talks you had with me trying to make me understand that we were just two ordinary people and I'm so ashamed I couldn't see it or understand." Iris' words tumbled out expressing all the feelings and emotions that had been burning in her heart for these months of separation.

"Does that mean you're ready to come back with me?"

"After you came all this way to find me I guess I better not disappoint you. Still, thinking about that big kiss I planted on you, maybe I better try playing a little more hard to get." Iris' smile widened at the intense look of happiness on Milo's face. "Maybe I should go ahead and confess something right now. I already gave notice on this house and made arrangements to go back home. I'm so homesick and lonesome for you I like to went crazy these last few weeks. I been staying awake nights wondering how I was going to get you to take me back after the terrible way I treated you."

"If a person ever had a good reason to run away from an intolerable situation I think what you were up against in Sheila's Tree would about top the list. Every nightmare you had about your relationship with a black man came true in spades. No pun intended. How could you not run?"

"I could have done what I'm going to do now—just go back and marry you and live life as normally as we can. If we have any friends—like Ryan, here— they'll show it soon enough and if somebody wants to take offense then to Hell with them!"

Ryan finally spoke up. "Iris we were kind of expecting more persuasion might be needed to talk you into coming back with us. Milo was even ready to move over here if you felt like you couldn't go back to Wyoming. What changed your mind other than not being able to live without the poor guy?"

Iris frowned and tears came to her eyes. "I spent a lot of time traveling around and looking at things. The Negroes here are treated so badly you would hardly think it's possible. In Wyoming we just don't know what it's like. They have separate toilets, separate drinking fountains; they can't eat where they want to or join clubs and organizations. They ride in the back seats on the bus. Everything good is 'whites only'. The black kids even go to different schools, mostly without books and normal equipment. The Negroes don't even vote because it is so hard to register—and even if they do vote, half the time it never gets counted. Seeing what people live with here opened my eyes to what my stupid attitude was before. It was just an ignorant idea I had left over from what my drunken Daddy believed in and talked about all the time. He grew up right here in Midlothian and I can see where he got it from. It's not like the white people don't know what they're doing is wrong and unfair. They do know. It's just that there are laws on the books; they all do it and so it's accepted by everybody—even the Negroes for the most part. I've got a feeling things might be changing someday, though, because a few ladies were willing to talk to me about it when I asked the right questions. There is a deep, deep anger in these people. I don't know—I feel so bad about how it is here." She wearily shook her head in frustration and sadness.

"Maybe these folks feel about Georgia the way I feel about Wyoming," Milo said. "I guess I'd live there just because I love the country and the lifestyle and the big outdoors. I'm sure glad you feel the same way. But the truth is some of those laws are on the books in Wyoming, too. If we go ahead and get married there are going to be some rough times, Iris. You know we will catch all Hell from some people who don't believe in interracial marriage."

"I don't care anymore. I hope we have a dozen little brown cowboys and cowgirls crawling all over the place in a few years. Maybe when we all look the same in five hundred years from now people won't know who to pick on."

"Right now I feel like anything is possible," Milo glowed. "Lets get loaded up as fast as we can and get out of here."

On the long drive to the Atlanta airport Milo and Iris dreamed their future.

"The first thing I'm goin' to do is see if ol' Ballard will sell me the D-Z. He's gettin' so stove up he can hardly get around and I reckon he would a lot rather be in town with Miz Castle than out there on the ranch. He's got no family 'cept that brother of his and Ray surely wouldn't have no use for the place. If we had that spread we could be on our own place and not have to worry about nobody."

Iris sighed with contentment. "We couldn't think of anything that grand, but I got a lot of money for the Bull Run when I sold it to Juno. We can buy a little place and run a few cows and horses. Maybe we can start up a kind of a dude ranch for kids and have poor children come for the summer and learn how to cowboy."

Milo and Ryan looked at each other and erupted in gusts of laughter. At least Milo could be sure that Iris wasn't marrying him for his money.

NATURAL
CONSEQUENCES

Ryan was glad to be back in Wyoming, however, he felt a new and unsettling awareness of conditions in his adopted state after being away for a few days. There was a hectic pace of activities in and around Sheila's Tree and the mining district that effected everything about the formerly sedate lifestyle and local culture. After having spent a week traveling far from his home territory, Ryan observed with new and critical insight the alarming and disintegrating effects of the new economy. People were making more money, which was good, and new influences from outside the provincial rural agrarian traditions of the state were enriching the knowledge and experience of everyone. But schools were becoming crowded, vehicle traffic was developing in areas that had never even seen a paved road before, and folks everywhere were encountering more strangers than friends and acquaintances. Crime statistics were up and, as Ryan's eyes were more and more opened by Collie and Milo, there was obvious degradation of the wildlife, waterways and prairie landscapes. These cumulative effects had gradually built up over a period of two or three years and there was no social or political system in place to ameliorate the pernicious invasion of the physical environment and altering of traditional folkways. System wide consequences were analogous to the introduction of a foreign weed or insect which spreads and prospers to the detriment of existing flora or fauna because of the absence of natural enemies or other environmental controls. From the perspective of a conservative, long-time resident's viewpoint, the state was suffering from a foreign invasion. Ryan felt it too, though, as a newcomer himself, he could easily be classified as one of the invaders. He decided to take steps to eliminate the unsightly and perhaps dangerous discharge of radioactive minerals in the mill effluent.

"Sean, the mill is humming like a top. We seem to be producing yellowcake faster than we can ship it out. Our profit margin hit a new high last week. You have done a splendid job with the design and operation of this process. I've got a problem, though, that we are going to have to face. I think there must be ways to clear up or clean up some of the visual problems of the yellow lake and maybe even get rid of the tailings pond and the discharge of chemical contaminants in the long run." Ryan hesitated with a slight frown and then an oblique grin. "Of course anything we do is going to cost money and, perhaps, effect the efficiency and smooth operation of the mill. Are you ready for that?"

"There may be some modifications in process that could be factored in, but you must consider, Ryan, that we are currently operating according to the strictest government standards and are in complete compliance in all things."

"I don't believe the government standards were written to cover this kind of operation. Mine safety is one thing but the radioactive waste we are piling up out the back door here was never a consideration when those regulations were put in place. What is the half-life of the gamma radiation from these minerals and chemical compounds we are discharging? What if that poisonous brew were to spill over into the Powder River? I think we have to take a responsible position and make sure that some catastrophe can't happen even if it costs us some real money."

"You aren't the only one affected here, you know. We have a government contract with production standards that must be met and there are some other investors in Wyo Nucleonics who may have some opinions."

"If we don't, at least, look at the engineering and design of some safeguards, we're not going to know what the cost is," Ryan pointed out.

"I designed this mill with the latest and best features available anywhere in the world. Now you are telling me at this late date that my efforts were not good enough for you? I am operating the mill at the absolute maximum economic efficiency, as well. You are not complaining about the revenues, I notice."

This remark stung Ryan to the heart and voices began to rise.

"Look Sean, I'm not criticizing your design or operational parameters at all. It's simply that I and everyone else in town can observe just by looking at this yellow waste pit that a lot of hot radioactive material is coming out the exhaust pipe of this mill and some of it may be harmful to folk's health. We have to look at that whether it's a requirement of the law or not. Maybe economic efficiency and uranium recovery efficiency and responsible public policy are not the same thing."

The South African shook his head in amazement. "I can't believe you would even think of tampering with this operation. You employed me to bring everything I had to this project to design and operate for maximum efficiency and profit. If that is no longer your aim, Mr. Baker, then you need a different kind of engineer than myself."

There were not many options available at that point. Ryan was extremely disappointed and unhappy at the fallout with the admitted creative genius behind the highly successful uranium mill but he felt strongly that changes must to be made. Both men reluctantly faced up to the consequences of their positions on the continuation of the milling process and the focus of its operation.

"I'm still an eighty percent majority stockholder in Wyo Nucleonics. If you can't, or won't, meet my expectations on this then I'll have to get somebody who will."

"I can't believe you are so improvident and foolish about this. Hell, Ryan, just buying out my contract is going to cost you over one hundred thousand dollars. What do you think Ray and Ballard are going to think when you spring this on them?"

"I'd guess they are probably as concerned about this town and the environment here as I am," Ryan answered. "I've already heard of cleanup programs going on down in Colorado and New Mexico where the mines have been operating longer than here. There are things that can be done even though it's expensive. We're going to start exploring some of those options around here."

THE LAST SUPPER

Ryan and Collie were deep in conversation as they sipped fragrant goblets of cognac following a robust and delicious steak dinner at the Cielo Grande hotel.

"I have to win this lawsuit against New Mexico Mining Corporation to set the stage for changing and improving the whole spectrum of problems that are developing in Sheila's Tree. The outcome of this trial seems to me far more important than just the impact on Palmer ranch and my own affairs. Somehow people must be made aware of the extent and consequences of these terrible things that steal our heritage and change the world forever," Collie observed. "Men like E. L. Palmer and Deuteronomy Zwitzer and others put down roots here and created something that, at least in part, should be preserved and protected. I feel like the Native Americans must have felt when white men came along and destroyed their old way of life. Is it too late to make any difference? Are we doomed to just go on forever ruining and changing the natural world and traditional cultures just because we can think of ways to do it and make some more money?"

"Collie, I'm well beyond my depth here. I am a career geologist and engineer who has been trained to devise new and better ways to extract minerals and natural resources from the earth in order to make things easier and more comfortable for human beings. I certainly see the bad side of what has happened to the Bench and the rest of this area since the uranium boom started, but would it be better to forego nuclear power and all the benefits to civilization that may result? The nuclear age started because we were fighting to preserve freedom and autonomy for half the people of the world. Surely it was important to win the war?" Ryan had not yet revealed to Collie the extent of his commitment to change things at his mill. He wanted to test her rational by playing the Devil's Advocate for a moment.

"All I can do is what I can do," Collie stated firmly. "I imagine myself like a pebble tossed into a large pond of water. I can make big ripples near at hand and influence things fairly effectively close to home but as the ripples get further away they gradually die out. I intend to start making waves that may stir things up for the whole country but will certainly begin here in Wyoming."

"You mentioned the other day that you may have higher political aspirations than Mayor of Sheila's Tree," Ryan prompted.

Collie smiled conspiratorially. "I've already quietly contacted Colin Gervais in Cheyenne about a possible switch to the Democratic Party and a campaign for the Senate next year. He was ecstatic about the idea, though he cautioned me to go easy and let him do some ground work with the party faithful before I make any public announcements. I've been such a staunch supporter of Wyatt and the Republicans that I may have to reach out rather dramatically to win any confidence. If Gervais, as the Democratic Party Chairman, can't convince their folks of my viability as a candidate then I guess nobody can."

"It's after 10:00 pm, are you ready to call it a night and head for home?" Ryan's eyebrows went up questioningly and his smile became a bit of a leer as he glanced at Collie. He reached for the leather folder containing the meal check. Collie smiled playfully and touched his hand.

"You don't seem too interested in my political career. What is on that evil mind of yours?"

"Oh, I'm just tired is all, it must be hours after my bedtime," he grinned salaciously. Ryan's eyebrow went up in earnest as he looked at the dinner bill. "My heaven, this comes to almost sixteen dollars with the wine and cognac. How can people afford to eat out these days?"

Collie laughed without any detectable sympathy. "Ryan, you could buy this restaurant on a week of income from that radioactive factory of yours. Don't be so cheap."

They drove to Collie's secluded townhouse atop the bluff overlooking Chopstick reservoir and walked hand in hand up the long flagstone walk.

"You know, I was supposed to be down in Denver at the Western Mayors Conference this week but I skipped out just because we were celebrating your birthday tonight. I haven't missed one of those meetings for the last four years so you can be proud of yourself for distracting me from my life's work," Collie teased.

She turned the key in her front door and they entered the foyer.

CRY "HAVOC!"

Shug and Pronto were feeling good about the trip to Wyoming and their work for Marion Reinhardt. Pronto was never happier than when his talent for destruction and rampage was unleashed. The hard work of claim staking that had been their first mission was not the sort of opportunity they were looking for. Only excellent pay had kept them interested in the hard manual labor. In the present case they were getting well paid for the chance to satisfy brutal passions and express contempt for order and normal society. Shug Brown was not prone to psychopathic rage as was Melindez, however, their long partnership had bred a certain amount of tolerance for Pronto's unpredictable destructive attitude. They made a good team for the type of work they followed. The County courthouse job in 1954 had been relatively easy and straightforward because their goal had been clear and directions were given in a very specific manner. Find the document exactly where Frailey told them it would be; tear the place up and get out. Nice and neat with no ambiguity. The hasty call from Reinhardt eighteen months later offered a job more difficult but no less satisfying for the irrational and demented Pronto. The pair had found it easy to break into the unoccupied ranch house but the search for a piece of paper that may or may not have been there in an unknown hiding place required more imagination and talent than either of the two criminals owned. The search rapidly degenerated into a furious whirlwind of ravaging destruction.

The current job was a duplicate of the instructions given for the Palmer canyon ranch house. The homeowner was out of town and the house was isolated and empty. The two were directed to break into the Mayor's townhouse, make a thorough search for the Cielo Grande easement document in every possible corner and, if found, bring it to Reinhardt. Shug and Pronto knew what the paper looked like, having seen it before in the courthouse affair, but the significance of the document for their employer was quite lost on them. From their viewpoint there was only vague continuity in the Wyoming action and Reinhardt's motives were of little interest. They were aware, however, that another mission remained after this one. A certain downtown law office was next to be targeted for search and destruction. There was a lot of money to be made and some barbaric satisfaction in destroying valuable property at the same time. Pronto was feeling powerful and almost omnipotent. He was in control.

Shug easily jimmied the backdoor lock and they slipped into the house with no trouble. Both men were equipped with miner's headlamps and thin cloth gloves. Working with quiet efficiency, the two criminals opened every cupboard and drawer, dumped contents on the floor and rummaged thoroughly in all possible hiding places. Books were tossed out of shelves, sofa and chair cushions ripped open and paintings removed from the wall. They were almost finished with the main floor living room, kitchen and dining room when Shug heard the sound of voices and a key in the front door lock. By the time Collie and Ryan were in the entryway and flipped on the overhead light Pronto and Shug had positioned themselves. As the light came on Shug struck Ryan in the forehead with a lead filled leather cosh, dropping him to his knees in a concussed daze. Pronto seized Collie and waved his knife menacingly in front of her eyes before placing the blade against her neck. The surprised victims were overpowered and helpless in seconds. Ryan made an attempt to resist as Shug tied his hands behind his back with an electric power cord. He was still seeing double from the blow to his head but swung an elbow hard in Shug's face. He caught Brown squarely in the mouth and gashed through the lower lip. Shug kneed Ryan viciously in the kidneys as he lay on the floor.

"Lay still son-of-a-bitch or I'll knock your Goddamn head off."

"Hey," Pronto barked, "Nobody s'posed to be aroun' here. W'at the hell we goin' do now?"

"Tie her up and we'll figure it out. Hurry up, Goddamn it."

Pronto found a roll of black friction tape on the littered floor in the kitchen and used it to bind Collie's wrists tightly behind her back. She was shoved violently to the floor beside Ryan who lay bleeding, near unconsciousness, and in obvious pain.

"That bastard, Frailey, said the place was empty this week," Shug growled, wiping streams of blood from his chin. "I should have known that fat cock wouldn't know what he was talkin' about."

"Sheet, how we goin' feenish theese job now? They seen our face an' prob'ly get us caught up good by the law. Theese woman is beeg Alcalde an' nobody's goin' mess around weeth us if we gets catch."

The two men looked at each other with emerging comprehension that there was only one way to avoid the consequences of having been caught in the act.

"This aint so good," muttered Shug. "I never figured on nuthing this serious."

"Don' worry, I know how to take care of thees. Why don' you go on down in the basement and start goin' through all those boxes an' sheet." He glanced at Collie lying on the floor, her black evening dress riding high on her thighs. "I know w'at to do up here."

"Jesus, Pronto, you make me sick." Shug hunched his shoulders and gave an almost pitying look at the two prostrate figures. He was only too glad to turn away and go down a nearby basement stairway from the kitchen to continue searching for the fatal document.

Pronto gave Ryan a vicious kick in the ribs and he rolled over against the wall with a weak groan, drawing his legs up and curling into a fetal ball. With hands tied securely behind him, eyes squinted shut in white-faced pain, it appeared that he was totally incapacitated. "I be right back to take care of you' Gringo ass."

The Mexican yanked Collie to her feet and pushed her upstairs ahead of him to the upper floor with the master bedroom, guestrooms and family room. In the bedroom Pronto slapped her viciously in the face, right, left, right, left, until her head flopped and she felt that her senses were leaving. He grasped her clothing at the front and ripped downward stripping her bare to the waist, then flung her backwards on the bed. Her head struck the oak headboard with a thud and stars sparkled behind her eyes with crackling strokes of pain.

"Wait for me, chiquita, I go take care you' frien' down stairs and then I come show you a real good time. You gonna like it." He flipped open the switchblade knife and turned back to the stairs. The words burned in Collie's ears. She had heard them before during Louise Greene's long debriefing by Wilbur Shliefsanger.

The moment Ryan was left alone he brought his bound hands under his drawn up legs and feet and scrambled upright. Though he was dizzy and in pain his condition was not nearly as bad as he had pretended. He ran to the kitchen and grabbed the wall telephone. There was no dial tone. The first thing Shug had done upon arrival at the property was to cut the phone line. The thought of Collie in the power of Pronto Melindez was piercing Ryan's brain. Both he and Collie had immediately recognized that this man was no doubt the long sought attacker of Louise Greene. What could he do? What to do? On the floor amid the mess at his feet was a long carving knife dropped from its wooden holder on the sinktop. Ryan grasped it in his tied hands and ran for the stairs. There stood Melindez, glittering black eyes filled with hate and murderous rage.

"Hey you gringo dog," he snarled, "you think you gonna fight me with a knife? I goin' to cut you. I goin' to take out you' eyes and cut off you' cojones."

He flourished the knife like a rapier then held it low in his right hand and advanced with a gliding, bouncing motion, balanced on the balls of his feet, eyes focused intently on the butcher's knife grasped in Ryan's fists. As he got almost within striking distance Pronto feinted rapidly at Ryan's head. When Ryan raised his arms to fend off the blow Pronto swept his right leg at Ryan's left calf and dumped him squarely on his backside. No sooner did Ryan hit the floor than the Mexican danced forward and kicked him hard in the left ear. Pronto laughed shrilly.

"Come on, Gringo, get up. We gonna have some more good times."

Ryan lurched to his feet and tried to present some semblance of defense as a lightening fast strike gashed his upper arm. Almost casually Pronto flicked the blade towards Ryan's face and sliced to the bone through the cleft chin. Ryan was getting soaked in his own blood.

"Sheet, man, theese fun. Where you gonna hide now, knife fighter?"

Ryan stood grimly erect, backed up against the entryway wall. He was woozy and weak but all fear had evaporated in the fury of action. He managed a rictus grin.

"Come on you little murdering devil, I can take you down in a heartbeat. You can't kill me without getting closer than that."

Pronto's face turned cold and empty. The black eyes were flat and devoid of human compassion and feeling. He moved in for the kill.

"OK, knife fighter. I wanna get back upstairs and go to work on you' girlfrien' anyhow."

He slid forward with his unusual dancing gait preparatory for the final deadly thrust of a cold blade into Ryan's stomach. The parquet-tiled floor of the entryway was pooled with Ryan's blood and as Pronto pushed off for the final swift lunge his feet betrayed him. Lost traction from slippage on the bloody floor caused the forward leap to fall short and Melindez was exposed for a moment almost on his hands and knees in front of Ryan. With all of his remaining strength Ryan plunged the kitchen knife in a convulsive double fisted blow between Pronto's shoulder blades. Ryan toppled forward across the dying man's body then rose shakily, staggered through the kitchen and out into the back yard where he collapsed.

"My God, what a mess," exclaimed Shug as he emerged, seconds later, from the basement doorway. "How did the Mex get hisself done up like that?" Shug had always imagined that Pronto was invincible in a knife fight.

He ran out of the house close behind Ryan and found his limp form on the dark lawn not far from the edge of the rocky bluff overlooking the reservoir.

"I don't know how you did it, asshole," Shug grated, "but it didn't buy you nuthin'."

He jerked the thick leather belt from his ample waist and slipped it over Ryan's head and around his neck. He sat on Ryan's chest and began to tighten the belt.

There was another person unaccounted for in the blood soaked household. Perhaps Shug Brown thought that, because she was a woman, Collie need not be reckoned with at the same level of caution as a man or perhaps he assumed that Pronto had already disposed of her. It was a grave mistake to underestimate or ignore Collie Palmer.

When Pronto left the bedroom to deal with Ryan, Collie struggled, hampered by the shredded remnants of her dress, to pull her taped wrists under her feet and bring them in front of her just as Ryan had done. Without hesitation she rolled over and pulled back a sliding panel in the headboard of the big double bed. There was a .32 semi-automatic pistol fully loaded in its accustomed place. Collie knew how to use it. She strode bare-breasted down the staircase like Liberty at the gates of the Bastille, ready for battle. She, as well as Ryan, had identified Pronto as the attacker of Louise and she was bent on vengeance.

As Collie reached the foot of the stairs she could see Melindez' bloody form in the foyer lying in a shapeless sprawl with the knife protruding from his back. Ryan was nowhere in sight and she felt a surge of panicky anxiety. Then she noticed the spattered trail of blood leading to the kitchen and followed, fearing to find Ryan mortally hurt. From the kitchen she could dimly see dark forms struggling on the back lawn. Collie flicked on the electric porch lights and illuminated the macabre scene of Shug sitting on top of Ryan with the belt firmly in his grasp.

"Stop! Stop what you're doing or I'll shoot," she screamed.

Shug yanked on the belt and began to pull with all his weight. Ryan's tongue protruded from his bleeding mouth creating a shadowy grotesque mask.

Collie was standing on the back deck with the pistol in both hands leveled at Shug Brown's heedless form.

"Stop I tell you, stop!"

The first bullet caught Brown in the left temple and no more were needed. Collie didn't know that, however, and continued to fire two more rounds into his slumping body. Only when she realized that her target was lying almost on top of Ryan did she stop shooting. She ran out to loosen the belt from Ryan's neck and then pounded on his chest with clinched fists trying to restart his breathing. For the second time in her life Collie saw awareness stir in his eyes and heard his rasping gasps for oxygen. This time she tenderly embraced him in her still bound arms, weeping tears of relief and hugging his limp body unashamedly to her naked bosom.

Collie and Ryan would never know that they were huddled on a spot no more than ten feet from where the Wagon Master, Dorsey Fuller, some one hundred and three years earlier, had single handedly driven off a war party of savage Indians who were in the act of brutally murdering his daughter. It was brave ground; the site of courageous acts borne of desperation in response to brutish violence.

CLOSING IN

Both Collie and Ryan spent the remainder of the night of terror in Mercy Hospital under the care of Doctor Hysett. They were found to be in good physical condition despite Ryan's deep cuts and bruises and Collie's lacerated mouth and cheeks. They were tentatively placed under criminal investigation, though the physical evidence at the scene and their standing in the community precluded being arrested or held in custody. After an hour of individual and separate interrogation by the County Sheriff shortly after police arrived at the violent crime scene, it became clear that both homicides were in self-defense of home and personal safety. The Sheriff made a statement to the local press later in the early morning hours and national news syndicates immediately picked up the story.

The next day saw a bedlam of activity, questioning, well-wishers and news media attention nation-wide. It was all city Police Chief Bertie and Denton Eldring could do to get the pair out of the hospital and safely into the Lawyer's private home without being mobbed by reporters. Collie could not bear to go back immediately to the terrible bloody mess of her town house and Ryan was still weak from loss of blood and sedation. Milo Harris and Iris Patton were early visitors at the Eldring residence.

"I went down to the Sheriff's office the minute I heard the radio report this morning," Milo related. "The first thing they wanted for me to do was identify the bodies. They sure enough were the same two hombres that were in the Bull Run the night of Miz Greene's attack. I gave 'em the names they called themselves by that night and told 'em about Pronto making a telephone call to Mr. Frailey, too."

Denton was taking notes on the conversation. "Do you realize this is a direct connection to the New Mexico Mining Company, Collie? Reinhardt and Frailey are related by marriage and according to gossip it was George Frailey who got NMMC interested in the Canteen claims in the first place. I can't wait to see the information we subpoenaed from the mine the other day. Now I'll know exactly what to look for."

They were interrupted by a telephone call for Collie from Cheyenne. It was Patrick McCall.

"Colorado, you sure know how to make the newspapers. How do you think your sharp shooting is going over at the breakfast tables of the Wyoming voters this morning? About the only thing missing is a front page picture of you standing there with your shirt off holding the smoking gun."

"Shut up McCall, you're not funny. I will have nightmares about last night for as long as I live. The last thing I'm thinking about right now is the stupid election."

"Well, you better think again. You're as good as elected right now. Talk about an American heroine—you may be up for a civilian medal of bravery. I could probably get you elected President if you wanted to run. By the way, I was just kidding about the picture, right? Please tell me nobody got a shot of your boobs."

"You have a dirty mind, McCall. I was fully dressed before the first policeman even got to the house last night. Listen, your pathetic cheeriness and Irish humor are too much for me this morning. I'll call you back after we settle a few things around here. You'll hear from me next week sometime."

"OK. I know it must have been a hell of an ordeal. Just be very careful what you say to the press and keep the heroine image in mind. Don't let on about your political situation just now. We'll save that for a big play when the time is right."

Collie hung up the phone with her mind in turmoil as she remembered the terror and desperation of the night before compared to the optimistic opinion of her campaign manager about the public impact of the story. Her primary thought was simple thankfulness that she and Ryan had both managed to survive the deadly events of the attack. She experienced no deep regret at having struck down Brown. She knew she would do it again under similar circumstances.

JUSTICE SERVED

Several weeks later Denton Eldring was explaining to Collie and Ryan how the legal intricacies of New Mexico Mining Company's trespass and damages to the Palmer ranch were going to be redressed.

"We got Perlmutter to concede to everything. They obviously couldn't go to trial after we started subpoenaing mine pay records for Brown and Melindez and finding people like your friend Milo Harris who could put them near the scene of several of these crimes. The District Attorney never even considered anything other than self-defense for you two after they went over the house and put together what happened. Once it was clear that Reinhardt actually employed those two degenerates we pretty much had them. The clincher was when our forensic expert was able to show that the 1895 Cielo Grande easement agreement had been tampered with. I knew old E.L. would never be dumb enough to make a contract like that. It explained the courthouse vandalism and the other break-ins. Oh, and then the best part, the breakthrough on the criminal prosecution was when we tracked down that forger in San Francisco through Reinhardt's private office records. I'm sure the grand jury will indict both Reinhardt and Frailey and they should get to spend a few years breaking up rocks that have nothing to do with a uranium mine."

"And you also got NMMC to agree to pave Pass Road?" Collie asked.

"That was no problem. The new manager out at the mine, Ed Cholick, said they wanted to do it anyhow to save maintenance on the haul trucks."

Denton continued, "Your damage settlement will be around a hundred thousand dollars after legal fees, plus three thousand a year for future commercial use of the haul road through your ranch. That ought to help finance a few radio spots for your Senate run. Down in Denver they're starting to talk television as the next big media factor for elections. I hear your campaign manager is the fast talking Mr. Patrick McCall. He is a genuine Irish swashbuckler. I sincerely hope you run that pompous old hack, Paige, out of Washington. He should be ready to retire anyway."

"We are certainly going to go all out on this campaign and there is no better man to manage it than Patrick McCall. I can't thank you enough, Denton. This whole affair has been a nightmare experience but I learned a lot about myself. Sometimes you have to be tested before you find out what you're really made of. There were dark times in the past couple of years when I let my imagination run away with me but reality can be more frightening than our worst fears. I'm ready for the future now and its going to be a grand adventure."

Collie put her hand in Ryan's. "Ryan and I have big plans and, together, I think we can make a few ripples on the pond here and there."

They walked out of the Attorney's office, hand in hand, under the wide blue sky of Wyoming.

THE END

EPILOGUE

—————————— ▼ ——————————

AUGUST 2003—*50 years after the story ends*

Colorado Palmer Baker reached her eightieth year but was only three years retired from the legislative branch of the United States government. She delivered her last speech at the Wyoming State House in Cheyenne on her birthday to celebrate and commemorate her long life of public service. Though a few men had seen elective service exceeding forty years duration, she was, by far, the longest serving woman in the honorable history of the United States Senate. She was also one of the most respected and popular lawmakers in the history of the state. In the late Nineteen-sixties, with husband Ryan Baker at her side, she had campaigned for the United States Presidency and come within seven convention votes of becoming the Democratic nominee. She always thought that she might have beaten Richard Nixon in a national contest and saved her country the traumatic debacle of his resignation had she been the chosen candidate. Seven times she had campaigned for the Senate seat and seven times she had won easily. The first contest in nineteen hundred and fifty-eight had been much the closest. Wyatt Paige had conceded her victory early in the evening, however, with a somewhat bitter comment about beauty coming before wisdom and experience to the detriment of the great state of Wyoming. The home invasion episode and deaths of Melindez and Brown had never been mentioned by the candidates during the hard-fought 1958 campaign but the public had been exposed to every detail of the terrifying story for weeks following the incident. The separate trials of Reinhardt and Frailey were still going on as the Senate campaign began. Collie's most difficult hurdle had been the switch in politics from Republican to

Democratic registration. Patrick McCall had candidly spun the change in party affiliation as the only avenue by which Collie could pursue her ambition for national office. Patrick claimed, with obvious justification, that the Republicans would never have abandoned Wyatt Paige for another candidate no matter how suitable that person might have been. Collie represented this position openly from the start, preserving her moderately conservative positions on many issues, and then laid out her ideas and goals for balanced national supervision of looming environmental issues. At that time no one dreamed of anything so Draconian as the Environmental Protection Agency or an Endangered Species Act for which she later spearheaded support, however, Collie repeatedly pointed out the dangers of ignoring consequences to the natural world as the growing U.S. economy matured. The best selling book, Silent Spring, by Rachel Carson, published in 1962, lent a certain validity and urgency to Collie's arguments before her first term reached its six year conclusion.

Uranium mining essentially ended in 1983 in the United States when Uncle Sam stopped buying yellowcake. In the decade of the nineties Senator Baker got the Wyoming Uranium pits in the Canteen district listed as a Super Fund reclamation site and reconstruction of the old mines returned the Bench to a close semblance of its former pristine state. Her husband, Ryan, made sure that his processing mill was completely cleaned up and the site sanitized shortly after the mining stopped. Used to a frame of reference in terms of the slow rhythms of the geologic time scale, Ryan felt that all traces of the frantic uranium rush would soon be obliterated and forgotten along with the ephemeral men and women who participated in it. His life's work was mostly spent in studying and writing about geo-ecological systems and commercial implications for the mineral industry around the world.

Milo and Iris developed the D-Z ranch into a haven for their own children and other deserving or needful youth of all races. They became affiliated with the juvenile justice system in California and many young lives were salvaged as a result of exposure to the cowboy way of life. They found happiness and fulfillment in a life together and were deeply involved in the racial struggles of the late fifties and following decades. Milo never raised his hand against another human being for the remainder of his life though he fought hard for his beliefs in every other way.

Denton Eldring became a national figure and participated in a number of celebrity criminal cases. He retired at Jackson Hole after many productive years practicing law.

Sean Mochery became a well-known figure in the mineral industry. His interest turned to gold production and economic recovery of ultra-low grade ores in the western United States. He and Ryan met often over the years and even worked on a few projects together, however, it was difficult to forget their basic philosophical differences from the Wyoming days.

As the new millenium relentlessly rolls up on the calendar, Wyoming back-country is once again broiling and seething with a new rush to exploit mineral wealth. This time it is natural gas but, just as during the years of the Uranium boom, many of the same problems with human and environmental safety still remain to be resolved.

Every life is a story—every character deserves a book. Life goes on.

ABOUT THE AUTHOR

Malcolm Crawford is a retired mining engineer living in Las Vegas, Nevada. Graduating in 1958 from Stanford University in his native state of California, Crawford's first job was working in the uranium fields of Wyoming where he saw most of the events and encountered many of the characters found in the fictionalized historical novel, *Sheila's Tree*. Most of Crawford's career was devoted to the management of irrigation districts and municipal water districts in the northwest and California.

Crawford is a life-long outdoorsman and conservationist. He has climbed Mount Shasta in Northern California, hunted and fished throughout Alaska and the western states and pursued his hobby of bird watching around the world. He married a Spanish girl, Londa Iriarte, in Casablanca, Morocco and raised a family of four children. The Crawfords recently celebrated their 50th wedding anniversary on a cruise of the western Caribbean with all of their children and grandchildren in attendance.

0-595-32963-2

Printed in the United States
27452LVS00003B/283-360

9 780595 329632